ONE STEP AHEAD

Detectives hunt a serial killer who knows all their moves

DENVER MURPHY

THE
BOOK
FOLKS

Published by The Book Folks

London, 2019

ISBN 978-1-7956-3952-1

www.thebookfolks.com

One Step Ahead is the first book in a trilogy featuring retired detective Jeffrey Brandt. Details about the other books can be found at the end of this one.

Chapter One

'Over at last.' Former Detective Superintendent Jeffrey Brandt sighed, opened his front door and was greeted by the silence and stillness inside. The evening had been his retirement party; a forced and turgid affair, full of awkward speeches and false promises to keep in touch. Yet Brandt had accepted it with apparent good grace, conscious that it was a necessary process in his metamorphosis.

No longer with a wife to insist he remove his shoes, he merely shrugged off his coat; heading into the sitting room and straight for the drinks cabinet. At the party he had resisted the temptation to over-indulge but now safely home, he could celebrate in earnest. For despite his feigned sadness at leaving the police, he could remember little in his life more worthy of celebration than this.

As relieved as he was to finally be embarking on a more rewarding path, it wasn't as though Brandt wanted to forget the past. Not only would it serve as a reminder of how far he had come, and what he had sacrificed along the way, he would need to draw on the skills he had honed over his long and distinguished career if he was to be successful in this new one.

When he started in the police, Brandt viewed the job as a crusade for good and righteousness. Of average height and build, he had always looked unremarkable but, stood in his uniform at the passing out parade, his dark hair swept back with the aid of Brylcreem, and with his parents and girlfriend proudly watching on, his blue eyes had sparkled with anticipation of what was to follow. His enviable service record and reputation for solving even the most complex of cases suggested his vocation had been a success.

But Brandt knew the truth.

Over time, the crimes he was investigating, the affronts to decency and humanity, had come to be viewed as unpleasant and inconvenient by-products of the modern age. Society had become so desensitised to violence, be it real or fictional, that what he was doing hardly seemed to matter anymore. That it mattered to the victim and their close friends and family, only made it worse when some kid out of law school was encouraged to pick holes in each bit of evidence he had gathered, and every investigative method he had used. With juries seeming increasingly unwilling to reach guilty verdicts, and with many of those few convictions made being subsequently overturned, Brandt's job had become increasingly difficult.

And yet the same determination that had seen him enter the police force had driven him on for a while, encouraging him to bury himself deeper in his work. He had obsessed over every detail, certain that he could make the case for the prosecution water-tight. But at the same time as his marriage failed, he came to understand that he was becoming a lone voice; the decline he was seeking to reverse had already been accepted. Society had entered a slumber of indifference and, worse still, so too had most of his colleagues. Overworked and underpaid, they had taken the route of least resistance; regarding what had once been a calling as a job much like any other.

Unable to find meaning in his work, he began to look forward to his impending retirement, but not because it would allow him to escape his troubles. He had already paid the ultimate price in his personal life and, unless he found a purpose to his continued existence, all that awaited him was more opportunity to reflect on a life wasted.

The only chance Brandt had to reconcile all that he had given to society with everything it had cost him in return was to tip the balance in his favour. Now destined not to leave a legacy through fatherhood, he could at least make his mark by reversing the decline that had seen all his hopes and aspirations unfulfilled.

Freed from the shackles of the rule of law, he could channel all his knowledge and experience in a more effective direction; one that would force people to see how bad their apathy had allowed things to become. For Brandt had a particular talent, one that could not be taught and one that was ostensibly in contrast with a conviction to do good: the ability to connect with the murderers he hunted on an emotional level. His empathetic understanding of what drove them to kill had allowed him to establish motive in the most apparently random of crimes. Spending so much time consumed by the dark thoughts of others had the combined effect of eroding Brandt's morality, and allowing him to learn from their mistakes.

Chapter Two

Living in Nottingham for the past three years had allowed Sarah to carefully perfect her Saturday routine. Although keen to punctuate the end of the working week like most of the young teachers at her school, she resisted calls to have the typical late, alcohol-fuelled Friday night. However, far from being puritanical it was because Sarah believed that Saturday should be a day for action and activities, whilst Sunday was best suited to hangovers, television and, if one could summon up the energy to cook, roast dinners.

Braving her top floor apartment's balcony with some freshly brewed coffee, Sarah waited for the sun to rise over the trees of Victoria Embankment Park. She knew that caffeine wasn't the ideal preparation for a session at the gym but found the stimulant, combined with the biting air of a pre-dawn Saturday, invigorating. As she sat there watching the first rays dapple on the River Trent, it was only the longing for the cigarettes she had given up three months previously that prevented the scene being perfect in her eyes. Whilst no longer craving the nicotine, it was times like these that forced her to remember the pleasurable routine of smoking.

In an effort to distract herself, she decided to have a quick scan of Facebook to see what she had missed the night before. Despite the school having a strict policy on staff use of social media, it only took a few moments for her to gain a comprehensive picture of the events. With the final posts not until after 3am, and involving a dubious looking kebab shop, Sarah doubted she would hear from that particular group of friends again until much later in the day.

With the sun now fully visible, the coffee finished, and the cold having managed to penetrate the layers of both her white dressing gown and black padded jacket, Sarah knew it was time to go back indoors and get changed. She would save showering until she had finished at the gym, so it was just a case of throwing on some of her exercise gear. Nevertheless, she decided to remain outside for the moment and read once again the unexpected text she had received on Thursday. It was from Josh, a man she had dated briefly the previous November. There had seemed to be some potential there and Sarah had invited him round for dinner. Knowing where this might lead, she had gone to tremendous effort, not just with the food, but with a beauty regime that had lasted most of the previous day. His failure to show, or provide any sort of explanation, was first met with anger. When days followed without contact, her emotion turned to confusion and, finally, worry when the message she sent enquiring what had happened, at great personal cost to her pride, was not replied to. Later, the mutual friend who had first introduced them confirmed, somewhat awkwardly, that nothing untoward had befallen him. Determined not to humiliate herself any further Sarah had left it at that and tried to cast him from her mind. She'd be lying if she suggested she had not thought of him on occasion but when the text came through it had been met with genuine shock.

*– Hi Sarah, hope this is still your number. Sorry
about before, can I make it up to you? Josh x*

She didn't want to respond and give him the
satisfaction of showing she cared, but she was curious to
find out why he had stood her up in the first place, and the
reason he was making contact now.

One of the things she loved most about going to the
gym was that it gave her space to think. Visiting there on
her way home from school every Tuesday and Thursday,
on those nights she slept better than she did the rest of the
week. Perhaps it had something to do with the exercise,
but she believed it was more of a result of being able to
process the things on her mind. However, the ability to
think clearly was less welcome on this particular Saturday
morning because her thoughts kept returning to Josh. It
was troubling her sufficiently to see her typical routine cut
short by electing to skip the twenty minutes on the cross
trainer she usually finished with. Having showered and
now sitting on one of the benches in the changing room
with a towel wrapped around her, she started punching in
a reply.

– I doubt it.

Sarah convinced herself that there was nothing wrong
with typing it, so long as she didn't send it. Although the
message itself was suitably cold, she knew that regardless
of its content, the very act of replying would imply she was
bothered by what had happened. Then again, it would
serve to bring some form of closure and allow her to
continue her weekend as normal. So engrossed was Sarah
with her thoughts that she failed to notice that the towel
had come undone at the top and was gradually slipping
down her front. As her index finger hovered over the send
button, she promised herself that regardless of what he
might text back, this would be the sum total of her
communication.

Despite hearing the ping of the incoming message tone barely a minute later, she continued to dress, feeling that the show of strength by not immediately checking her phone vindicated her earlier decision. The same part of her that had dared her to send the message now challenged her to wait until she returned to her apartment. This was something she was prepared to do, and had started walking home, until the weaker part of her convinced her that the message probably wasn't from him and might be important.

Without breaking stride, she removed the phone from her coat pocket and a single press of the home screen lit up the display, revealing the message contents.

– Do you still have the Saturday routine of some pre-lunch shopping? I'll be in the coffee shop at midday.

The blast from a car horn alerted Sarah to the fact she had stopped dead in the middle of the side street she was crossing. Partly through shock and partly through anger at Josh's presumptuousness, she gave the driver the finger; immediately regretting it. Although her school was the other side of town, which meant it was unlikely a parent would be driving out of this particular residential street, she understood the hypocrisy of this indiscretion given her earlier thoughts regarding her colleagues' Facebook antics.

* * *

Nottingham city centre is suitably large, containing no fewer than two shopping malls, and if Sarah didn't want to be spotted by someone, she knew she could continue with her Saturday routine unimpeded. If she wanted a coffee at midday there were plenty of other places she could choose from. Sure, they might not have the lemon tart she so enjoyed but this could be her penance for not earning the treat via the cross-trainer.

As she walked into town she could feel her resolve gradually crumbling. Defiant, she convinced herself that it was her inner-strength that was preventing her from wanting to be driven out of her favourite café. When she passed the station car park and turned from Queen's Street into Carrington Road, the Broadmarsh Shopping Centre was firmly in view. She knew then that she would go and listen to what Josh had to say. However, in order to keep the last of her dignity she would pick up a couple of items on the way, so it wouldn't seem that she had gone into town specifically to meet him.

From the main entrance of the station, a large group of people suddenly appeared. Sarah professed to know little about football and didn't recognise which team the blue shirts belonged to. However, the sheer number of them suggested they were probably here to play Nottingham Forest rather than their lower league local rivals, Notts County. Clearly this was a team who had played here regularly because few stopped to get their bearings, and most were heading in the same direction as her towards Castle Wharf's waterfront bars.

Sarah was swallowed up by the crowd, only to feel herself being nudged by someone overtaking on her left, swiftly followed by contact with the lower right of her abdomen. Concerned that was where her handbag hung, she instinctively moved her hand to the area to check it had not been snatched. As she padded the region, she could feel moisture. Holding up her fingers to the sunlight revealed blood. Almost simultaneously she felt an excruciating pain rise from her side, and her legs crumbled. As Sarah sunk to the floor she was accidentally kicked by the person directly behind as he attempted not to trip over her. Looking up at the blue sky from the cold concrete, the edges of her vision began to narrow. Concerned shouting could be heard, accompanied by a woman screaming, but the noise seemed distant and muffled to Sarah. Darkness gradually crept in and it was with gratitude she observed that the pain was now fading.

Chapter Three

By the time Brandt arrived at Nottingham Castle he could feel his pulse returning to normal. He paid the entrance fee in cash and proceeded around the exhibits, taking little in, and settled on a bench towards the back of the site. He wanted the opportunity to rest before embarking on the remainder of the walk back to his car but, more than anything, he wished to take some time to reflect on what he had just achieved. Brandt had little interest in anything he had seen at the castle but had chosen this location as a suitable point between where he had parked and where he carried out his task. Despite being confident that he had escaped the scene without suspicion, he thought it wise to provide himself with a reason for visiting the area. The few people who knew him would be surprised to hear he had made such a trip in order to shop, but someone who had recently taken early retirement could quite conceivably wish to visit some of the country's historical sites. That he had chosen match day would bear no significance, especially as the city having two league teams meant there was a game each Saturday throughout the football season.

Certain that the day would represent the first episode in a long and successful new career, Brandt had decided to keep his first act simple. In America they talk about a defendant needing means, motive and opportunity. By keeping it so simple, including the use of a generic steak knife, he had made it so that virtually every able-bodied adult could be seen to have the means to commit the crime.

In terms of motive there was absolutely none. In fact, Brandt would barely be able to describe his victim, much less have any link to them. For this was what he believed to be the single greatest factor in how he was going to escape detection. The randomness of his selection meant it neither fitted into the category of a crime of passion, nor did it suggest any real planning. As a consequence, the police's typical lines of enquiry would prove fruitless.

Opportunity had been dealt with by linking an entire train's worth of people with the crime. Brandt knew that they would be looking for someone on the 10:19 direct from Birmingham New Street, which arrived in Nottingham at 11:28. Their profiling would suggest a white male in his twenties or thirties with previous convictions for violence. Possible mental health issues. The police would start with CCTV footage, train ticket sales made by card, and they would probably ask for the parent club's assistance in matching these against their records of who had acquired tickets for the match. Brandt was willing to bet that, in any train full of ardent football fans, it was likely there would be a number of people who fitted the profile. The supposed simplicity of the investigation would prevent them noticing that one more person exited the station than went through the ticket gates.

It was not so much the pangs of hunger but the desire to get home and watch the news that prompted Brandt to leave the comfort of his bench. As he exited the castle grounds, he observed that the sky was becoming overcast and he could feel the temperature dropping. Yet nothing would spoil his mood as he made his way back to his car.

Much in the same way that the internet had proven useful in helping him establish which train would contain the bulk of the away fans, Brandt had used Google Maps to identify a residential street just outside town that was quiet enough not to have CCTV, but sufficiently busy that no one would consciously observe him parking. The width of Lenton Boulevard meant that cars could park on either side without disrupting the traffic. Brandt had stopped at the foot of one of the large horse chestnut trees that lined the road, making his movements even less noticeable.

Within a couple of minutes Brandt was on the A52, following signs back to the M1 motorway. He didn't tune into one of the local stations in case it would spoil the evening he would spend watching the various news channels on his large television. He had planned to indulge in a late lunch at Leicester Forest East Services but his impatience to return home outweighed the hunger now firmly rooted in his stomach.

Chapter Four

'What the fuck?!' Brandt cursed loudly from his armchair. He had arrived home just before 4pm and had made himself a quick sandwich to tide him over before the Chinese takeaway he intended ordering later. On the side table to his right stood a freshly opened bottle of his favourite whisky, a twelve-year-old Glenfiddich, already with a quarter of its contents gone. Having tuned his satellite box to the correct BBC channel for the East Midlands, he had happily sat through the national news knowing his actions would not yet merit this level of attention. However, when the local news started with the planning of a proposed wind farm near Loughborough, Brandt lost his patience.

'And that's the problem with this fucking country!' He shouted, berating the newsreader. He could not believe that the potential spoiling of the view for a few residents was deemed more important than the fatal stabbing of a woman by a gang of football hooligans. The truth was, though, he could well believe it. When he first started investigating murders it was big news, if not at a national level, certainly locally. He would be able to go home once his shift was finished and relive what had happened on television or read about it in the morning's newspaper. Nowadays, unless it was someone famous, involved children, or there was something particularly gruesome or perverse about it, barely a ripple was caused in the media.

Almost as though responding to Brandt's criticism the newsreader moved on. 'In other news, police are investigating the stabbing of a woman outside Nottingham train station just before midday. She was rushed to the Queen's Medical Centre and is thought to be in a critical condition.' After a brief pause she continued. 'With around sixty minutes gone Nottingham Forest are...'

'Is that it?!' Brandt switched off the television.

With prior thoughts of Szechwan beef and egg fried rice cast from his mind, he proceeded to work through the bottle of whisky in earnest. 'Heartless bitch!' he slurred at the blank screen. More than the mere two sentences afforded to what had happened, it was the monotone and passionless delivery by the newsreader that offended Brandt most. The more he thought of it, the more it reminded him of the way his wife had told him she was leaving almost three years before. The way she had said it – the tired, resigned delivery that morning over breakfast, devoid of any feeling – told him all he needed to know about his chances of convincing her otherwise. Rather than say anything, he had simply left for work only to find her, along with her personal items, gone when he returned. There had been little contact and none face-to-face since then; the ease of their parting after fifteen years uncomplicated by their lack of children.

Brandt knew it was their failure to successfully reproduce that had caused the most damage, even before the one message from her since which wasn't purely about money.

> – *It's not as though I didn't have offers. I gave you the best years of my life and you gave me nothing.*

They hadn't planned to have children straight after they got married but neither did they attempt to prevent it. It was only after a few years, and once all her friends of roughly the same age had families, that she convinced him they should see a doctor. Although the instinct was not as strong for Brandt, he was not averse to becoming a parent and, more than anything, he wanted his wife to be happy. He was sure any man would only be too pleased to have their sperm count come back as healthy, and was similarly relieved to hear that his wife was not suffering from any complications herself. They had been told to *just give it time* and to *not put pressure on themselves*. However, Brandt soon felt the pressure. The more often he received that accusing stare over breakfast following coming home too late from work the night before, falling asleep in his chair after too much whisky, or offering some kind of explanation why he wasn't in the mood, the less he wanted to make love. By then it had become a biological process anyway, devoid of passion. Any suggestion of foreplay was just there to get him to the stage where he could perform. With her lying motionless and silent beneath him he could sense her impatience when the task took longer than normal. The combination of the reducing number of occasions and the frequency with which Brandt was unable to finish, conspired to make the time that had still seemed so abundant when in their mid-thirties, run out.

There was nothing Brandt could do to correct that now. Sure, he was probably still able to father children but there was only one woman with whom he had wanted to start a family. Nevertheless, he was certain that he could fix the other problem that troubled him. What he intended to do was to shock England to its very core. He would make the people sit up and pay attention; they would no longer ignore or gloss over the darkness that blighted society.

As he neared the bottom of the bottle and could feel sleep washing over him, Brandt's thoughts turned to the girl. When he plunged the blade into her kidney it was with the intention of creating death. Despite his intoxicated state, he could recall the moment with vivid clarity. The sun glinting on her golden hair as it bounced on her shoulders and the way she indicated where she wanted the knife to go as she moved to counter the glancing impact of the person passing her on the left. Brandt had been surprised by the ease with which the knife entered her body, all the way to its hilt. He had detected the fragrance she had applied that morning and instantly decided the visceral brutality of twisting the knife to open up a hole would be unfitting of the beauty of the moment.

Closing his eyes, Brandt hoped that final decision would go on to save her life.

Chapter Five

Josh entered the interview room convinced he was in some form of nightmare from which he would soon awaken.

'Thank you for coming to help us with our investigations Mr Ramage,' Detective Chief Inspector Stella Johnson said, sitting down and gesturing for Josh to do the same. DCI Johnson was the same woman who had knocked on his front door a short while earlier and was leading the team investigating the stabbing of Sarah Donovan.

She was in her mid-thirties, athletic and sharply dressed in a trouser suit. With resources in the department stretched, owing to the number of lines of enquiry being pursued, she had been irritated to find even her newest detective, DC Hardy, unavailable. She punished DI Fisher's presumptuousness in allocating him a task without her permission, by having him go and get the duty sergeant to spare her an officer from uniform. PC McNeil was new to the force and Johnson had made it clear to him on the journey over that he was there merely to make up the numbers; his role simply to observe.

'Look, don't I need a lawyer or something?' Josh asked. Although not prone to claustrophobia, he found the grey room oppressive. He could feel beads of sweat forming on his brow.

'At this stage you are just helping us with our enquiries. You came here voluntarily and are free to leave at any point.' Johnson paused deliberately. 'But you can have a lawyer if you feel you *need* one.'

'Okay?' enquired McNeil.

Josh, staring at his hands, missed the swift glance of admonishment Johnson gave her colleague. 'I guess so,' he responded, lifting his head and interpreting McNeil's nod as one of reassurance. The truth was he felt far from okay. When he observed the police car from his sitting room window, followed by the knock at his door, he knew he was in trouble. Although the news report he had seen the previous evening, whilst waiting to watch the goals from the Forest match, had given very few clues as to the identity of the victim, he now understood it must have been Sarah. Given he barely knew her, much less had seen her recently, he was sure that their call was not for the purpose of informing him. In a state of panic, he had decided to pretend that what they were telling him had come as a complete shock.

Johnson took a long draught of coffee from the Styrofoam cup she had collected on the way through the police station. 'Can you start by telling us about your relationship with Miss Donovan?'

'Relationship?' asked Josh in a louder and shriller tone than he would have liked.

'Yes. Relationship,' repeated Johnson evenly.

'We weren't in a relationship.'

Johnson sighed and avoided the temptation to roll her eyes. 'Your relationship with Sarah… meaning how you know her.'

Josh paused. 'We went on a couple of dates a while back.'

'And?'

'And that's it.'

'Why did the relationship end, Josh?' Johnson was doing her utmost to keep her increasing exasperation with this man hidden. She had completed a quick background check before they collected him. He had a professional job with an accountancy firm, having graduated from the University of Nottingham a few years before. His profile suggested that he was far from unintelligent. Johnson was finding it hard not to take Josh's incomprehension as him being deliberately obtuse. She believed that the more likely culprit was one of the football fans but there was something about him that didn't add up.

After a long pause he responded. 'It just didn't work out.' He had decided on the ride into the police station that his best course of action was to say as little as possible.

He was mistaken.

Johnson rose from her chair and planted both hands firmly on the desk. Had McNeil not been so taken aback by the tirade that followed, he might have laughed. Josh, who had at least six inches on Johnson and approximately four stone, was physically cowering; his shaking causing the uneven chair leg to rattle on the floor.

'Time to stop fucking us around!' Johnson shouted, not minding in the least that some of her spittle had landed on Josh's face. She allowed her voice to drop a few decibels. 'If I ask you one more question and I don't get a full and frank answer, I am going to arrest you on suspicion of attempted murder and have you thrown in the cells until I build up the patience to listen to more of your bullshit. On your way down the corridor I'm going to have McNeil here conduct such a thorough search of you that he's going to be concerned he may lose his arm, given how deep he will check for contraband in your rectum.' Johnson allowed a pause to enjoy the look of horror on Josh's face. She sat down with a smile that did not reach her cold, piercing eyes. 'Now do we understand each other?' she added calmly.

'Yes,' murmured Josh feebly.

'Sorry, I didn't quite catch that?'

'Yes!' he cried in distress.

'Fine. So, where were we? Right. Why did the relationship end?' As Josh opened his mouth to speak, a quick raise of Johnson's index finger caused his voice to die in his throat. 'But before you answer, I'm going to ask PC McNeil to roll up his right sleeve to reveal how long and broad his forearm is.'

'I had started seeing someone else,' came the instant reply. He then hastily continued, having read in Johnson's eyes that she did not see this as sufficiently upholding his end of the bargain. 'When I first met Sarah, I had also started dating someone else and decided my prospects with them were better.'

'Did you have sexual intercourse with Miss Donovan?'

'I'm sorry?' Josh stammered, stunned.

'Don't make me repeat myself,' responded Johnson flatly, exaggerating the look she gave McNeil's bare arm that was now resting on the table.

'No, I didn't.'

'And did you have sexual intercourse with this other woman whilst you were dating Miss Donovan?'

'Excuse…' Josh didn't finish the question. Instead he gave a resigned sigh. 'Yes.'

'I see,' Johnson said, nodding. She did not add anything but remained motionless with a stony expression on her face.

'But that's not the reason I chose her,' continued Josh when he could bear the silence no longer. All he received in return was a raised eyebrow.

'And how did you break the news to Sarah?'

'Erm, I didn't.' Another raise of the eyebrow motioned for him to carry on. 'I… I just stood her up.'

Johnson smiled triumphantly. She had known exactly what had happened, having already seen the unanswered texts Sarah had sent Josh last November. She took his admission as an indication that her earlier performance had succeeded in making him compliant. She was so pleased with herself she didn't even mind when McNeil decided to brave another contribution. 'Real charmer with the ladies.'

'Okay, let's fast forward to today,' she continued. 'I don't think I need to ask about what happened with the other woman. However, do correct me if I am wrong in thinking that relationship ended recently.' She took his silence as confirmation her assumptions were accurate. 'You were in Nottingham city centre at just before midday?'

'Yes.'

'Why was that?'

'I had arranged to meet Sarah for coffee.'

'And did you meet with Sarah?' Johnson was pleased that the pace of the conversation had picked up considerably.

'No.'

'So, she stood you up. Payback was it?'

'Well, she didn't exactly stand me up.'

Johnson couldn't help but allow a laugh to escape. Even now, despite everything that had gone on in the last few minutes, Josh could not entirely abandon his pathetic male pride. Sarah's phone records had revealed that she had not responded to his invitation, even if her movements that morning suggested she was planning on meeting with him. Johnson decided now might be the time to try a bit of tag teaming. 'What do you make of all this then, McNeil?'

'Well, ma'am. I reckon Josh wouldn't like being stood up.'

Pleased with his response, she decided to continue. 'But Josh, here, says that she didn't *exactly* stand him up.'

'That's true, ma'am. So maybe when she didn't respond he decided he would go and see her. Take the initiative.'

It was with his mouth agape that Josh observed this exchange.

'Ah… but you see, McNeil,' she replied theatrically, 'Josh wouldn't have known that Sarah would have been on Carrington Street at that time.'

'Well, perhaps not the exact time, ma'am, but he would have known the location,' McNeil replied.

Clever boy thought Johnson. He hadn't even seen the messages from Sarah's phone. Johnson had read them to him on their way to pick up Josh, though as more of a means to remind herself of the key details, rather than to brief McNeil. It also meant he knew the area well if he understood Carrington Street to be the most direct route into the centre from where she lived.

'Can you confirm your whereabouts at approximately 11:45am yesterday?' Johnson asked Josh.

'I was most likely on Market Street on the way to the coffee shop.'

'So, nowhere near the station then?'

'No, it's the other side of town. I guess there must be CCTV there which can confirm it?'

'We'll see,' said Johnson standing up, again impressed that McNeil understood that he should too. 'Thank you for your time, Mr Ramage,' she smiled warmly.

'Am I free to go?' Josh asked, unable to hide his relief.

'As you always have been,' Johnson replied in a friendly manner, moving in the direction of the door. She stopped and turned. Josh shuddered as he witnessed her face become stony once more. 'Just one last thing.'

In the silence that followed Josh could hear his pulse throbbing in his head.

'When we told you what had happened to Miss Donovan…' Johnson's voice was barely above a whisper, '…why did you pretend that you didn't know?'

His mouth flapped open and closed. He was almost relieved to see her index finger rise once more to indicate he wasn't to speak.

'Tell you what, don't answer that now. I'm sure we'll be talking again soon.' She turned and opened the door. As she strode through she called over her shoulder, 'PC McNeil, would you be so kind as to show Mr Ramage out?'

When McNeil returned to the duty area, he couldn't hide his surprise when Johnson offered him a cup of coffee. She was pouring herself one from the percolator in the corner. He chose to decline, believing that he would be dismissed long before it would cool sufficiently for him to drink it comfortably. He would rather risk offence turning down the offer than demonstrate ingratitude by leaving the mug untouched.

'So, ma'am, do you fancy him for it then?'

'How about you?'

The ambiguity of her response didn't come as a surprise. 'Nah. He's too much of a pussy.' McNeil immediately regretted using a word most women, in his experience, took offence to.

'I entirely agree,' Johnson replied with a smile.

'So why did you sweat him so hard, ma'am?'

'His type makes me sick. What I suspected of him, having read his misogynistic and narcissistic messages to Sarah, was confirmed the moment he opened the door. He couldn't give a shit about what happened to her, only how it might inconvenience him. I bet he's never seen the inside of a police station and yet he walked in here thinking he could dick us around. That's why I gave him that little parting gift. I want him to think it's us back to arrest him every time he hears the doorbell.' Johnson gently shook her head. 'No. I want him to think it's us every time a car pulls up in the street.'

'Remind me not to get on the wrong side of you, ma'am,' McNeil said with a smile. When it was reciprocated, he noticed for the first time that, despite being fifteen years his senior, there was something quite attractive about DCI Stella Johnson.

Chapter Six

Brandt pulled up in his driveway and switched off the engine. He observed that the steam emanating from the plastic bag on his passenger seat had fogged up the side window and the section of windscreen immediately above it. The aroma in the car had been building throughout the short journey. Although reluctant to open the door and allow it to escape, Brandt wasted little time exiting his vehicle, so keen was he to get inside his house and reveal its contents.

He stood in the porch fumbling for the correct key with his head obscuring the beam from the automatic security light. The sudden ringing of the telephone from inside caused him to swear under his breath. Not concerned that he might miss it, his outburst was due to annoyance that someone wished to interrupt his carefully planned evening. Bet it's that prick Franklin, he thought. And yet a sigh of relief escaped him as he first selected and then slotted home the key. The warmth of his house met him as he pushed open the door.

Ignoring the continued ringing, he headed past the phone, shaking off his coat on the way. He did not mind in the least that it fell into a heap on the hallway floor, such was his keenness to get into the sitting room. In there was his familiar armchair with all three of the nest tables positioned around it. On the middle one was set out a plate and a selection of cutlery. He placed the bag on the table on the left and dashed into the kitchen to collect a beer from the fridge. He poured the amber liquid into the pint glass which he sat on the right.

Brandt switched on the television but paid little attention, such was his focus on the bag's contents. He chuckled to himself when he realised his order was far too large to fit on to the plate. He dished out just a spoonful from each container. Since his wife had left him, Brandt had become a frequent customer at his local Chinese takeaway. If asked, he was sure the owners would consider him a *regular* but neither they nor he had chosen to strike up a conversation. Today had been no different except for the wink Brandt received as he was being handed his freshly prepared order. Unsure whether to respond he had merely nodded, understanding that the owner had assumed the size of the meal implied he was expecting company.

Entertaining that evening could not have been further from Brandt's mind as he started working his way through the various dishes. For what he had planned, it was far more appropriate that he would be home with the curtains drawn. As he merrily listened to the national newsreader discuss the impact of the falling value of Sterling, he considered the contrast with how he had felt the week before.

Although he had yet to see what the regional news had made of his endeavours that day, he was confident he would not wake up tomorrow feeling cheated again. It wasn't so much that he had been unsuccessful in killing the girl, it was more the dispassionate way it was reported and how his resulting overindulgence of whisky had brought a premature end to what should have been an evening of celebration. As he had lain awake the next morning, his hangover doing nothing to lighten his mood, he had resolved that not only would he plan this next job so that it would have more impact, but he would also put more preparation into ensuring the evening that followed would be similarly enjoyable. That it had meant adjusting the timing of his actions so that the Chinese restaurant would be open on his return only made him laugh again, this time causing shards of prawn cracker to spray on the carpet. He very much doubted the police would consider that when trying to work out the motive behind the time of the attack.

With smug satisfaction joining the warmth that the food was bringing to his stomach, Brandt returned his focus to the television. England had drawn away from home in what the reporter had described as *a dour match*. Brandt knew he had only a few moments to spoon some more Chinese onto his plate before the national anchor would announce the switch to the regional news.

He took a long draught of his beer and his self-chastisement at not having the foresight to collect two from the fridge was interrupted by the same newsreader who had caused him so much disappointment the week before.

'Our main story tonight is the brutal killing of…'

In that instant Brandt knew that this might be the best night of his life.

Chapter Seven

'Say that again?' DCI Johnson demanded, grabbing DC Hardy by the shoulders.

'The lab report shows traces of Sarah Donovan's blood on the victim's shoulder, ma'am,' he replied nervously.

Johnson relaxed her grip and screwed up her face in an almost-comic look of confusion. 'What did you just tell me?'

'I called the lab when the email came through and the pathologist confirmed that there had been a swipe of blood on the jacket inconsistent with what had come from the wounds. He had first assumed it was the perpetrator wiping the blade following the stabbing, but it wasn't spread in the same way as it would if it were fresh.'

'I don't follow,' Johnson said absently, her brain already in a whir as it considered the ramifications of this discovery.

'Erm, well, ma'am, if it was fresh it would have been more of a smear, whereas the pathologist said this was more, er, sporadic. As though dried blood had been loosened with a bit of water and then wiped on the jacket.'

'Fuck me, just what we need at the moment with our case load, is a serial killer who thinks he's a clever dick,' murmured Johnson, who turned and paced down the corridor leaving DC Hardy stood there unsure what to do next.

* * *

'Wait a…' Detective Superintendent Potter did not have time to finish before Johnson burst into his office. He was about to admonish her for the interruption but could see by her face that it was important.

'Guv, it's the same one,' she blurted out.

Potter held up a hand to calm her. 'What is the same one, Stella?'

She shook her head in frustration, not with the DSI, but that her rush to get the information out had only created delay. 'The killer is the same perp as before.'

'What before?'

In a final effort to control herself she sat down. 'The stabbing of that mother yesterday was done by the same person who knifed Sarah Donovan last week.' Had DC Hardy been there, he would have noticed the same expression of incomprehension on DSI Potter's face as he had seen on Johnson's earlier.

She explained what had been sent through from the pathology lab, before moving on to highlight the similarities in the instances. The size and serration of the murder weapons were consistent, as was the location of the injuries on the victims.

'And it's not the man you arrested for the first one?' Potter asked as soon as she was finished.

'No, guv,' Johnson said. Although the man hadn't been charged, he had fitted the profile of the person they were looking for. He had been on the train that had arrived from Birmingham and had a history of violence towards women, including two stints in prison. What had made his presence in Nottingham particularly suspicious was that he was currently serving a football banning order, following his involvement in ugly scenes during his team's home match against Forest the previous season.

'How can you be so sure?' Potter asked.

'We didn't release him from custody until later that evening,' she added quietly.

'Oh Christ, who else knows about this?'

'Just you, me, and DC Hardy at the moment.'

'Right, let's keep it this way for now. Cut that bastard loose but don't make it seem like he's in the clear. We need to control this until we fully understand it.'

Johnson nodded. 'I had better go speak to Hardy.'

'Hold on. He's a good lad; he can wait a moment.' Silence ensued as Potter gave the situation some thought. 'Could it be the boyfriend?' he asked hopefully.

'I don't see the connection, but we'll check it out.'

'We need to control this,' Potter repeated, as much to himself as to Johnson. 'If this gets out there'll be panic.'

'And that's not the worst bit, guv.' Observing his raised eyebrow, she continued. 'He wanted us to make the connection...'

Chapter Eight

'I don't know why you're looking so sad, it's your fault.' Brandt snorted at the newsreader, laughing. Oblivious to his accusations, she was explaining that the two young children were staying with their grandparents in another part of the country. 'I had to pick her, otherwise you would have dismissed it like the other one.' He raised his glass in a toast. 'Well I hope you're happy now!'

The repetitive nature of the news reports that Saturday evening had caused Brandt to lose interest in the channel quicker than he had imagined, but he did check back occasionally to keep abreast of developments.

Although the victim had been named within a few hours, a photograph was not released until the police press conference on Sunday afternoon. Back in his comfy armchair, he paused the television so he could study the features of the woman. The photo did reveal some of her beauty, but it paled in comparison to how she had looked in the flesh. Brandt cast his mind back to the previous day. This time he had identified his target as she walked towards him. She failed to pay him any attention even though he was the only other person in the alleyway that led from the housing development to some green space, presumably on the way back from the park. She had been preoccupied with encouraging her eldest child not to run his fingers along the wooden fences as she pushed the double buggy along. This had allowed Brandt more time to take in her features. As the gap between them closed he could see that the light makeup she wore had been hastily applied. He mused that its imperfectness only served to highlight the flawlessness of her face. When she absentmindedly twitched her head in an effort to move the ringlet of auburn hair that obscured her vision, he first glimpsed the deep blue of her eyes.

With less than twenty feet between them he put his hands into his pockets. His right instantly felt the comfort of the knife's handle beneath the glove and his left grasped the small bottle of spectacles cleaner. Brandt did not wear glasses and had bought the spray specifically for this purpose. He withdrew the items and swiftly moved them behind his back. A smile formed at the corners of his mouth as he considered the conclusions the police would jump to when they discovered the presence of this liquid on the woman. Brandt gave the blade two quick squirts of the solution on each side and then put the bottle in his rear trouser pocket.

He never glanced down at the children as he drew alongside the front of the pushchair. His right hand was already lifting towards her upper arm and, slowing his pace a fraction, he wiped the flat of his blade against her jacket. The pressure he applied was sufficient to make her look over her shoulder and up towards him. Their eyes locked and he paused for an instant, enjoying this moment of tenderness before plunging the knife into her side. He barely allowed it to ram home before withdrawing and stabbing a further three times. Each occasion causing her eyes to widen further with shock.

As her legs collapsed from under her, Brandt had to restrain himself from attempting to catch her, such was the synergy he felt with this woman. The spell of their encounter was broken when her head bounced violently off the fence and Brandt heard himself whistle tunelessly as he walked away.

With the photo on the television screen causing him to relive the events in such vivid detail, Brandt could feel a stirring within, unfamiliar to him for so long. Initially surprised by his arousal, he rationalised it as perfectly understandable given the moment of deep intimacy he and the woman had shared.

Brandt sat motionless for a time, wondering whether to acquiesce to his urge. Using his remote control to pause the screen, he gazed at the image, curious to find that it was not the man sat on the platform who was disturbing him. He was DSI Potter, someone he had met on occasion whilst still in the force. In contrast to the familiar sight of the balding middle-aged man, the person sat next to him was youthful, if not young, athletic and with long golden hair. He could almost believe it to be the woman from his visit to Nottingham train station were it not for the name plate indicating she was one of the leading officers. In fact, any similarity to what he had seen of the woman the previous week would only heighten his stimulation. DCI Johnson's face, although far from unattractive, possessed a harshness about it. Combined with her piercing eyes it served only to unsettle him.

He decided to resume the broadcast, hoping that moving it on a few moments would see an appropriate change in her expression. But as Potter proceeded with his standard spiel about lines of enquiry, DCI Johnson's stare continued to bore into him.

Distressed by the feeling of being watched, Brandt turned off the television. Without the inspiration of the photograph he realised that any yearning had now passed. Instead he got up to retrieve the whisky bottle from the drinks cabinet. He poured himself a generous measure and sat back down to contemplate the specifics of his next *job*.

Chapter Nine

'I don't understand.' Sarah winced as she attempted to sit up.

'Please don't stretch yourself,' PC McNeil protested, glancing anxiously at the door. 'As I said, it's just a precaution.'

'But the doctor said I may be able to go home in a few days. It makes no sense to move hospitals.' Her mind suddenly cleared a little. 'You said *precaution*. Precaution against what?'

McNeil shifted his weight from one foot to the other. 'We just think you would be safer that way.' He could see tears welling in Sarah's eyes. He had always considered himself a hard person and his family had been far from surprised when he entered the force. Although he had been in more challenging situations before, including informing people that their loved one had died, there was something about this case that resonated with him.

'But I already have a policeman outside my door all the time; surely that gives me enough protection?' Sarah was almost pleading.

'I know but…' Suddenly McNeil's phone rang. He was relieved by the interruption. 'Please excuse me,' he said, stepping outside the room.

'McNeil? It's DCI Johnson,' came the voice on the other end of the line.

'Oh, hello, ma'am,' he replied, trying to conceal his shock at her calling him directly.

'You're at the hospital, yes?'

'Yes, seeing Sarah Donovan. I was…'

'Have you told her yet?' Johnson interrupted.

'Well, I was sort of telling her when you called.' McNeil didn't really know why he felt nervous.

'Right, well go and explain that you're mistaken and there is nothing to worry about.'

'But, ma'am…'

'Concerned for your precious ego?' Ordinarily McNeil would have been offended but he could hear a playful tone entering Johnson's voice.

'No, I just wanted to know why.'

'You don't need to know, *Police Constable* McNeil.' Again, harsh but still playful.

McNeil decided to push his luck. 'Is it because you've caught him?'

His question was met with laughter. 'Afraid not. Quite the opposite in fact.'

McNeil paused for a few moments. 'Ah, I see,' he responded.

'Do you?' The playfulness had gone.

'Well, I think there are only three possible reasons for the change in plan. You've just ruled out the first. The second would be to save resources but it's not that either.' He deliberately paused.

'And why not?'

'Because someone else would be calling. Someone… *lesser.*' McNeil could almost hear the smile at the other end of the line. He smiled himself, thinking it was only a few moments ago that it was her who was making accusations regarding people's egos.

'Go on then McNeil, impress me with your acumen.'

'You don't want her to be safe.'

'That's a terrible thing to say.'

McNeil paused, worried. If misinterpreted, his last comment could be seen as gross insubordination. His instincts told him to apologise and to qualify what he had said. It wasn't as though he had a problem with authority; as an ambitious young officer he fully embraced that he would need to do his fair share of brown-nosing to get on in the force. But he sensed that wouldn't work with Johnson. Any respect he had gained in their short time together had been a result of him being bold.

In for a penny, in for a pound he concluded. 'You want to use her as bait. You think the killer will come back to finish the job.'

The silence that followed was oppressive.

'PC McNeil, you are to report to my office the moment you return to the station.'

The line went dead.

Chapter Ten

As McNeil arrived back at base, he realised that he didn't technically know where DCI Johnson's office was. The building had three floors and, until now, he had yet to venture to the Criminal Investigation Department at the top.

'McNeil, over here!' The duty sergeant that day was a grizzly veteran of twenty-five years' service called Bob Andrews. Happy to consider himself old school, his uniform was always freshly pressed, and he took pride in polishing his shoes each morning. The other officers had a tremendous respect for him despite his unwillingness to socialise out of hours.

'Yes sir?'

'I need you to take a run over to the city centre. One of the shop owners thinks he had an attempted break in last night.' Andrews had yet to make eye contact, instead diligently filling in his logbook.

'I'm sorry, sir, I've been requested upstairs.'

Andrews carried on writing until he finished his sentence. He placed his ballpoint pen neatly on the desk and then looked up at McNeil with a smile. 'Does the DCI want her plaything back?' It was Andrews whom DI Fisher had come to see in order to find someone from uniform to accompany Johnson.

McNeil wondered whether he already knew of her alterations to the arrangements for Sarah Donovan's protection. 'As it happens Sarge, it is her that I am going to see.'

Andrews leaned forward, his voice now hushed despite no one being in close proximity: 'Just be careful McNeil, you're a promising young officer and I don't want to see you get into any difficulties.'

'Sir?'

'Let's just say they're awfully stretched up there, what with that madman running around. When CID gets stretched, they get stressed. When they get stressed they are more likely to make mistakes. Plain clothes think they're better than us and it's an illusion they wish to maintain.' His voice was nearly a whisper now. 'Just make sure that if things go tits up, they're not able to make you their scapegoat.' And with that the duty sergeant picked up his pen and started writing again.

'Thanks, sir,' McNeil replied before making his way to the staircase. The truth was he felt anything but grateful for the advice he had just received. The apprehension he held that he was getting into something over his head had seemingly been confirmed. He tried to dismiss it as inter-force rivalry. He didn't really understand people like Andrews. Clearly more than competent, he had chosen not to move into CID. To McNeil it was like a talented footballer refusing to move to a Premiership club. He saw it as a natural progression for his career and welcomed that his association with DCI Johnson might bring it about far quicker than he had ever hoped.

Feeling a little more confident, he took the final flight of stairs two at a time, only to be dismayed to find that the keypad to the door didn't accept the code he used for the rest of the station. Having pressed the buzzer, he moved anxiously from one foot to the other, waiting for a reply.

When none was forthcoming, he apprehensively pressed it again. Almost instantly he heard a shout from the other side of the room: 'For fuck's sake, Hardy, you lazy berk, see who that is.'

Moments later the door opened, and McNeil was met by a detective in a cheap suit, looking not much older that he was. 'Yes?' Came the impatient enquiry.

'I'm here to see DCI Johnson.'

'And you are?'

'Never mind introductions, get back on the blower!' It was the voice who had instructed DC Hardy to answer the door, and belonged to DI Fisher, a tall man who had recently started shaving his head in order to disguise the natural baldness that had developed since he had hit forty.

'Yes, guv,' Hardy responded, rolling his eyes good naturedly.

'Think you can find your own way sweetheart?' Fisher called across to McNeil sarcastically.

Taking this to mean he was invited to enter, he stepped through the door and proceeded to scan the area. Most of the space was open plan and housed a number of desks, all with their own computer and telephone. Very few were occupied and none of the people looked up at the visitor. He headed for the closed off rooms at the back and saw Johnson's name engraved on a metal plate on one of the doors.

He was about to knock when he was startled by a voice directly behind him. 'McNeil, what are you doing standing around?'

'Er, I just got here, ma'am.'

'Perfect timing, I've just been with the DSI.' She rolled her eyes, in an uncanny copy of Hardy's, moments before. 'Head on in, there's something I need to discuss with you.'

When he opened the door, he was met with a plain but tidy room consisting mainly of a desk with a high-backed chair on one side and two smaller seats on the other. Johnson pushed past him and sat down elegantly, adjusting her skirt as she did so. He took the right hand of those opposite and observed that the only thing on the desk, aside from the obligatory computer, was a silver photo frame; its contents pointed at Johnson.

'Nosey, are we?' She had caught him looking. Before he could answer, she turned the frame around to reveal a small boy in a school uniform of a purple jumper and grey shorts. His blonde hair and prominent cheekbones closely resembled Johnson's.

'Your son?'

Johnson let out a sudden burst of laughter. 'My nephew,' she said. McNeil hoped that she didn't notice his smile that greeted her reply. He briefly wondered whether she had intended this exchange from the moment he noticed the frame.

'How did she take it?'

McNeil was instantly shaken from his thoughts. Assuming Johnson was referring to his conversation at the hospital he replied: 'Fine. To be honest she seemed quite relieved.'

'When do you think she'll be released?'

'Friday at the latest.'

'I see.' Johnson leaned forward on her desk. 'What I am about to tell you is to remain strictly between us. Only you, me, and the DSI are aware. And he wasn't exactly thrilled by the idea.'

McNeil wanted to find out more about the DSI's reaction but didn't think Johnson would welcome the interruption.

'So, this is, sort of, off the books. Officially unofficial, if you like. You okay with that?'

'Sure,' he lied.

'Good. I need you to be my man on the ground. We can't have CID there as it'll look like overkill and we don't want to unsettle Sarah.'

'She's been through enough already,' McNeil said sincerely.

'Yeah,' replied Johnson, dismissively. 'I'm going to give you my mobile number and you call me if you spot anything suspicious. I don't care whether it's a dog taking a dump; if it looks odd, you call me. Understood?'

'Yes, ma'am, but we're going to be terribly short of manpower out there if something goes down. Standard procedure just has one car maintaining surveillance. There's also the added complication of her living in a block of flats. The number of people coming and going...'

'That's why I picked you,' she interrupted.

'Ma'am?'

'That's the closest to a compliment you're going to get from me. For now. Help me catch that bastard and I'll make sure you get a desk up here. But for now, you follow my instructions without hesitation. Deal?'

'Deal.' As the implication of Johnson's offer sank in, McNeil noticed his excitement was tinged with a sense of unease. 'Do you really think he's going to go after her?'

'I think there's a chance and, to be honest, we've got sod all else to go on at the moment. He's arrogant and he's enjoying himself. He wanted us to make the connection between the attacks, which means he wants us to chase him. He thinks he's invincible so what better way to show it than to finish off what he started. Right under our noses.'

Chapter Eleven

Brandt was singing.

He had never liked listening to the radio and failed to understand why it was so popular. Why would you spend your time hearing a bunch of songs you didn't like on the off chance something might be played that was bearable? Worst of all was those annoyingly cheerful DJs, so stuck for something to say, they invited contributions from dim-witted listeners who had nothing better to do than to call in and share their inane anecdotes. The only time he tended to switch on the radio was to listen to the news, and for that he deliberately selected a station which didn't play music at all.

But today was an exception. Today he was in a good mood. As soon as he turned on the ignition, he had surfed through the pre-programmed stations on the car's stereo and had quickly settled on Radio 2. Most of what was being played was modern stuff he didn't recognise but currently it was David Bowie's *Let's Dance*. Having never bought a Bowie track in his life, he was surprised to find how many of the words he knew. For those he didn't, he was quite happy to mumble his way along until the chorus came around. His singing continued with the next song:

Lady In Red. It was one of his ex-wife's favourites but even that didn't bother him. She had loved *Stars In Their Eyes*, an irritating 1990s so-called talent competition where people got made over to supposedly look like the artist they were going to attempt to perform as. Soon after they had started dating, he remembered her crying when the real Chris De Burgh surprised some loser in the middle of the song and turned it into a duet. However, he doubted if his bitch of a wife or if any of the morons who watched it were hearing the lyrics in the same way he did today:

The lady in red is dancing with me, cheek to cheek
There's nobody here, it's just you and me
It's where I want to be
But I hardly know this beauty by my side
I'll never forget the way you look tonight

Brandt could feel tears forming and decided to pull into the next service station. He was currently wearing his typical post-retirement outfit of a jumper and chinos so that any of his nosey neighbours would think he was off to a museum or visiting a friend. Going back to the scene of a previous crime would require a disguise, especially because he was intending reaching Nottingham by train. He felt it was prudent not to arrive by car for a third time, but public transport was not without its own risks. To minimise these, he would start his rail journey at nearby Loughborough, hoping that there would be plenty of other people making the relatively short trip in on a Saturday to go shopping. He would be wearing a hat with a brim to obscure his face from CCTV and would park in a residential street near to the station. That way, if for some reason someone did decide to track his movements, they would assume he had walked to the station from his house.

Watford Gap services had received something of a makeover since his last visit a number of years ago. Originally planning to get changed swiftly in one of the toilet cubicles, he stopped off at Costa for some coffee and cake first. He had no set time for where he needed to be and, in some respects, the later it was, the fewer people would be around to witness it.

He settled into one of the café's soft armchairs to read a complimentary newspaper whilst waiting for his drink to cool. The front page was devoted to a scandal regarding a Premier League footballer. He mused that if someone having sex with a stripper merited top billing then surely it wouldn't be long until he was the main headline. *Today might be the day*, he chuckled to himself whilst taking a bite of his millionaire's shortbread.

Brandt wondered what Sarah was doing at this exact moment. She was rarely far from his thoughts. They say you never forget your first love and, whilst he saw the parallels, it reminded him more of when he lost his virginity. It was a moment he felt he had been building up to his whole life and was as thrilling as he had hoped, even if in reality it was rather clumsy. From what he had gathered from the various news reports, she typically walked to town on a Saturday morning to visit the shops. He very much doubted she would be doing that today. The website of a local newspaper had informed him of her release from hospital and, in their usual intrusive style, had photographed her being helped out of the car close to where she lived. Brandt used to despise the press and it was always the locals who angered him the most. You could usually keep the nationals on a leash by feeding them just enough information to satisfy them, with the threat that the flow of information would dry up entirely if they printed something that might jeopardise the investigation. But the local hacks didn't give a shit about protocols or trying to form a workable relationship. All they cared about was finding a career defining story; a break that would pave their way to the nationals. Now, though, he was finding their indiscretion advantageous.

Brandt was feeling a little self-conscious as he emerged from the public toilets, but his new clothes made up for the psychological discomfort with how they felt on his body. Since his wife left, he had consciously dressed to give the impression he was doing well for himself. He had even upgraded his suits from his usual supermarket items to those from designers with foreign names he could not begin to pronounce. Not that he actually needed a smart casual wardrobe since the endless dinner parties that punctuated his marriage had instantly dried up. He tucked his plain black polo shirt, with small contrasting-red symbol where the breast pocket should be, into his jeans. With the early spring temperature relatively high on that Saturday, he had forgone a jacket in favour of a vest underneath.

As he stepped outside into the sunlight and carefully placed on his head a baseball cap he had picked up at the last minute from a charity shop near home, he could feel the buzz of the caffeine working through his system. Much as he welcomed the extra sharpness he felt it was giving to his senses, he knew this was a pale imitation of the thrill that was only a short time away. He wondered how the dump of adrenaline would feel to DCI Johnson when she was informed of his latest exploits. Whereas some colleagues used to feel sick when something big went down, others, like him, were energised. He realised that he had become addicted to it but the highs he was chasing now were a lot greater. Having spent a career being reactive to the actions of others, he was now forging his own, spectacular trail.

Chapter Twelve

'You coming down the Cross Keys tonight?' PC Strachan asked, whilst attempting to stretch away the numbness in her limbs within the confines of the unmarked Vauxhall Insignia. The Cross Keys was one of the more traditional pubs in the city centre and had plenty of space. They found it an ideal meeting point on a Saturday night; appealing to officers of all ages. With a few drinks inside them they usually split into smaller groups, depending on where they wanted to finish the night.

'Should be good,' she continued, without waiting for a response. 'Some are talking about heading on to Gatecrasher later because that DJ is in town tonight.'

'Yeah, probably,' McNeil responded absently, without knowing who she was referring to. He was busy trying to concentrate on what was outside the windscreen but with lots of things going on, and yet nothing specific, he was finding it hard.

They had arrived at 8am, replacing the squad car that had been there overnight. The parking space had an uninterrupted line of sight to the entrance to Sarah Donovan's block, along with a good view of the general surroundings. Having stopped for a drive-thru

McDonald's breakfast en route, the first hour or so had passed quite pleasantly and the scene had remained quiet until the residents started heading out.

'I don't mind shifts like these,' Strachan said. 'It's kind of like getting paid for sitting around and having a chat. Which is probably what I would be doing this afternoon anyway if I was off duty. Except my mum is way more talkative than you and our sofa is way more comfortable than these seats.'

McNeil did not dislike Strachan; they had even shared a drunken snog a few Saturdays ago. McNeil had thought it might go further but, when she was struggling to walk as they attempted to switch nightclub, he convinced one of the other female officers that it was probably best if they took her home. Nothing had been said since, but McNeil wondered whether her talk of going out tonight was with a view to continuing where they had left off.

Regardless, McNeil very much doubted he would be seeing Strachan tonight; promise of a drunken fumble or not. He hoped to be spending his evening with Johnson. If the day proved successful, it would probably be back at the station amid a flurry of paperwork and interviews. He fully intended being there, if for no other reason than for her to keep him in her mind given what she had said about providing his career a leg up. If the killer didn't turn up, as was looking increasingly likely, he would suggest they drown their sorrows together. He intended sounding sufficiently casual so that any reluctance on her part would not make things awkward in the future.

He had only spoken to Johnson once so far that day. Strachan had gone to use the toilet at the nearby pub, and no doubt to smoke a crafty fag, and he took the opportunity to provide her with an update. Their conversation was brief, and she was clearly irritated, although whether it was because he had disturbed her unnecessarily or she was frustrated with the lack of news, he couldn't tell.

Chapter Thirteen

He anxiously pulled the baseball cap a little further down at the front. He doubted that anyone would recognise him, but it paid to be cautious. He knew what he was doing was risky. There was every chance Sarah wouldn't open the door to him or, worse still, she would have visitors. Her parents maybe. He felt confident he could deal with whatever situation arose, but he didn't like uncertainty.

At the last moment he had decided to pick up some flowers at the railway station. Although carrying them would draw more attention, he believed it would back up his explanation for being there – should someone ask.

Crossing the River Trent, he could see the block of flats matching the address he had for Sarah. He could feel the mixture of nerves and excitement build as more adrenaline was dumped into his system. This was different to his previous encounters with women. He wasn't used to doing the chasing, merely reacting to those who were in the right place at the right time. It certainly raised the stakes, but Sarah had never been far from his mind since that Saturday a couple of weeks ago. One way or another, this would bring some form of resolution.

As he crossed the car park, he sped up a little. Pausing at the entrance door, he read the labels on the different buttons. None had the names of their occupants, but he knew that Sarah was in Apartment 84; top floor. His hand moved to press the buzzer but stopped just short. What would he say? *Oh, hello Sarah, I'm really sorry about what happened. I bought you some flowers…* Not likely. He stepped back rethinking the whole thing. It wasn't too late to back out; not too late to go home.

His indecision was interrupted when he heard the door's latch click. A multitude of thoughts crossed his mind in that instant. *What if it is Sarah? What would I do? Do I have time to run away or will I have to confront her?* As the door opened, he was startled to see a small dog emerge. It did not even glance in his direction, so keen was it to be out in the open. At the other end of the lead was a plump middle-aged woman.

'Calm down, Pickles,' she said good-naturedly, giving a gentle yank back on the lead. She was holding the door open.

Stood there, awkwardly clutching the bunch of flowers, he felt he had little choice but to enter. He reassured himself that he would just wait a minute for the woman and her dog to go and he could exit again. He could just ditch the flowers here and head for home.

Whether it was their cost, the effort he had gone to in order to get there, or the effect failure would have on his ego, he used his last shred of courage to press the button for the lift.

Chapter Fourteen

'Isn't that sweet?' Strachan said, pointing.

'Must be feeling guilty for something,' McNeil replied grumpily.

'It will be something lovely,' she continued, ignoring his comment. 'Perhaps he and his wife found out she was pregnant.'

'No, he looks nervous.'

'Becoming a parent is quite a…'

'Shut up!' McNeil shouted abruptly, reaching for his phone. He hit the redial button. He heard the ringing tone just once.

'Yes?'

'Ma'am, I might have something.'

'I want you to describe everything.' Her voice was calm and controlled.

'There's man with a bunch of flowers stopped by the main entrance. He's looking around nervously.'

'Delivery guy?'

'No, no van. On foot.'

'What does he look like?'

'Hard to tell, he's wearing a cap. Erm, he has blue jeans and a black hoodie. Hold on, he's reaching out for one of the buzzers. Wait. He hasn't pressed it. He's just looking around again.'

'Man with a hoodie, cap and flowers,' McNeil heard Johnson repeating quietly. 'Go, go, go!' He instantly realised she wasn't talking to him but, instead, relaying orders. Her voice returned to normal volume. 'Backup is one minute away. What's he doing now?'

'He's still just stood there looking around. Hold on, he's stepping away.'

'Don't lose him!'

'No, someone's coming out… Ah, shit! She's holding it open for him. I'm going in!'

'Don't! Wait for backup!' But McNeil didn't hear the order. He was already opening the door, not caring that it slammed the side of the car next to him.

'Madam, wait there!' He shouted across the car park at the resident who had emerged from the building. He knew he would have little chance of breaking down the door. She either hadn't heard him or didn't think he was calling to her.

'Police! Stop right there!' He bellowed this time. It had the desired effect. The woman froze on the spot and the lead to her dog dropped to the floor. Moments later her hands rose in the air in what, under less serious circumstances, McNeil might have found comic.

He had closed half the distance to her, and was about to issue the instruction to return to the door, when a screech of tires distracted him. He turned in the direction of the noise just in time to see an unremarkable white van bearing down on him.

McNeil's brain was screaming at him to leap to the side, but his legs would not obey. The screeching began again as the van locked its tyres under braking. He closed his eyes waiting for the inevitable.

When it didn't come, he opened them again and looked up through the windscreen, into the equally terrified face of the driver. Before he could think what to do next he heard the side door slide open.

'Go, go, go!' came the command from within. Out leapt three male and one female specialist firearms officers. They were dressed in blue overalls with body armour and helmets, both made from Kevlar. None of them looked in his direction, instead heading straight for the entrance to the flats in parallel pairs, their Heckler and Kock MP5 carbines sweeping in front of them.

As McNeil started to follow, he was overtaken by another officer who was hefting a long metal cylinder with handles, known in the police as The Big Red Key. The man had barely stopped in front of the door before making a short back-swing with the object and then thrusting it at the lock. Despite the loud crack, the door remained shut.

'Again!' Shouted the commanding officer next to him. This time a longer swing had the desired effect and, in a crash of metal and plastic, the door gave way. 'Go, go, go!' Came the familiar order and the four officers with MP5s filed in, heading for the stairs. Although breathing heavily following his exertion, the fifth dropped the battering ram, drew his Glock 17 self-loading pistol and followed.

McNeil listened to the thunder of feet in the stairwell and glanced at the lift doors. The electronic number above them moved from six to seven, before finally resting on eight. A feeling of dread swept over him as he imagined the doors opening and the man heading for Sarah Donovan's flat. Yes, he would be caught, of that McNeil was certain. But would they get to him before he got to Sarah?

As he headed for the stairs McNeil was disgusted to find that his thoughts were moving away from what might be happening to Sarah and to what would happen to him when it was over. Far from being celebrated for helping catch the killer, serious questions would be raised regarding his professional judgement. Sure, he was only there because of orders from above, but the fact remained that he was the man on the ground and he had not stopped the suspect, despite spotting him long before he entered the apartment block. What's more he had a suspicion that DCI Johnson would gladly use him as a scapegoat, as Sergeant Andrews had warned, if it prevented any of the shit for this being chucked in her direction.

Now a third of the way up, he heard the door at the top being flung open. Wondering how long it would be before there were any shots, the first he would have witnessed on active duty, McNeil reached for the phone he had stuffed in his top pocket whilst getting out of the car. He nearly tripped as he glanced down at the display and was surprised to see that the connection to Johnson had not been severed.

'Ma'am?' McNeil called in the direction of the microphone. He jammed the device to his left ear whilst using his right hand on the banister to pull himself up the stairs quicker. He did not receive a response. As he rounded the penultimate flight of stairs, he heard shouts, muffled by the fire door which had now self-closed.

As McNeil burst through, his first sight was the fifth officer turning around and levelling his pistol at his chest. For one sickening moment, he thought he was going to be shot, sure he could see the pressure of the man's index finger being applied to the trigger. Their eyes locked and McNeil was relieved to see recognition dawn. The gun lowered.

'Down on your knees!' Both McNeil and the officer turned to the owner of the voice, but his back was to them. 'Hands behind your head!'

He moved his position to get a better look at where the commands were being directed, whilst remaining conscious not to draw any more unwanted attention to himself. Between the tangle of legs, he could see flowers strewn across the hallway and an officer crouched, cuffing the man he had seen walk across the car park.

Chapter Fifteen

Brandt exited the ticket barrier knowing that if he looked up beyond the peak of his cap, he would be faced with a number of CCTV cameras, even more than would have tracked his progress from when he got off the train. If he needed any more reassurance that his choice of outfit had been correct, he noticed that the young man stood at the florist stall looked remarkably similar. It seemed that a hoodie and jeans was the default clothing for the male weekend shopper and the wearing of some form of hat was far from unusual.

Although his destination was to the left, Brandt turned right as he emerged from the station. Should anyone choose to look at the footage from that afternoon, he wanted to be eliminated as someone heading for the shops rather than the river. He deliberately passed the spot where he had stabbed Sarah Donovan and it took him all his willpower not to slow his pace. He would have loved to linger there for a while and relive that tremendous moment of a couple of weeks ago. Instead, he gazed at the Broadmarsh Centre in front of him.

Ordinarily the thought of going shopping with so many people on a Saturday would be horrifying, but today the anonymity it gave him was welcome. He kept the leisurely pace of those around him and pretended to glance at the various window displays. Although he saw nothing that remotely interested him, Brandt was satisfied he had played the part sufficiently well as he started heading away from the busiest parts. He moved along some narrower streets, looking to pick up the main A60 road and start heading in the correct direction for his adventure that afternoon.

It was not long before Brandt found himself crossing back over the railway and at the next junction he could see Hooters: a bar and restaurant from America where the waitresses wore tight tops and skimpy shorts. Much as he thought he would enjoy the view inside, what he hoped awaited him further on would be a far more intimate experience. He quite liked Nottingham and was sad to think this would probably be his last visit. Naturally it held happy memories for him, but it was also the area itself he liked. It didn't have the intimidating size of London but retained that impersonal quality where it felt you could go about your business without anyone paying attention. Similarly, one minute you could be on a packed city street full of shoppers and a few minutes later be somewhere quiet and discreet.

Whereas his two previous encounters had been meticulously planned, right down to the very spot where he would complete his task, he had only settled on a general area for this one. He did not believe it to be the trap of complacency that serial killers sometimes fell into once they thought they were too smart to get caught. On the contrary, Brandt knew that the police would be looking for meaning; for patterns. They would be trying to understand the thought process behind the specific location and would be developing all kinds of hypotheses. He was certain that this latest act would all but convince them he was a resident of Nottingham. They would be marking the three locations on a map and would be trying to work out the region in which he lived. That he knew he was heading in the general direction of Sarah's place only helped reinforce it. They may well come to the conclusion that he had followed her from her home and decided to stab her once there were sufficient people around at the station.

Deep in thought, Brandt didn't even notice the white van that sped past him, even though the draught of wind almost dislodged his hat. As the gradient of the road increased in order to cross the river, Nottingham Forest's football stadium loomed large on his right. Further along the road he could make out some of the floodlights from Trent Bridge cricket ground. There weren't any matches scheduled at either venue, but he was concerned that there might be increased CCTV if he should continue any further.

He stopped on the bridge and surveyed the area around him. As he looked south, away from the City Ground, he contemplated detouring onto the path running along the river. This would mean he would be away from the traffic and, having selected an appropriate candidate, he could wait until the way was clear in both directions. It troubled him slightly that the river was overlooked, not least by the nearby apartment blocks, but he might find a spot further along where their view was obscured.

Brandt took out his phone and brought up the now familiar Google map of Nottingham. He saw that the river meandered, and he wanted to make sure that it wouldn't take him so far away from the station that he may be forced to double back on himself. He knew from experience that, unless given sufficient cause to, people would rarely even register passing someone once. However, some sort of impression would be left on their memory because, should they encounter that person again within a short space of time, it tended to leave an imprint.

He worked out that he would need to follow it for about a mile before there was a tree-lined route that would lead him pretty much straight back to the station. Satisfied that a mile should give him sufficient opportunity, he started down the path to the riverside. Believing fate to be with him, he was delighted to see a blonde woman, walking a pug, emerge from under the bridge and end up in front of him just a few feet ahead.

His early years as a detective had taught him how to follow people discretely without drawing attention to himself. Approximating that he had twenty minutes until his turn off, Brandt felt quite relaxed as he set a gap of around ten metres between him and the woman. His only real concern was what would happen if the dog decided to stop, perhaps needing to empty its bowels. He figured that if that happened in a sufficiently secluded spot he would just have to get on with his task. But he did not want that. This was to be his decision. His timing. It was to be on his terms, not a fucking dog's!

Acknowledging that his mood was darkening unnecessarily, Brandt tried to stop his train of thought and focus purely on the woman ahead. The whole purpose of this exercise had been to enable him to enjoy the moment more. He was not going to allow concerns about things he couldn't control spoil that. Although he had only caught the merest glimpse of the woman's face as she had emerged from under the bridge, he knew straight away that she was beautiful. The way her hair was now glinting in the sunlight and bounced in time to the movements of her slim but curvaceous body, seemed to confirm this to Brandt. He had never pigeon-holed himself as favouring a particular hair colour, but he was sure a woman such as this could turn him towards blondes.

Almost as though drawn by the intensity of his thoughts, the woman glanced behind her. It was brief; fleeting even, and her gaze never even made it as far as Brandt. He knew, ultimately, that this was a good thing but a part of him regretted being denied the intimacy it would have brought.

Nevertheless, he had seen enough to confirm that fate was on his side. This was his calling; this was what he was meant to do. His whole life, even his two previous acts in Nottingham, had merely served to bring him to this point. Despite being brought up in a Catholic household, his family's religion had not rubbed off on Brandt. His time in the police had only served to solidify the feeling that such acts of violence and depravity as he witnessed almost on a daily basis, demonstrated that either God didn't exist or was not the sort of god Brandt could love. But now, today, on this river path in Nottingham, he had something of an epiphany.

Brandt had always seen death as destructive but now viewed it as quite the opposite. This woman presumably led a mundane life and her impact, however positive, would only have been on those immediately around her. What Brandt was just about to do would spread her influence far and wide. The media coverage this would undoubtedly provoke was Brandt's gift to the world. Her face would be everywhere; her beauty distributed for all to enjoy. Her life would be eulogised by those who knew her and, perhaps, even by many who didn't. Her funeral would be far better attended than she ever could have expected. This outpouring of love was his gift to her; the reward for her sacrifice. And to Brandt's mind, it was a sacrifice worth paying many times over. In the city of Nottingham in particular, but all over the country, loved ones would hold each other a little closer tonight. Less would be taken for granted and more would be appreciated. Who could put a price on such a tightening of the fabric of society? But if one could, it would certainly be worth more than the cost of an individual.

Brandt's commitment to his new career had never wavered but these thoughts certainly helped to galvanise his resolve. The fact that he was gaining such satisfaction from his work was just a fortunate by-product. He did not feel guilty for it. In fact, he saw it as entirely healthy. He had always accepted that the immediate pleasure derived from procreation was not its primary purpose but when it was overlooked, deliberately ignored, suppressed even, that was when things had gone wrong in his marriage.

Brandt had grown sick and tired of feeling guilty for things. By the time his wife had left him it seemed as though he was responsible for anything that happened that was less than ideal. Such was his sense of guilt that he often believed himself to blame for two conflicting things at once. He had felt wrong to want so much more from their sex life and yet he had believed he was to blame for his wife's inability to get pregnant. It had been the same with work; although widely admired for his gift to spot the lead in a case where all others had failed, this only served to heighten the guilt he felt when there was a crime he couldn't solve.

That's why he knew his latest endeavour was right. There had not been one minute, not even a fleeting second, where he had questioned the purpose of what he was doing; much less consider that it might be wrong. When he had first plunged that knife into the girl outside the station, the release he had felt was so much more than a chemical reaction started in his brain. It was almost physical, like a snake shedding a skin, perhaps even more transformational – an insect emerging from a pupa. Much as this change is the last stage of creation for the insect, so too Brandt knew that he was now becoming the ultimate iteration of himself.

As if to provide a physical confirmation of his psychological musings, Brandt could feel himself begin to stiffen. A quick glance at his phone confirmed that he had been following this woman and her dog for half a mile now. The noise from the main arterial roads through Nottingham had faded and it was only the occasional vehicle in a side street that was noticeable above the indistinct hum. The meandering of the river meant they were no longer visible from the blocks of flats built near

Trent Bridge, and the numbers of walkers had dwindled to the extent that there was no one but the woman and her dog on this stretch of path.

With the strain in his trousers becoming uncomfortable at his current speed, Brandt was pleased to see the dog pausing to take a particularly long sniff at some foliage on the grass verge. He wondered whether he should take the opportunity to close the distance and complete the act. The conditions were as good as they were likely to get but unconsciously he could feel his pace slowing. Any apparent hesitancy was not due to having second thoughts. Whereas his encounters with the other two had been momentary, with every passing minute, his affinity with this woman grew. The longer he spent staring at her from behind, the more he yearned to add to the fleeting view of her face from first spotting her. Much as he was caught up in the thrill of the chase, he had not lost the cold logic that had served him well during his previous career. He knew that, when the time came, he would have to act fast. Whilst no one else was currently in sight, at any time someone could walk or, worse, jog or cycle around the corner. Therefore, he would need to make his getaway as quickly as possible. But then again, Brandt was feeling somewhat fatalistic. The chances of someone witnessing their moment of intimacy were the same whether he did it now or further along the path. Consequently, he would take his time building up to it to ensure that today's events would be etched on his memory forever. He would not need any visual stimulation back in the confines of his home. That hard-nose bitch, DCI Stella Johnson, wouldn't be able to unnerve him with her dead-eyed stare. He knew her type back when he was in the force. So determined were women like that to get on; so determined were they to prove they could make it despite the gender-biased odds they fabricated in their feminist, no doubt lesbian, minds, that they ended up conforming to every male stereotype they were supposedly fighting against.

Although these dark thoughts had only lasted a few moments, they had two unfortunate consequences for Brandt. Firstly, he no longer felt physically aroused. He only had a moment to mentally curse DCI Johnson for once again seeking to spoil his mood, before the second consequence became all too apparent. The woman was now only a matter of feet in front of him. Brandt had just a couple of seconds before he would pass her. He hated the fact that he was being rushed but, seeing no sensible alternative, he thrust his hand into his pocket and felt the now-familiar comfort of the steak knife's hilt.

Whether he had fully explored the various scents, or sensing the growing impatience at the other end of his lead, just as Brandt was about to brandish the knife, the pug started trotting back to the path. Aware of Brandt's proximity, his owner glanced up. Brandt stopped as their eyes locked. She was quite simply the most beautiful woman he had ever seen. Knowing that he would rather die than break the connection, he was dismayed when, after the merest of smiles formed on her lips, she started turning her head.

Desperate to restore the moment, Brandt went to speak but all that could escape his mouth was a hushed 'Um.' Nevertheless, this had the desired effect and, whether involuntarily or not, the woman turned back to face him. Her smile remained but was now more quizzical than when it first appeared. Brandt returned the gesture and was about to attempt talking again when he saw her glance down. As the sun once more glinted off the exposed blade, the woman's eyes widened and the lead dropped from her hand to fall silently to the ground.

Chapter Sixteen

Duty Sergeant Andrews glanced up from his logbook. McNeil could see the look of pity on his face. He would rather anything but that; a sanctimonious smugness followed by an *I told you so* would have been preferable to his disappointed expression. But McNeil didn't have time for this now. As soon as Josh had recovered from the shock of being wrestled to the floor by five heavily armed specialist firearms officers, he had started ranting about police brutality and civil law suits. Whether the massive dump of adrenaline in his system had provoked the outburst of aggressive masculinity, so absent in his interview with DCI Johnson a couple of weeks before, or whether it was an act put on in an attempt to mask the embarrassment of having voided his bowels, McNeil didn't know. All he did know was that Josh calmed down considerably once led away from a stunned Sarah Donovan, who had opened the door to find out what the commotion was outside her flat.

McNeil had yet to see Johnson, and their last contact had been by phone; confirming that Josh was not to be arrested and could be released. It had been a brief conversation with none of the playfulness and intrigue of the call when he had been at the hospital a few days earlier. As if McNeil needed reminding, Sergeant Andrews seemed to endorse his suspicion that he was going to be made the scapegoat for this bungled operation. His mood hadn't been helped by the firearms officers beating a swift retreat as soon as it was clear that Josh wasn't a suspect. McNeil had been left to deal with the mess. By the time he had failed to reassure Sarah that what had just happened didn't mean she was in any danger, Josh had left the area. PC Strachen, more than a little shaken up herself, had observed him walking back towards the city centre around about the same time the van containing the other officers had sped away. In a way he was grateful that Sarah decided she was going to stay for a time at her parents' house. Although he had to endure their vehement stares as they came to collect her, it did mean that he wouldn't have to spend the remaining few hours of his shift sat with Strachen making inane small talk.

All McNeil now wanted to do was get this day over and done with, and go home to drown his sorrows. For a few hours the alcohol would allow him to take his mind off thoughts of his stalling career and what mundane tasks awaited him when he returned to work on Monday morning. Although the murder investigation would continue as before, he very much doubted that he would have a role to play in it any longer. He sighed as he looked at his watch and realised he still had a little over three hours remaining until he could clock off. He was going to find a quiet spot to complete the mountain of paperwork associated with events from this morning, and attempt to keep as low a profile as possible.

He was about to head off to the vending machines to grab a coffee before starting, when he heard an all too familiar voice.

'McNeil. My office. Five minutes,' barked DCI Johnson from across the room.

By the time he looked up she was already heading towards the main exit.

Well this is it, thought McNeil. Any hopes of being allowed to quietly slip back into the anonymity of his old role had been dashed. He would now have to face the humiliation and injustice of being blamed for merely following orders. Whilst he knew that he would want to stand up for himself and argue that any fallout from that day was Johnson's responsibility for hatching the risky, not to mention ethically questionable, plan, he also still felt somewhat intimidated by her. Even if he could brave the inevitable wrath that would immediately meet his accusations, he could do nothing to stop her exacting revenge by ensuring he was given nothing more high profile in the future than shoplifting. He could of course make a formal complaint but as modern as the police was in the 21st century, and as much as official policy endorsed whistle-blowing, the truth was tradition came above everything. A grass was still a grass, and a grass could not be trusted; shunned forevermore by his colleagues.

If Sergeant Andrews had an opinion on how best to handle the situation, he clearly wasn't keen to share it and maintained his focus on completing sections in his logbook. All that remained for McNeil was to get this over and done with, in the hope that he might be allowed to leave early and crack on with his plan to quickly fall into an inebriated oblivion.

It was as he neared the top of the stairs that he remembered he still didn't know the code to enter the plain clothes' floor. Just as he was about to gingerly knock, like a school pupil at the door to the staffroom, he heard footsteps behind. Without greeting, Johnson brushed past him and started punching numbers into the keypad. McNeil was hit by the strong aroma of fresh cigarette smoke mixed in with whatever perfume she had applied that morning.

Although she held the door open behind her, she did not look in McNeil's direction and strode across the floor towards her office. That none of the few detectives in the room glanced in either of their directions was small comfort. He walked into Johnson's office and turned to close the door, having resolved to speak first; hoping that a heartfelt, in tone at least, apology might go some way to fixing things.

Nevertheless, it was she who spoke first: 'Who shat in your cornflakes?'

'I'm sorry?' Not quite the apology McNeil had intended.

'I said, why are you looking so glum all of a sudden?'

'But, ma'am, the flat… Sarah, Josh…'

'Ah, bollocks to that. So what?'

'But I thought you would be…' Was all he could manage in reply.

'Nah, it was a long shot anyway.' She smiled and eased back in her chair. 'And as for that contemptuous little twat, I would love to have seen the look on his face when he saw all those automatic weapons trained on him.'

McNeil felt himself relax. More out of relief than becoming emboldened, he sat down before being invited. If Johnson had a view on this, her expression did not reveal it. She continued: 'One of the officers said he literally shat himself.'

When McNeil couldn't manage to suppress a laugh, Johnson followed suit. Her smile completely lit her entire face; her usually cold and piercing blue eyes positively swimming with the mirth that lay behind them.

'But what about the press?' McNeil asked, as soon as he had calmed down. He instantly regretted the question. So far, the exchange had gone far better than he could have wished for. Why did he have to say something that might cause Johnson's mood to sour?

'Again, so what? The fact is the papers are always banging on about public funding cuts and fewer officers on the streets. At least it shows that we were out there, looking after the first victim. And if I know anything about Josh, he'll keep quiet. His ego won't want any uncomfortable questions about how he reacted, or even why he was there in the first place. Besides,' she continued thoughtfully, her tone becoming more serious. 'We still have a killer on the loose.'

'So, what now?' McNeil enquired.

But before Johnson could reply, her office door was flung open and DI Fisher rushed in. 'Ma'am, there's been a fatal stabbing!'

Chapter Seventeen

DCI Johnson was not aware that DSI Potter was on the phone when she burst in; yet showed no remorse once she realised. Potter, placing his hand over the receiver, was about to admonish his subordinate but something about her intense, not to mention impatient, glare caused him to change his mind. Instead he uncovered the mouthpiece and said, simply, 'I'll have to call you back' before hanging up without waiting for a reply.

'Guv, it's him!' Johnson declared, her voice almost shouting.

'Stella, slow down. What's him?'

'He's killed again.'

'Oh.' No further explanation was necessary; DSI Potter knew who was being referring to. His heart sank. Immediately his mind flooded with the implications of this news. Beyond the natural concern that yet another of his citizens had fallen victim to this perpetrator, he was conscious of the enormous pressure that would come from his superiors. That there had been no leads so far of any worth was bad enough, but another murder so soon after the last, had the whiff of a serial killer about it. The media would go into a frenzy and the spotlight would fall firmly on him, despite Johnson as DCI having the lead role in the investigation.

Yet Potter was very much of the old school and firmly believed in maintaining a calm demeanour in front of his team. Over his thirty-year career he had gradually worked his way up to the position he had now held for the past seven. He had no desire to rise any further, believing the job of Chief Superintendent was the perfect balance between authority and remaining grounded in day-to-day police work. His success and the respect he had gained along the way was not down to the impetuous enthusiasm and commitment shown by promising officers such as DCI Johnson, but by a steady and methodical approach. That way he could be always relied upon to do a solid job, and his logic and eye for detail, along with his willingness to nurture a diverse team of differing talents, ensured that few crimes warranting their attention went unsolved. Although what faced him now was looking likely to be his biggest test so far, he was not going to abandon the professional approach that had served him so well in the past.

'Give me the lowdown,' he said, using his right hand to indicate that Johnson should sit in the chair opposite his desk.

Continuing to stand she replied, 'Stabbing on the Trent, mile or so west of the cricket ground, past the memorial gardens.'

'Same weapon?'

'Not confirmed yet, guv, but it was a woman in her late twenties.'

Much as Potter wanted to raise a note of caution and to tell Johnson not to jump to any unnecessary conclusions, he knew such comments would be born out of hope more than expectation.

'Right then, we need to meet this head-on in the press conference.' His voice now had the steely resolve of someone who had decided on an appropriate course of action. 'The public is going to want answers so I'm going to get it delayed until Monday morning to give you time to work on any lead. If, as I suspect, an arrest hasn't been made by then I will make an appeal to the public. We need them to be more vigilant moving forward. At the very least, if another attack cannot be avoided, someone might see something.'

'Okay, guv, do you mind if I make the appeal?'

'Sure, but why?' Potter was surprised that Johnson would want the negative attention that would be associated with, to all intents and purposes, admitting that the people of Nottingham were no longer safe.

'No offense, guv, but I think it will have more impact coming from a woman.'

Potter paused for a moment, raising an eyebrow and selecting his words carefully: 'I didn't think you had any time for gender stereotyping?'

'I don't sir; I hate it, but that doesn't mean it doesn't exist. If just one woman takes extra care as a consequence of me making the appeal, then it's the right thing to do.'

'Fair enough,' Potter replied evenly. It never ceased to amaze him how complex Johnson's character was. Each time he thought he had her worked out, he found another facet. He cast his mind back to the waves she had caused when she first made detective. It wasn't so much burning ambition, more a determination to prove herself that had caused her to appear so abrasive to her colleagues. Potter suspected that, despite nothing pertaining to this being on her file, she must have faced some form of discrimination earlier in her career. The way she had dressed, so determined to hide her femininity and natural attractiveness, added credence to his thoughts. Understanding the politics of policing, just as much as the procedures, Potter took Johnson under his wing and mentored her in finding a balance to her approach. He had explained that if every crime she solved came at the cost of alienating a colleague, she would soon find herself isolated and marginalised. Potter had been concerned that such a warning could be misconstrued by Johnson as a threat, but it had very much been taken in the spirit that had been intended. Moreover, whilst Johnson had learned to play the game, superficially at least, she never lost the quick-witted tenacity that had ensured her rapid progress. If the reputation and respect, if not popularity, she had gained with her subsequent promotion, was not sufficient proof of her successful transition, her change in appearance was. Gradually make-up, almost imperceptibly subtle at first, had been applied, and her hair had changed from always being scraped back into a ponytail to typically flowing half way down her back. So too followed an all-year-round tan and clothes that, whilst remaining entirely professional, accentuated her athletic figure rather than attempting to hide it.

'You never know, guv,' Johnson said, rousing Potter from his reminiscences. 'Perhaps we'll have him nicked by Monday anyway.'

'Do you think so?'

'No,' she replied flatly. 'I think he's enjoying himself too much to let a stupid mistake spoil things.'

Chapter Eighteen

'You lying bitch!' Brandt shouted at the television screen, whilst sat in his familiar armchair. Any similarities to previous outbursts over the last few weeks were just superficial. Whereas before they had been filled with venom and vitriol, this was laden with glee.

As planned, DSI Potter handed over to DCI Johnson after outlining the main points of Saturday's murder and stating that a number of leads were being followed. Brandt had observed this with only mild interest, having already gleaned the information from press reports over the weekend. This was to be expected and Brandt knew that even if they did have some key evidence that might lead to his capture, the last thing they would do was share it publicly. But it was of little concern because, once again, he had given the police very little to go on. Reflecting once more on means, motive and opportunity; things had changed little since Brandt had started on his new career. He was still using the same ubiquitous steak knife, but he knew the police would have attempted to draw some conclusions regarding his motive and opportunity. Clearly the three attacks would lead them to believe that he either lived in Nottingham or close by. Any suspicion someone was travelling from further afield, like he was, would be countered by the variety of locations used. By not only spreading out across the city but also using different settings, from a busy train station to a river path – via a housing estate alleyway – the police would see this indicating solid contextual knowledge.

That the victims were attractive women overwhelmingly indicated the motives of a man, was not a worry. He certainly didn't see the narrowing of the profiling to a specific gender mitigating against the subterfuge created by the incorrect radius of their search area. Brandt knew that the vast majority of murders committed by women were crimes of passion and therefore his victims being unconnected was enough alone to point towards a man.

The bit of their thinking he could not follow was the consequence of something deliberate on his part. He assumed that by this third act they would know they were dealing with the same man, but Brandt had been keen for that connection to be made earlier. Of all the things he would have loved to understand, it was what they had made of the swipe of Sarah Donovan's blood on the second victim. It was without question they would know he had deliberately done this, but they would not know his reasons why.

Regardless, the fact remained that the police would have made the connection after the second woman, and here was DCI Johnson implying that it was only now, one death later, that the parallels were clear. It wasn't even as though he had left them such a clue this time. Sure, he had used the same steak knife, but he hadn't felt it necessary to flag up the link. Brandt would have been willing to bet that, no sooner had they heard the news of what had happened along the River Trent, they had immediately known he had struck again.

'Liar!' Brandt repeated. It amused him that they had not wanted to reveal this sooner. Was it that they were confused why such a deliberate clue had been left? Perhaps, but from experience he guessed it was because they would not have wanted to alarm the public until it was apparent that a pattern was emerging. That, and the fact that the pressure on the police to make an arrest would increase tenfold now this was in the public domain.

Brandt watched with keen interest whilst DCI Johnson appealed for people to be vigilant. She sounded genuinely concerned, but the warmth of her words did not stretch to her eyes. They remained as ice cold as ever. Yet Brandt no longer found their stare unsettling. The news conference confirmed that they were nowhere near to catching him, despite what DSI Potter had said about following *a number of credible leads*. There was no way they would have come out with such an appeal, such an admission of the inability to keep the public safe, if they thought they were even part of the way towards catching him.

It was the timing of the press conference that had caused Brandt a moment of panic. Given the killing had hit the national news on Saturday evening, the delay until Monday seemed unusual. For a while on Sunday, Brandt had been concerned that its absence had meant he had made some sort of mistake which the police were following up. He knew his planning had been sound, both in terms of how he had travelled to Nottingham and not leaving any unintended clues at the scene. However, he also knew he could not have legislated against everything. Perhaps someone else had come around one of the bends just as he was fleeing the scene and had provided a good enough description to allow the police to pick him up on CCTV later in his route. Perhaps there had been a building somewhat obscured by the trees with a window that someone happened to be looking out of. Perhaps there had been a homeless guy foraging on the other side of the bushes. All increasingly unlikely but still, technically, *possible*.

Brandt had even toyed with the idea of making his getaway on Sunday evening but had decided against it, having not given the slightest bit of thought to it in any of his previous planning. He concluded that if the police were on to him, the worst thing he could do was something that would be seen as out of character. The quiet road on which Brandt lived had a sufficient number of nosey neighbours that his departure on a Sunday evening would probably not have gone unnoticed. Instead he had decided to sleep on the problem; reasoning that, if he felt the same the following day, he could ensure a more anonymous departure. It gave him enough time to work out where he would go and, more crucially, how he would get there. He would set different timers on his house lights and leave his car on the drive. Brandt knew that taking public transport held many risks but the Automatic Number Plate Recognition cameras scattered across the road network made car travel equally perilous.

However, the next morning he had felt calmer and somewhat fatalistic about events. As he lay in bed thinking about the women with whom he had formed such a special bond, he had been reminded of the signs he had received that suggested he was being supported by a higher power of some kind. How with the first, as he had exited the station, he immediately had seen her long flowing hair. Sarah Donovan had seemed to indicate, by a simple body movement, where she had wanted him. Then a voice in his consciousness had prevented him from twisting the knife and thus saved her life. When he had revisited Nottingham, he had decided that whoever had entered the alleyway next would become his second act. The fact that it was another attractive young woman had suggested more than a coincidence, seemingly confirmed by his third victim emerging from under the bridge over the River Trent, just as he was about to take to the path.

It would appear he was destined to focus on attractive young women. This was something he felt entirely comfortable with, even though it would be causing a number of conclusions to be drawn by the profilers at the police. Brandt surmised that, given he hadn't deliberately targeted young women, they would end up coming up with someone different. Not only had Brandt never intended for there to be an apparent pattern to his victims, it was something he had planned against. This was one of the reasons why he had gone to such lengths in the alleyway to highlight it was him striking again. If the person had been a middle-aged man, the chances of the police making the connection with Sarah Donovan would have been particularly slim. Perhaps it would have taken quite a few more acts before they knew they were dealing with one man. Brandt didn't have the patience for such a wait. He had wasted the best years of his life in a marriage and a profession that had given him little satisfaction.

So what if he got a particular thrill from these women? He was not oblivious to this; in reality he embraced it. How could he not when they had aroused feelings forgotten since the first years of his failed marriage? Though being responsible for the life seeping from another human created a euphoria beyond anything sexual, causing Brandt to believe it would remain the same regardless of gender or age, he was sure that reliving these moments back at home, whilst still gratifying, would clearly not have the same erotic thrill. Far from making him a pervert, Brandt thought his victims might even be grateful. Surely, just like him, they wanted their lives, no matter how short, to have meaning. To leave a legacy when they died. Although primarily that would be them immortalised in media, print, and the spoken word, the contribution of their existence would live on in Brandt.

Therefore, to run away now and, more crucially, to abandon such an important project would be an injustice to their sacrifice. They deserved the snowballing of exposure that his repeated acts would bring. He didn't want them consigned to the regional news and the odd fleeting mention in the nationals. Brandt realised he had a duty to create some serious waves; they, along with him, were ready to become the most talked about people in Britain. Today's press conference marked the start of that journey and Brandt could barely contain his excitement with what the forthcoming Saturday might bring.

Chapter Nineteen

The frustration and boredom that DCI Johnson had felt earlier in the week was now turning into anxiety. Even though she knew that the killer would be mad to strike again on yet another Saturday, all the same, she found it a distinct possibility; one that was growing every minute it got closer to the weekend. Not that she thought for one moment the killer was mad, at least not in the traditional sense of the word. Far from being a raving lunatic, this man was cold and calculating. Up to this point he had managed to avoid leaving any evidence of worth, and yet had the confidence to highlight the link between his victims. Whilst DSI Potter believed it was the killer's way of taunting the authorities, perhaps trying to show an air of invincibility, Johnson was not convinced. There had been no attempt by him to contact the police, nor did she think there would be. Far from making some kind of statement or seeking notoriety or infamy, Johnson believed that the killer was doing something he simply enjoyed. The fact that he was selecting attractive young women only supported this by implying a sexual dimension. That they had yet to find any evidence of physical interference pre- or post-mortem made Johnson believe they were dealing with a sexually repressed individual. For the level of bitterness and loneliness to reach murderous proportions, whilst at the same time avoiding either the levels of violence demonstrating a hatred of women, or the molestation associated with acting out one's fantasies, suggested the work of a middle-aged man. Having already demonstrated confidence as well as competence, Johnson only believed it a matter of time until the perpetrator lost whatever inhibitions were currently holding him back.

She shuddered at the thought of the consequences for those who would be subjected to his perversion, but then also for the backlash it would bring the police. If what Johnson had told the people of Nottingham on Monday had not caused sufficient fear, when it transpired that the killer in their midst was a sexual predator, it would doubtlessly cause panic. The upshot would make this week, so far full of following up hollow leads from hundreds of phone calls and watching hours of CCTV footage, feel like a holiday in The Bahamas.

The reality was that Johnson could have skipped most of the mundane tasks, and left it to her team, along with McNeil who had remained keen as ever to help. She could have spent the time going over the little evidence they had, working up theories. It wasn't so much that she knew that there was little to go on, more a sense of responsibility to muck in with the others. She knew that she often appeared aloof but was equally conscious that, if they were going to get a result from this, she would need the team galvanised and the best way was to lead from the front. Much as she felt that she had been successful in hiding her increasing frustration, it would seem that McNeil was able to read her moods better than most.

Johnson had been certain after the mix up at Sarah Donovan's flat that McNeil would try and distance himself from the CID investigation. She would not have been surprised, much less blame him, if he had requested to move back to his usual work. That he had asked to stay and help meant something to Johnson, even if she had been determined not to show it. Unless things made a dramatic change for the better, she doubted any of them would come up smelling of roses, but she did feel that McNeil was starting to fit in with the rest of the team.

'You don't think he'll bother tomorrow do you, ma'am?' McNeil enquired, as though reading her mind. They were both studying the board in the main area; a network of photographs, maps, and pieces of information associated with the case.

'What do you think?' came Johnson's now familiar response to his questions.

'He'd be taking a huge risk if he did so.' Not only would the press conference have served to make people extra cautious, but Saturday would see the largest visible police presence in Nottingham since Forest were in the top division in the 1980s and football hooliganism was at its height.

'So?'

'He doesn't strike me as the sort of person who would take such a big risk.'

'And stabbing three women in broad daylight is the work of a cautious man?'

'No, ma'am, I think they were carefully planned and, although carrying inherent risks, he had worked to minimise them. Tomorrow contains too many variables I think he will feel he cannot control.'

'So perhaps he's decided to retire then?'

'No, ma'am, I don't think that either. As things stand, I can't see him stopping until we catch him.' McNeil's tone had taken on a sombre note.

'So, what then? Lay low for a while and wait for the dust to settle?' Johnson had only kept this conversation going in an attempt to alleviate some of the tedium but, the more McNeil spoke, the more interested she became in what he had to say.

'I don't think he is going to do anything tomorrow, but I reckon he's going to be out and about taking everything in.'

'Oh really?' For the first time Johnson's question was genuine. Whilst she also believed that there would not be an attack tomorrow, she had not considered the idea that the killer would be in public.

'Yes, I think he will be keen to know what difference he's made.'

'And what do you base that on?'

'Well…' McNeil thought carefully. 'This is probably because of the blood swipe on the second victim. He wanted us to know it was him striking again. Plus, I think it shows some ego. Also, he will probably know about us waiting for him at Sarah Donovan's flat.'

'Go on…'

'So,' McNeil said pensively, 'whilst I don't think he is stupid enough to do anything, with everyone on high alert, he'll want to see how everyone's acting and, in particular, us.'

Johnson stopped to consider this for a moment. 'If you're right, how can that help us?'

'Well, I'm not sure, ma'am,' he conceded. 'I suppose if that were me, I might check out the places I had been before because that is where I would be able to notice the differences.'

'So how do we turn that to our advantage?'

'What I would do is tone back the uniform presence in these areas, so as not to spook him, but deploy some plain clothes to keep an eye out for him.'

Clever, thought Johnson. Not only might McNeil be onto something, but the way his mind worked suggested he was cut out for this line of policing. She was similarly pleased that this had been witnessed by the rest of the team. No more bullshit photocopying and filing for him; she no longer cared if he might be seen as the teacher's pet. He had faced her line of questioning with honesty and a refusal to be intimidated that few of them possessed and, although a long shot, what he was proposing was the first bit of genuine proactive thinking since she had made the call of using Sarah Donovan as bait.

'Very well, McNeil, go and make the necessary arrangements.'

Chapter Twenty

Brandt was in a particularly good mood on this dry, clear morning. Once again the weather was in his favour, something he appreciated all the more because he intended driving the whole distance this time. He started wondering whether today's candidate had even the slightest inclination that this would be a Saturday unlike any other – their last. It might be as small as giving their loved one a longer kiss goodbye that morning, or unconsciously taking a glance back at their house as they left it for the final time. Brandt liked to think they did because, again, it would fit his belief that he was doing something preordained; something with purpose.

It made him contemplate how the residents of Nottingham were feeling this morning. He guessed that there would be a number of apprehensive people, many of whom would have woken up thinking of him. How many had changed their plans and altered their typical routine given what DCI Johnson had advised earlier in the week?

He knew the atmosphere in Nottingham that day would be a little subdued, but people had a defence mechanism whereby, no matter what they heard, they never truly accepted that bad things would happen to them. Yes, some of the women would avoid taking short cuts through alleyways or walking their dogs along secluded sections of the river, but would they do the truly safe thing and stay at home? He very much doubted it. Similarly, their limited attempts to minimise the risk would lack any true thought of the extent of the danger. Brandt had grown tired over recent years of seeing the same pointless knee-jerk reactions to terrorist attacks. If it had been something on the airlines then extra security measures would be put in place, inconveniencing and delaying countless passengers, before gradually being relaxed once the dust had settled. Even if permanent changes were made, like they had with bag and body searches at major events, the manner in which they were administered changed in the weeks following an attack. The staff responsible for carrying them out, so invasive in the immediate aftermath, soon became far less thorough. Anyone who wanted to smuggle in something illegal had to do little more than conceal the item somewhere less obvious.

Brandt supposed that the counter argument to the apparent futility of all this, was that people felt safer; happy to buy into the illusion. But this was why he couldn't let up, couldn't allow himself to be caught. Selflessly and relentlessly he believed himself duty bound to continue until the illusion was shattered and human nature's natural complacency was driven from the public.

Chapter Twenty-one

'Do you want me to take over?' Johnson said, as she nearly got whiplash for the third time following McNeil's jerky acceleration.

'Sorry, ma'am, it's just I haven't driven this particular model before.'

Johnson knew that he had never driven anything as powerful as the Audi S4 she had chosen this morning from the impounded stock. The police were allowed to keep and use those vehicles that had been proven to be purchased with the proceeds of crime. Johnson, a secret petrol head, used any excuse to dip into this more exotic motor pool rather than the usual dull collection of Vauxhalls and Volvos. Although preferring the BMW M4's additional performance, the Audi S4 still had a more-than-adequate 340 BHP and was, crucially, more understated in looks, especially in this metallic grey paintwork and estate body style. Appearing to the untrained eye to be just another junior executive's company car, the engine mated to its Quattro four-wheel drive system ensured that in the right hands, it could keep up with almost any vehicle on the road.

Although Johnson enjoyed banter with McNeil, she knew that today would be long and stressful. With other things playing on her mind, she had decided she would start as gently as possible. So, as well as allowing him to drive to their first location, she did not comment that, unless he was willing to pay astronomical personal insurance premiums, his age meant he was likely to be restricted to owning little more than a Ford Fiesta for a while yet.

Johnson, unshackled by the burden of being a young adult, owned a faster car than the one she was being driven in that morning. Also an Audi, her TTRS had more power and was lighter and nimbler, whilst retaining the security of all-wheel drive. Far from understated, she had ordered hers in bright red and loved, not just driving it, but also the attention it drew. Unconcerned by the stereotype of an attractive blonde driving a red sports car, she even wished she had gone for the convertible version. Although the extra weight applied to strengthen the chassis would blunt the performance a little, being open to the elements and that warbling five-cylinder soundtrack would heighten the sense of speed.

Yet today, zipping along Nottinghamshire's country roads couldn't have been further from Johnson's mind. All she wanted was to get to the train station and check her teams were set up exactly as instructed. She figured the railway was as good a place as any. As well as being the location of the first attack, it might also be the route by which the killer would arrive. Logic dictated that he was a resident of Nottingham, but Johnson had always worked on the principle that nothing should be ruled out until done so by the evidence.

'You've done well so far, McNeil,' she said, somewhat out of the blue.

'Nah, let's be honest, ma'am, I'm no Lewis Hamilton,' he replied.

Johnson let out a louder laugh than she would have expected. She put it down to the tension. 'No, I meant so far with this case, not your awful driving. And you can call me Johnson when we're not with the rest of the team.' As though suddenly aware of the potential shift in relations the informality both statements brought, she jumped straight onto the radio. 'DI Fisher can you update me on your position?'

They both waited whilst her second in command gave a detailed description of where he was and what he was doing. With his officious tone offering no sign that he would stop talking any time soon, Johnson leaned forward to turn down the volume. McNeil's sudden gear change caused her to require two attempts to find the relevant knob. Facing him again she added: 'But your driving's shit. I'll take over later.'

'Yes, ma'am,' he replied with a wry smile.

Chapter Twenty-two

As Brandt switched off the engine, he closed his eyes for a few moments, enjoying the quiet; punctuated only by the small pings and ticks coming from the engine bay as it cooled. Once again conscious to avoid places where CCTV was installed, he had decided to leave it near the university campus and walk the remainder of the way. At this time of day things were quiet, to the extent of rejecting the original parking spot he had selected from Google Maps for being too empty. Where he was now, struck a fine balance between being somewhere secluded but sufficiently populated by other vehicles that his car's presence would go unnoticed for a few hours.

As he stepped out into the still cool morning air, he began to stretch his muscles, enjoying the freedom of movement after the journey. He heard another car coming up the road and, before it came into sight, Brandt started walking. When it was gone, he doubled back so he could retrieve his jacket from the car and lock up. With no one else on the road he paused, wondering whether this wait alone would change today's fate for a particular individual. Would these few seconds mean that he would encounter a different person when he arrived at the location he had selected? Perhaps. Perhaps not. He contemplated waiting a little longer but then cursed himself for indulgent thoughts such as these; reminding himself that he had a job to do.

Within a couple of minutes, he was on the main road headed into town. Here it was much busier with both traffic and pedestrians, but he felt comfortable in such surroundings; his anonymity assured by being one of a number of people making the journey to the shops. Having been overtaken by a bus, he paused at the next stop to study its route. Just like him, it was heading straight into the city, but Brandt didn't contemplate catching the upcoming one. The presence of cameras on board ruled out the possibility, and Brandt was genuinely enjoying the walk. It allowed him time go over his plans and for the thrill of anticipation to build.

His mind drifted back to DCI Johnson, wondering how she was feeling at this particular moment. He suspected that she would still be calmly waiting for the day to play out, with it still far too early to fear something had gone wrong. That would come much later and, by then, he would be back in his car, possibly even home. More than anything he wished he could see her expression change from the initial frustration of believing today had been a washout. He wondered what would happen to that cold, icy stare when she realised that not only had she been outwitted, yet again, but also that what they were dealing with was far greater than they had anticipated.

Chapter Twenty-three

'Shall I nip in there and grab us some lunch?' McNeil asked, pointing at the branch of Subway just down the road from where they were parked. They were positioned near the station, having spent most of the morning moving between the main sites, checking that everything was as it should be. From a policing perspective, it was all as planned. There was an increased and overt presence in areas like the shopping centres, where the greatest concentration of people was, along with a discreet but focused force at the previous crime scenes.

'What?' Johnson asked absentmindedly. 'Erm, no. I'm not hungry.'

'Well, I'm starving. Got to eat, all that nervous energy...' McNeil trailed off, undecided whether or not to push the matter. 'Something small?'

'Ok, I'll have a coffee,' Johnson replied, still staring at the entrance to the station.

McNeil's laughter was loud given the relative quiet of the interior of the car. 'That's not exactly food.'

'Surprise me,' Johnson managed with a weak smile. In truth she hadn't paid attention to what type of food McNeil was proposing. For all she knew, he might come back with a kebab or something equally frightful. Regardless, she was relieved to have a few moments to herself.

She hated this part of the job and the waiting around was one of the reasons why she had sought to join CID. Being a detective was both reactive and proactive: something would happen that they would then investigate, whereas uniform would spend a fair portion of their time waiting for something to happen. At least then she hadn't necessarily known what that something would be. Today she knew all too well. The longer she spent in the car that morning, the more convinced she was that the killer was going to strike again. Perhaps it was happening now, in some secluded part of the city and it was just a matter of time before she got the phone call to confirm.

'God, I need a cigarette,' she mumbled to herself and unconsciously started drumming her fingers on the top of the steering wheel.

'Here,' McNeil said a few minutes later as he got back into the car and handed her a wrapped cylindrical package. 'I went fairly plain with turkey and ham because I didn't know what you like but, if you'd prefer my teriyaki chicken, I'm happy to swap.' He sounded genuinely cheerful and either the fresh air had done him good or he was simply excited at the prospect of addressing his hunger.

'Thanks,' Johnson said, placing the sandwich on the dashboard and opening the door before adding, 'I just need to check on something.'

Johnson walked up the street in the casual style she had been taught. Totally observant, constantly scanning her surroundings with her eyes, but with limited head movement. Her pace was nondescript; neither appearing in a hurry, nor slow enough to lack purpose.

She was heading for one of the policemen whom she had occasionally shared a cigarette with outside the station. His name escaped her and, as she approached, she witnessed his demeanour change from someone apparently waiting outside the bookmakers to alert and ready for instruction.

He relaxed back into character as Johnson leaned on the ledge next to him and he looked into the street with the same vacant expression he had shown a few moments earlier.

'Got a smoke?' She asked, without looking in his direction.

He didn't reply but, instead, reached inside his jacket and handed her the packet of cigarettes. Lambert and Butler were far from her preferred brand, but Johnson could feel the nicotine receptors in her mouth come alive in anticipation of the forthcoming first drag. She smiled as she noticed one of them had been turned upside down; the white paper contrasting with the orange-brown of the filters. 'Lucky fag,' she murmured. If her colleague heard her, he didn't respond.

Johnson decided that she needed all the luck she could get and withdrew the upturned cigarette from the packet. Without needing to ask, she was handed a lighter and, having applied the flame and taking a long, satisfying drag, she waited whilst he lit one of his own before beginning the short walk back to the car.

It was with a mournful look she observed that there was still a third of the cigarette left as she neared the Audi but, not wanting to draw attention to herself, she quickly flicked it into the roadside gutter before getting back into the vehicle.

If McNeil minded the stench of the fresh smoke as it enveloped the car, despite the open windows, he didn't say. He remained concentrated on finishing his roll, having demolished most of it in the time Johnson was away. She took a sip of the coffee McNeil had placed in one of the Audi's cup holders and then proceeded to open her sandwich.

Her appetite was even less than before thanks to effects of the nicotine and the sight within the wrapper. Although packed with salad, there was far too much bread for someone who was so carbohydrate conscious. Unless she was having a blow-out, Johnson was careful what she consumed, and wished she had paid more attention to what had been proposed for lunch.

Gingerly raising it to her mouth, she took her first tentative bite. Her slow chewing action soon became more rapid and she had barely finished her mouthful before she went in for seconds.

Johnson's, previously absent, eagerness for lunch did not go unnoticed. 'Good huh?' McNeil said. He didn't wait for a response. 'I find the plainer ones like turkey and ham require a more exotic cocktail of sauces. I didn't risk the hot chilli but, instead, asked for a combination of chipotle southwest and sweet onion.'

Johnson had to swallow quickly before the laugh escaped her. 'Quite the connoisseur, aren't we?' She managed to keep her tone the right side of mocking.

'Well, there's not a whole heap of choice when you're out on the beat and you don't want to get fat on burgers and chips.'

'You could make your lunch?'

'But that would just be replacing a sandwich with a sandwich…'

'Good God, I forget how young you are sometimes,' she replied good-naturedly. 'There are so many things you can have. What about leftovers from the night before, or brown rice with vegetables? How about some couscous or even some quinoa?'

'*Good God,*' McNeil mimicked. 'I forget how posh you are sometimes. Even if I knew what quinoa was, you're assuming I could cook the stuff.'

'Nah, it's simple. Even you couldn't fuck it up,' Johnson said, smiling.

'I wouldn't be so sure.' Before thinking through the possible implication of his next statement he added, 'perhaps you'll have to show me sometime.'

The silence that followed was uncomfortable, bordering on oppressive. The seconds that passed seemed like hours to McNeil. Desperate to end it, he was deciding whether to qualify his statement or just try and change the subject, when Johnson added in low and thoughtful voice, 'Perhaps I might.'

Chapter Twenty-four

Johnson slipped the key into the lock. Her house was empty and lifeless, save for the lamp that had been switched on by the automatic timer. As she took off her shoes, a noise from her stomach reminded her it was over eight hours since lunch. However, as she approached the refrigerator her hand veered down at the last moment and opened the freezer instead. Collecting the bottle of vodka from the bottom drawer, she slammed the door shut and selected a simple glass tumbler from one of the kitchen cupboards before making her way into the sitting room.

She had a headache from her constant vigilance throughout the day, and decided against putting on the television. Instead she used her phone to play some Emeli Sandé through the room's Bluetooth speakers. Johnson closed her eyes and could soon feel the effects of the soothing music and the vodka, which she was sipping neat.

As the weariness faded a little, she was frustrated that it was replaced more with disappointment than relief. The afternoon had proceeded like the morning and, save for a few anxious, and ultimately fruitless, phone calls made by members of the public, there had been nothing to report. By 3pm Johnson had started to suspect that nothing was going to happen and two hours later she had become convinced of it. Yet she had held on for a further three hours, having stood down most of the officers once the majority of the shoppers had gone home. McNeil had refused her attempts to send him away and even offered to stay out later in case something happened with the evening's revellers. Notwithstanding that, he had not protested too much when she had declined his offer, having also believed this wouldn't really fit in with the style of the killer.

The absence of food in her stomach was causing the vodka to have a quick effect. If she were going to be able to function properly in the morning, she knew she would have to nip the drinking in the bud. She wanted to believe that the feeling of disappointment that remained was because they would need to be vigilant tomorrow in case their murderer had merely moved his schedule back a day, hoping for an easier time of it. Therefore, any feelings of relief that he had not struck again would be premature. The truth was that a part of Johnson wished something had happened. Although unlikely to be fortunate enough to catch him in the act, at least that would have given them another crime scene and, consequently, more clues as to his identity. Sure, he had been careful and cautious so far, at least when he had chosen to be, but sooner or later something would slip. Irrespective of whether it was through carelessness, arrogance, or perhaps some unforeseen bad luck on his part, eventually Johnson would have a decent lead.

With her thoughts returning to work once more she poured herself one last vodka in the hope it might settle her mind again. Finding that it didn't, she resorted to a hot bath in the hope that the combined effects of it and the alcohol would allow her a reasonable night's sleep.

Regretfully placing the bottle back in the freezer Johnson trudged upstairs and turned on the taps. She applied a liberal amount of her favourite bath oil, watched the water turn into nourishing milk, and inhaled the scent of argan and sweet almond. Although her choice of outfit for the day had proven comfortable, it was a relief to cast it off and put the items in the laundry basket.

With the water still running Johnson didn't hear her mobile phone's ringtone and it was only when she switched the taps off, and she was swirling the bath's contents as a final check of the temperature, that she noticed the caller's third attempt at reaching her.

Cursing that she may miss it, she lunged for her towel to dry her hands and just managed to answer it before it rang off again.

'Yes,' she barked irritably unto the mouthpiece. Having not programmed McNeil's number into her contact list, she hadn't recognised the number on the display.

'Sorry, ma'am, I didn't mean to wake you.'

'I wasn't asleep, I was…' Johnson didn't finish, for some reason uncomfortable with the idea of sharing her current location. Although her body was dry, and she was perfectly warm within the confines of her bathroom, she wrapped a towel around her.

'I emailed you a link,' came the barely concealed command.

'Look it's late McNeil, get to the point.'

'It's our man…'

'What?' Johnson asked, but before receiving a reply her mind was already going ten to the dozen, trying to decipher McNeil's last statement. *Had he been caught? But how? Had he handed himself in? But why? Had he made contact?*

'Down in Kent.'

Johnson's thoughts suddenly ceased. 'I don't understand…'

'Around lunchtime today a girl was murdered in Canterbury. Er, it sounds like our man. Same sort of woman attacked. A stabbing…'

Chapter Twenty-five

Brandt was in his armchair, his usual brand of whisky next to him, with the television on. He was watching an old comedy on an indistinct satellite channel that relied on repeats to fill the airtime. On any normal day he would have switched over long before now, lamenting how the programme was nowhere near as funny as it had seemed at the time of original transmission and how people's enduring fondness for it was based more on nostalgia than actual taste. But today, in combination with a few generous measures of alcohol, Brandt found himself hooting with laughter in tandem with the canned background audience.

When he had returned home earlier that afternoon, Brandt had only briefly turned to the news channel. Unperturbed by his day's exploits making it no further than a brief mention on the South East local news, much in the same way his first act in Nottingham had done, he merely thought to himself: *Give it time*. Whilst surfing the channels until something took his fancy, he contemplated how long it would take the authorities to establish the connection. He hadn't wanted to make it too easy for them; he wanted to give them the opportunity to reveal how good his foes were. Were they so focused on their immediate vicinity that the connection would only be made once they discovered the cunningly concealed murder weapon or was Johnson casting her net sufficiently wide? If it was the former, they would only ever see what he allowed them to see. However, if the latter, then maybe he wasn't as many steps ahead of them as he had suspected.

As the catchy end credits music started, Brandt decided he would treat himself to an early night. The improvised plan he had made regarding the murder weapon and its implications had taken up most of his thinking that afternoon. A part of him regretted it because today, as with the others, he had achieved something beautiful. He wanted a chance to relive it, free from the distractions of the television and made his way upstairs with a final refill of his whisky glass.

Settling into bed, Brandt closed his eyes and thought of the girl. She had raven black hair, worn a summer dress, and had been barely protected from the chill of the spring air by a light denim jacket. She was taller than average but, despite this, she walked with an air of lightness and careless abandonment. She wasn't the first girl he had selected; he had followed the original as she had veered from the high street onto the back roads. As before, he had enjoyed following her; soaking up the thrill of anticipation, safe in the knowledge she was oblivious to his presence. As they moved further away from the main part of the city, she had even stopped in a street free from any pedestrians. Believing this to be his moment, Brandt had quickened his pace and had almost closed the distance when he saw the glint of metal being withdrawn from her handbag. Despite believing it could be a blade, Brandt had continued walking, tightly gripping the handle of the knife in his pocket. It was just as he was about to pull his weapon free that he realised it was a set of keys in her hand; a fact confirmed by the sound of a lock being turned once he had gone past.

His immediate thought had been to double back and push through the open door to complete his act in the hallway. The impatient side of his brain had told him that this might even be better than doing it in the street. He could close the door to ensure they were in perfect isolation. He could take his time. Perhaps even enjoy the feel of her body, the coolness of her skin and take in her unique scent. Brandt had already started to turn when he suddenly came to his senses. This had not been part of the plan and there were so many variables that were unaccounted for, not least the fact, at her age, she was unlikely to live alone in a house that, notwithstanding its modest size, must be expensive given its proximity to the centre of Canterbury.

Brandt had taken a long loop to return to the high street, not just so that he didn't end up doubling back, but also to allow himself time to calm down. Disturbed that he had even contemplated taking an uncalculated risk, he promised he would keep things nice and simple, resolutely refusing to deviate from the plan unless strictly necessary.

As he lay in bed, still flaccid in his hand, he wondered whether it was the relative simplicity of the killing that was preventing him deriving any real pleasure from the day. For a fleeting moment he remembered the resigned disappointment etched onto his wife's face at those times when he had failed to either maintain an erection or achieve one in the first place. Determined to prove to that bitch it had been more the lack of stimulus she provided, than an inability on his part, he screwed his eyes shut and concentrated hard.

He brought back the image of the woman's widening blue eyes as she looked at him when he had grabbed her in the few long seconds before he drove home the knife. Yes, he had felt the same thrill as before; made euphoric when he had walked sufficiently far away to believe he had not been seen. At the very edges of his hearing, he thought that he heard the scream of the person who first discovered her, but that had only served to make his heart beat faster. Indeed, and despite the long walk back to his car, he could still feel himself shaking slightly as he had attempted to turn his key in the ignition.

On reflection, he wondered whether that sensation had been more down to the brilliance of his improvised discarding of the knife. As Brandt had approached the centre of Canterbury he had passed a local garage; busy with trade. There had been a number of customers' cars parked out the front and the open shutters revealed two vehicles on ramps, one having its underside inspected and the other receiving a change of tyres. Brandt approached it for a second time that day and smiled as he saw that it was now closed. A couple of vehicles remained in the car park, but he assumed they might belong to customers who had yet to receive the necessary remedial work. With a plan barely hatching in his mind he had gone up to the entrance and seen on the door that their opening hours were 8am to 6pm Monday – Friday and 8am to 12pm on Saturday. A glance at his watch revealed that it was nearly 12:50pm and Brandt surmised that the darkness inside meant the workers were long gone. Brandt opened the shutter of the letterbox and dropped the knife through, with barely a moment's hesitation to admire the blood, still wet on the blade.

Knowing that Johnson would have been on high alert up in Nottingham, he wondered what the look on her face would be like in a few days when she realised that he had well and truly outfoxed her this time.

It was with thoughts of DCI Johnson's humiliation that Brandt could finally feel himself harden.

Chapter Twenty-six

Johnson spent the morning at the station. There were ground crews out like yesterday but in a much smaller capacity. Although she had them check in from time to time, she wasn't that interested; much less expecting something to happen. Johnson knew that they were possibly clutching at straws with the girl down in Kent but what she had managed to get from the police station in Canterbury certainly didn't discount their guy. The victim was a seemingly randomly selected female in her early twenties with stab wounds to her torso from a serrated knife.

Johnson dialled the number again.

'Look, there's still no news back from the path lab,' was what she received by way of a greeting. It had only been 10 minutes since her last call.

'Just tell them to get a move on, will you?' Johnson hung up without waiting for a reply.

Even though maps on the internet were far more detailed, when Johnson was working a case, she liked to use a paper copy. She had a map of Nottinghamshire on a wall in her office and they had one of Nottingham itself in the main area, as part of their investigation board. It had a number of pins in it, but the three red ones were where the victims had been found. Johnson had spent countless hours staring at it, hoping that some kind of pattern would reveal itself. Although she believed that it would now have to be replaced with a larger one, potentially of the whole of the UK, she would not allow herself to tempt fate and take it down until something more concrete came through from Kent. If it did, then the case might even get reassigned to a different task-force; especially given the possibility that the killer may have committed more murders around the country that hadn't yet been linked.

She headed back into her office and pulled out the map of England and Wales that sat in her drawer. Her eyes looked from Nottingham down to Canterbury and back up to Nottingham again. It was the best part of two hundred miles. She studied the roads in between. Could be fucking anywhere, she thought, staring at all the major towns and cities along the way.

The ringing of her phone startled her. 'DCI Johnson,' she announced formally into the mouthpiece.

'I've heard back from the lab and there's no trace of any swipes or smears on the victim's clothes.'

'Shit. Okay.'

There followed a few seconds of silence.

'You're welcome by the way,' came the sarcastic response just before the line went dead.

If Johnson was bothered by the tone of a subordinate she had never met, her face didn't show it. She placed the receiver back in its cradle and looked at the map again.

'What are you up to?' she murmured before rising to walk out of her office. 'I'll be on my mobile if you need me,' she called out to no one in particular as she headed to the door.

Originally intending to go for a smoke and then decide whether to go home, as she opened the external door, McNeil was walking across the car park.

'Any news?' Johnson asked, more conversationally than anything.

He shook his head. 'No, nothing. Everyone's still in position though. Any news back here?'

'No, the path lab didn't find anything on the body linking her to our guy.'

'Oh.' McNeil sounded disappointed.

'That was good work though,' Johnson offered cheerfully.

'Just clutching at straws, I guess.' He seemed genuinely deflated.

'No, seriously, McNeil. That was really good work. How did you even find out about the girl? It's not made the nationals.'

'I was sure he would strike again yesterday. When we didn't hear anything, I decided to search the news for stabbings.' His voice was more animated than before. 'It's seriously depressing the number that come up but they're mostly gang related or muggings. This one just kind of stood out, despite being so far away.'

'Look, if it's any consolation I think it might still be our guy.'

McNeil shook his head. 'He'd have left a clue though, like with the second one.'

'Agreed,' Johnson said.

'It's not just because I thought of it, but I kind of wish we could see the body so we could rule out it being him.'

Silence.

'Perhaps we can,' Johnson replied eventually. 'Fancy a road trip?'

'Come again?'

'Assuming nothing happens here today, I'll leave DI Fisher in charge. He's gagging for a bit of extra responsibility, but he'll have to continue coordinating the door to door activity with uniform whilst Hardy carries on going through all of the CCTV. Apart from that, we've got nothing else to go on. Besides, I've got a contact down there who will only be too pleased to see me.' Johnson smirked to herself.

'What's funny?'

'Oh nothing,' she said. 'Go home and get a good night's sleep. I'll pick you up at 6am.'

'Erm, do you mind if I come around to your place?' He didn't know why but for some reason he didn't want Johnson to see that he lived in a shared house in a grotty part of town.

'Oh, I see, don't want me waking the girlfriend?' she said, already walking back towards the station before calling out her address over her shoulder.

Chapter Twenty-seven

The red Audi TTRS gleamed in the dawn light, squat and aggressive with its fixed rear spoiler and large diameter wheels. Although McNeil was seven minutes early, Johnson was already waiting by the car, finishing off a cigarette. He was relieved. The half-hour journey from Radford to Wollaton had made him cold.

'Nice walk?' Johnson called sarcastically as McNeil opened the door.

He didn't rise to the bait. Instead he made a deliberate appraisal of the car before getting in. 'I didn't realise you used to be a hairdresser, ma'am.'

'Fuck off, PC McNeil,' she replied, deliberately flooring the accelerator whilst he was still fumbling for his seat belt. 'You drive like a bitch,' she added, barely slowing as she entered the roundabout at the end of her road.

Not wanting to give Johnson the satisfaction of showing that her driving was scaring the life out of him, he casually poked at various points of the interior. 'Nice,' he said. 'It's remarkably clean. Did you get it washed especially for our trip?'

'Bollocks I did,' she lied. 'But if you so much as leave a bit of mud on my floor mats I'll kill you.'

'So, no drive-thru then?'

'What?'

'Come on Johnson, your morning bowl of quinoa isn't going to last you all the way to Canterbury. I fancy a Maccy D's and I could murder a coffee right about now. Does this toy car have any cup holders?' he said, peering around theatrically once more.

Johnson applied the brakes heavily, smiling to herself as McNeil was thrown forward. 'Sorry about that, the pedal is a bit all or nothing. Guess I could have a coffee and maybe a bowl of porridge or something.'

Twenty minutes later the Audi, following signs for the M1, was pulling out of McDonald's car park. A comfortable silence had descended as both of the occupants were enjoying the warm, full feeling brought about by their breakfast. Pulling up at the drive-thru Johnson had required little persuasion to copy McNeil's order of a sausage and egg McMuffin meal, only hesitating at the last minute to switch to an orange juice for the drink. 'That way we have a cold drink to share whilst we eat and can then have the coffee once it cools down.' She didn't think to ask whether McNeil minded sharing the same receptacle and he never even considered the behaviour unusual for two colleagues of very differing rank.

Their progress along the motorway had been good for the first hour and, for the most part, Johnson had maintained a steady 85-90mph in the outside lane. McNeil soon relaxed in the car, having realised that she was a more than capable driver – her inputs smooth and confident. Things somewhat changed when the traffic became heavier just outside Dunstable and the variable speed limits were switched on.

'Hate these things,' Johnson grumbled to herself, after having to wipe off a third of her speed as she passed the first 60mph marked gantry.

'It's to slow us down before we hit the bulk of the traffic. That way a jam can be avoided,' McNeil ventured.

'That's bollocks,' she replied coarsely. 'You're just meant to think that. If a mile down the road we hit congestion we're meant to be like *oh I'm pleased I slowed down* when it's not as if you wouldn't have braked when you saw the queuing traffic. Or if the traffic suddenly clears, you're like *oh thank goodness they slowed us down so to allow things to space out a little.*' Johnson paused for a moment, realising how animated she had just been.

'Erm, let me guess. You have a few points for speeding on your license?' McNeil said.

'You what?'

'I bet that you were about to follow that little speech of yours with the claim that the only reason why they turn on the speed limits is so they can switch on the speed cameras and make some money.'

'You can just...'

'And the only reason why you would do so with such depth of feeling is that you have been caught out by these before,' McNeil interrupted smugly, before adding, 'And more than once I would imagine.'

'Fuck off, McNeil, at least I'm old enough to have a driving license. Your provisional doesn't even allow you onto a motorway.'

Silence descended. The next gantry was looming into view, this one informing the motorists that the speed limit had now reduced to 50mph.

'Bet she slows...' McNeil whispered, supposedly to himself.

Almost instantly he could feel the car accelerating. He turned in surprise to look at Johnson. With metres to spare she jumped on the brakes and wiped off just enough speed that, after an agonising moment of waiting, they didn't see a double flash from above.

He looked back at her with a mixture of shock and relief. All the while her expression had not changed, and her eyes hadn't left the road. He was about to ask if she was okay when he saw her left hand leave the steering wheel and rise to her face. It looked like she might rest it against her cheek but instead she curled up all of the digits except the middle one and proceeded to make the remaining finger move back and forth between her and her passenger, all the while maintaining her focus on the other side of the windscreen.

'And you say I'm immature...' McNeil quipped whilst trying to make himself comfortable in his seat once more. With the hand now back on the steering wheel, he took the opportunity to take a long glance at Johnson, knowing that she was unlikely to turn. Without those eyes boring into him he was able to appreciate the structure of her face. She had prominent cheekbones, upon which was skin that was virtually flawless, with the merest hint of the crow's feet of age forming at the corners of her eyes. As he observed her lips and how the bottom one was slightly fuller than the top, he wondered what they might taste like.

'Shit!' The abrupt curse brought McNeil's thoughts back to the present. The deceleration of the car, more gradual this time, confirming what Johnson had seen up ahead. 'We've hit the traffic already.'

'Cheer up, it'll probably clear after a couple of junctions and you'll be able to drive like Sebastian Vettel the rest of the way to Kent.'

Chapter Twenty-eight

'It's a nice car and everything but, next time, let's take something a little more on the comfortable side of sporty,' McNeil suggested whilst trying to straighten out his back in the unfamiliar police station car park.

'It's not my fault we were virtually bumper to bumper all the way here,' Johnson said grumpily, also feeling the effects on her bones of the near four-hour drive.

McNeil looked at his watch, a simple Casio he had been given by his mother in the run up to his GCSE exams years ago. It was covered in scratches and the black paint had chipped off in places, revealing the metal underneath. He had planned to upgrade to something sturdier and chunkier, like a G Shock, when he first joined the force but, whilst this remained accurate, he no longer saw the need.

'Do you need some help with that?'

'Come again?' McNeil replied absentmindedly, looking up.

'You seem to be struggling. Do you need me to explain what the big hand means?' It was clear that Johnson's frustration with the journey had evaporated.

'It's digital.'

'Even more worrying,' she murmured.

'Why are you in a good mood all of a sudden?'

'Ah!' Johnson laughed. 'That obvious, is it?' She began walking to the station. McNeil started following and was about to ask her what she meant, when she continued, 'Do you remember me saying that we were expected?'

'Yes,' replied McNeil, not really understanding.

'Well, do you remember me saying we were welcome?'

'Er, no.'

'We're not,' she said, turning and smiling.

'And that is why you're happy?' McNeil was more confused than ever.

'You ever watched one of those American movies where a crime happens, the FBI arrive and the local cops get all pissy?'

'Ah I see,' he said, nodding. 'So, we're like the FBI then?'

'Bingo!'

'But that still doesn't explain why you're excited...'

Whether or not Johnson intended sharing, they were already at the door. Although they had needed to give their credentials when arriving at the secure car park, they faced another buzzer.

'It's DCI Johnson and Special Agent Starling,' she called into a small microphone, whilst depressing the button.

'Could you repeat that?' Came the crackled reply.

'Look, you already know who we are. You're the same voice as when we arrived. We're already running late because of the stupid traffic round here so let's skip to the part where I meet with DCI Marlowe, shall we?' There followed an awkward silence, eventually broken by the clicking sound of the lock release. Johnson winked at McNeil, pulled the door and held it open for him. 'After you, Clarice,' she said, gesturing at the dimly lit interior.

At the end of the corridor there was another door and McNeil returned the favour, less out of a sense of chivalry, and more because he did not want to be the first person to face the duty sergeant within.

Johnson seemed only too pleased to stride through. Before she had got halfway to the counter she was already shouting out, 'You made the call yet?'

Reminding McNeil of his many encounters with Sergeant Andrews back in Nottingham, this duty sergeant also seemed transfixed by something in his logbook and didn't look up. 'She'll be down in a minute,' he replied, pointing with his pencil in the general direction of a row of metal seats bolted to the floor in one corner.

'Some coffee whilst we wait?' Johnson asked, apparently not taking up the invitation to sit.

'No thanks, I've just had one,' the duty sergeant replied, still engrossed in what he was reading.

McNeil failed to stifle a snigger and received a quick glance of retribution. Johnson stepped forward, hands on hips but, before she could say anything, a door to their right swung open and in walked a woman in plain clothes.

'DCI Johnson, good to meet you, I'm DCI Stacey Marlowe,' she said, holding out her hand.

As Johnson accepted the invitation, any thoughts of one-upmanship immediately drained away. 'Very good of you to meet us in person. This is my colleague, PC McNeil. We apologise for being late.'

Marlowe waived a dismissive hand. 'No worries. I imagine the journey down here was a nightmare. I wish I could say we had more to go on...' Her tone had taken on a seriousness now, losing its previous warmth. 'What makes you think it could be your boy?'

'Is there somewhere we can go, where we can speak in private?'

'Sure, sure,' Marlowe replied immediately. 'Follow me.' Having quickly punched a number into the door's keypad she led them through into the CID offices. McNeil observed that they had a similar layout to Nottingham's with a number of open cubicles and private rooms in the corner, but with the whole area looking older and somewhat tired.

DCI Marlowe made a detour to the coffee percolator on the way to her office. 'Get you both a drink?' she enquired, already pouring dark liquid into three mugs of varying provenance. 'Milk, sugar?'

'No thanks,' replied Johnson.

'I'm sweet enough,' ventured McNeil, instantly realising the look on both the DCIs' faces suggested his attempt to be endearing had failed.

'So, what have you got so far?' Johnson enquired, turning back to Marlowe.

'Well, I suppose nothing more than you already know,' she replied, walking towards her office. As they entered, she pointed to some armchairs surrounding a coffee table. 'The victim is a young woman; a student at the university who was in town, presumably to do some shopping. Three stab wounds to the lower abdomen with a nasty twist of the blade each time; designed to open up the wound.'

'Any witnesses?'

'We don't think so, but she was still bleeding out when she was found. That person says she didn't see anyone but we're hoping that when she recovers from the shock, she may be able to remember something.'

'Boyfriend? Anything like that?' McNeil asked.

'No, no boyfriend as far as we can tell. She seems like a nice person by all accounts, nothing to suggest it was personal.'

'How's the CCTV looking?'

'Still trawling through it. It was your typical busy Saturday morning,' Marlowe said, shrugging slightly.

'But nothing on that street?'

'Nope. Just far enough out to be sufficiently quiet and not under CCTV coverage.'

'Hmmm,' replied Johnson. 'So, although the attacker might have been unknown to the victim, it does imply someone who knows their way around Canterbury?'

'Yes,' said Marlowe. 'Or someone who just got lucky.'

'But you don't buy that, do you?' McNeil asked.

'No,' said Marlowe, smiling and taking another sip from her coffee. 'Whilst seemingly random, when they are spur of the moment there is usually plenty to go on. Typically, we would have the murderer by now…'

A silence descended with the three police officers deep in their own thoughts. Marlowe put down her mug and straightened in her chair. 'Look,' she said, 'I'm sorry if it's been a wasted journey. When we get more information, I'll be sure to pass it on, one way or another.'

She leaned forward, about to stand and, although McNeil was beginning to follow her lead, something about the way Johnson remained motionless caused her to hesitate. With a slight sigh, she relaxed her posture. 'And yet you still think it may be your boy.' It was more of a statement than a question.

'Yes, even more so than before,' came the flat reply.

'I don't understand,' said McNeil.

'We're trying to find a connection between the two lots of killings,' Johnson started to explain. 'And whilst we haven't found anything that directly links them…'

'Yet,' McNeil interrupted.

'…there is nothing that doesn't.' A short pause. 'There is nothing about this case that suggests anything different. Until there is, I want us to continue to consider the implication this has on our guy, if it was his doing.'

Marlowe shrugged. 'Ok, sounds reasonable enough. Anyway, as I said, I have your number, so I'll give you a call when we have something more.' She got up from her seat.

This time Johnson did stand. 'There was another reason for coming down here. We want to see the body for ourselves.'

Marlowe gave a wry smile. 'Ah, a DC of mine suggested that may be what you were after.'

'Problem?' Johnson asked.

'Far less than I was led to expect,' came Marlowe's ambiguous reply. This time it was McNeil's turn to smile. 'Would you be terribly offended if I got one of the officers downstairs to show you to pathology?'

'No, not at all. You have been most welcoming,' Johnson said with genuine warmth. 'Thank you for your time.' She reached out to shake her hand once more. Again, the roughness of her touch both surprised and impressed her. 'We'll find our way down from here.'

'Great, I'll put a call down to the duty sergeant,' Marlowe replied, giving a slight wave as she picked up the telephone receiver.

Once out of the office and out of earshot McNeil said: 'I liked her. She kind of reminded me of someone.'

If Johnson had understood the inference, she did not take the bait. 'Now, when we get down there I want you to look for anything unusual. Anything at all. Pathologists tend to be very protective about *preserving the integrity of the body* or some such shit. But if we're both asking questions, we should cover every angle. Just don't touch the body unless instructed.'

'I didn't plan to!' McNeil replied, horrified.

Johnson stopped walking and turned to him. 'Is this your first dead body?' No hint of teasing in her voice.

'Er, no.' He reconsidered. 'Well, close up it will be.'

'Ok, look, it can be a bit creepy. Try not to think about it – *her*. It's just another piece of evidence for us to examine. We'll be thorough, but we'll also be as quick as possible.' She fixed his look with her ice-blue eyes and gave a slight nod of her head. 'You'll be fine, McNeil.'

With a uniformed officer already waiting for them as they re-entered the custody suite, Johnson completely ignored the duty sergeant. Whether their guide had been warned of her prior belligerence wasn't clear, but the young officer maintained a professional but distant approach; excusing himself as soon as they arrived at the morgue. Despite being caught up in thoughts of what was to follow, it did not escape McNeil that it was he who might have been performing a similar function a few short weeks ago. The next few minutes might reveal if his progress since then had been in the right direction.

What waited for McNeil inside was not what he was expecting, given his understanding of such places was heavily influenced by any number of U.S. crime dramas. There was no wall of individual metal hatches, each one designed to house a body, where one would open up the relevant door and slide out the corpse. It was a largely square room with two mobile metal tables spaced apart in the middle; one was bare and the other had the outline of a person, covered in a white sheet. Elsewhere there was benching down one side; home to the various microscopes, conical flasks and other laboratory equipment used to examine samples taken from the bodies. At the end was a free-standing American-style refrigerator which, although large, was presumably only used for storing samples. The double doors at the end of the room, designed so that they swung both ways, suggested the storage of bodies was through there.

The only living occupant in the room was a large woman in her mid-fifties with short grey hair and wearing blue scrubs. She was peering over her glasses at a pipette she was using to add drops of a solution to a test tube. Without taking her eyes away, she informed her guests that the girl was under the sheet and, if they didn't want to wait until she was finished with what she was doing, they would have to scrub up at the sink in the corner.

Johnson and McNeil rolled up their sleeves, applied the soap and washed their hands in silence. Having dried themselves with blue paper towels, which they discarded in the specifically marked bin, they moved over to the table. Johnson stared at McNeil once more and, when he nodded his head to indicate he was ready, she started lifting back the sheet, folding it on itself three times before resting it just below the woman's feet.

What struck McNeil first was the paleness of the body, with a blue tinge to her lips. Her hair was straight and tucked neatly behind her shoulders. She was slim but not athletic and, even lying on her back, her breasts protruded upwards in a considerable swell. As though reading his mind Johnson whispered softly: 'Implants,' pointing to barely perceptible thin white scars underneath each breast.

Uncomfortable with what he was seeing, McNeil's eyes moved on to the definition of the bottom of her ribs before the dip down into her flat stomach. There, to the right, and in stark contrast to the flawlessness of her skin, were three ragged holes, each roughly the size of a ten pence piece.

'Notice how it hasn't puckered in on itself like with a typical wound? There is a certain sawing of the flesh which suggests a serrated edge.'

'Like a steak knife,' said McNeil.

'Indeed.'

'So, like our guy then…'

'Yes, except for Sarah that is.'

'Sarah?'

'Her wound was singular and relatively clean. Although she lost a lot of blood, the nature of it and the fact she had immediate attention meant it was survivable. But yes, like the two murders. Right, let's check for clues.'

'That's exactly what I have done and am continuing to do DCI Johnson,' said the pathologist, from the side of the room, with irritation. 'I'm currently checking the deposits from under her fingernails.'

'Don't let us disturb you then.' The false lightness in Johnson's tone did not go unnoticed by McNeil. She lowered her voice: 'Any calling cards he has left us?'

'Not that I can see,' he whispered, having glanced quickly over the woman's neatly trimmed pubic hair and taken a more careful look down each leg. Her toes were painted the same iridescent silver as her finger nails. 'You know it's funny,' he said, as much to himself as Johnson,

'She clearly took a lot of pride in her appearance and yet she doesn't have any tattoos.'

'That's dangerous…' Johnson replied cryptically.

'What is?'

'You're allowing your personal preferences to influence your interpretation of a situation.' If this criticism was designed as an admonishment, the observational nature of the tone suggested otherwise.

'Come again, ma'am?'

'You are right. This woman did care about how she looked. But you are assuming she should view tattoos as a bodily enhancement in much the way you do.'

'How do you know I like tattoos?'

With the conversation now beyond a whisper, both Johnson and McNeil could hear the pathologist tutting at them. They ignored her. 'Well it's obvious from your original statement. Perhaps the last thing the girl would want is to graffiti her body.'

'So, you don't like tattoos then?' McNeil was now puzzled.

'I didn't say that,' she sighed. 'I'm saying that different things can be viewed by different people in different ways, so we have to keep an open mind.'

The blank look on his face suggested he was still lost.

'Look, it doesn't matter.' Johnson turned to the pathologist, 'Can you roll her over to her side, so we see her back?'

With a grumble she called for her lab assistant.

There was barely a mole on her entire body, never mind a tattoo; her skin was almost as flawless as the front, except for the usual pink and purple marks of lividity during the rigor mortis process and some bruising on her lower left back.

'Caused by the stabbing,' the pathologist said, who had loitered and was watching carefully to check they weren't disturbing the body and contaminating evidence. 'Went sufficiently deep for it to disrupt the flesh near the surface there.' Clearly now having had enough of their company, she continued, 'What exactly is it you are looking for?'

'Just looking,' McNeil said dismissively. This raised a smile from Johnson.

'We're going to need to see her clothes,' Johnson added as the assistant rolled the body back over.

Perhaps it was their refusal to engage with her questions, but the pathologist didn't respond. The three of them stood there facing each other in silence. The defiance of the pathologist's crossed arms was met by the confident posture of Johnson's hands on hips. With the tension in the room almost palpable, and sensing that Johnson was building up to deliver a withering, and no doubt inflammatory comment, McNeil decided to diffuse the tension by indicating to a plastic tub in the corner. 'In there are they?'

'Help yourself, we've been over them and taken samples, but haven't found anything that feels out of place. No alien fibres or fluids on these unfortunately, and there aren't any foreign skin cells under her nails either. She looked after herself and was clean, so if she had a chance to scratch or fight back, we would have got some good samples, but nothing, so it is likely that the attacker took her by surprise and it was over before she had a chance to defend herself.'

She gestured toward the lab assistant who then started wheeling the body, still uncovered, towards the double doors. Having used the front of the table to push them open, he didn't return in the few minutes that Johnson and McNeil remained in the room.

'You're also correct about the type of blade. I can confirm it was approximately 7cm long and with a serrated edge. So yes, it is highly likely that this was a steak knife,' the pathologist concluded.

'I really thought there would be something,' McNeil said as they made their way across the car park. 'If he went to the trouble of indicating the second attack in

Nottingham was linked to the first, surely he would be even more keen to show us this was his work?'

Johnson had not spoken since they had left the path lab, even choosing to ignore the duty sergeant's sarcastic farewell as they exited the building.

'You going to open up then?' he asked, pointing to the Audi's passenger door, after having stood there for a number of seconds. 'At least we'll have enough time to grab some lunch before beating the traffic back north.'

'I fancy some fresh air. Let's have a walk into town and see what they've got,' she replied.

Chapter Twenty-nine

The scratched digital face announced it was 16:58. The pint glass sat in front of McNeil had drips of condensation running down the outside. The head of the beer had receded in the time since poured, giving the impression of already having been started, but it was untouched by his lips, as it would remain for the following two minutes.

McNeil had never consumed alcohol whilst on duty and the enjoyment he was deriving from the anticipation of the cool liquid on his throat, would not see him fail now. Although the bar was quiet, its few patrons, along with the general décor, made him feel decidedly under-dressed and he was looking forward to finding somewhere more normal when Johnson arrived.

Given how disinterested in eating she had been when staking out Nottingham station on Saturday, he should have been surprised when, not only had she agreed to his proposition of lunch following the disappointment at Canterbury police station, she also suggested they walk into town to find some. It was only when she seemed to be detouring from the quickest route to the high street that he realised it had just been an excuse to visit the crime scene. With all the evidence having been collected, there was nothing to indicate it was the correct place except for the street name and photographs she had seen of the exact spot.

McNeil had quickly run out of things to interest him there and had perched patiently on a low wall, leaving Johnson to her erratic wanderings. It had been a full ten minutes before she sat next to him, still seemingly content to keep her own council. Eventually she shared that the place *felt like him*. McNeil had confessed that he didn't share the same feeling, considering how varied the previous locations were, but she managed to convince him that this was an ideal spot for the careful opportunist. It was only a few turns away from the main thoroughfare; yet sufficiently quiet to allow him the seclusion needed to both attack and slip away unnoticed.

Spending time at the scene, with the occasional pedestrian walking by, apparently oblivious to the act of evil that had been committed there, had pushed all thoughts of food out of McNeil's mind. It was only now, as the digits changed on his watch to 17:00, and he took his long-awaited sip of beer, that he felt the first pangs of hunger again.

Johnson had appeared similarly affected by the surroundings and, having also agreed that lunch was off the agenda, insisted that they walk the surrounding streets, so she could get a sense of which direction she believed the attacker had come from, and the way he would have escaped. For all her bluster and bravado, behind it lay a logical and methodical mind. He enjoyed watching her work and felt there was much he could learn from her approach to investigation.

It was McNeil who had first pointed out that they needed to hurry back to the police station if they were going to hit the road in time to avoid the bulk of the rush hour traffic later in their journey. Misinterpreting Johnson's reluctance, his offer to drive had the effect of snapping her out of her current mood and inviting the good-natured torrent of insults about her previous experience with him behind the wheel.

Although it had been him who first suggested he didn't fancy the journey back, pre-rush hour or not, McNeil suspected by the swiftness the statement was replied to, that he wasn't the first to think it. Johnson's apparent coyness about suggesting they stay the night –something that, she later revealed, had been pre-approved by DSI Potter in case they uncovered more evidence – was a source of intrigue for him. Naturally it could be for a whole host of reasons, not least the fact that the trip had been entirely fruitless, but the near relief with which she received McNeil's admission that he wasn't ready to go back to Nottingham, suggested a certain nervousness on her part. And yet, as soon as he had broached the issues related to them staying, Johnson had been swift and decisive in confronting each of them. The most immediate and pressing was ensuring approval for her not returning to continue heading up the Nottingham investigation. Whilst Johnson had been confident that, if subsequently challenged by DSI Potter, she could find an acceptable reason for not going back straight away, she admitted that they would both feel more relaxed if they knew he was on side.

What followed had been a masterclass in manipulation, all played out on speakerphone for McNeil's benefit; something of which Machiavelli himself would have been proud. She had tempered DSI Potter's initial expectation that, having chosen to call him from Canterbury, they had some concrete information, by appearing to be looking for guidance; as a student would from a mentor. She successfully played to his, admittedly small, ego then proceeded to talk about obstacles they had encountered; first with the traffic but also with co-operation by the Canterbury constabulary. She hadn't mentioned DCI Marlowe, nor had she chosen to share how open and helpful she had been, allowing her comments about the duty sergeant and pathologist to be examples that implied a trend with the rest of the staff. McNeil was sure it had been much to Potter's relief that Johnson had politely turned down the resulting offer for the matter to be raised with the station's superiors. After describing the examination of the victim's body and their study of the crime scene, she suggested that their initial thought this might be the work of their killer had been incorrect. With the DSI under at least as much pressure as she was to get a result, he reached the same conclusion she had privately that, although there was no clear evidence connecting the murders, nothing that had been described to him demonstrated that they weren't linked. Potter had stated they must keep an open mind.

Johnson had apologised, offering that she was tired, and then attempted to wrap up the phone call by explaining that they needed to get back to the police station to retrieve her car before the long journey back. Whether out of concern for Johnson's welfare or just a refusal to concede that nothing more could be done to link the two cases, DSI Potter suggested they stay over, have a fresh look tomorrow and, if nothing else turned up, they could then make their way back mid-morning. She had appeared reluctant and even went as far as to say she didn't know where to look to find an appropriate hotel given it would be secured on tax-payers' money. Potter had told her that now wasn't the time to worry about such things and to just head for the high street and find the first one that looked decent.

Impressed as he had been by the conversation, not for the first time, McNeil wondered whether Johnson would be only too willing to throw him to the wolves if it served her purpose.

It had been an interesting walk along the high street. Johnson had turned down some perfectly acceptable looking lodgings, the decisiveness of her dismissals almost implying she knew there was better further up. As soon as they arrived at a hotel with an imposing and traditional frontage made of stone on the ground floor and Tudor beams, with bay windows, on the upper two, Johnson had declared it to be the right one. They walked under the awning, above which were flag poles proudly displaying the hotel's brand name, and a doorman greeted them to reveal an interior design that was clean and modern, but also luxurious with its expensive brown leathers and dark woods.

They settled on two of the mid-price rooms and agreed to part company to meet in the hotel's champagne bar at 5pm. Whilst Johnson had gone out to pick up some *essentials*, offering to buy McNeil a toothbrush and whatever other toiletries he required, he had gone up to his room. The receptionist had described it as *enviable*, a fitting description given its large size, polished wooden floors and enormous double bed. He was disappointed to find his view was to the rear of the hotel and settled down on the leather sofa at the foot of the bed to see what was on the large television mounted on the opposing wall. With the imperfect signal quality a match to the attributes of the daytime programming, he soon became bored and headed down to the bar early.

It was now 17:09 and he'd drained most of his pint. Johnson had yet to arrive, and McNeil knew that if the barman was half-way competent he would soon be enquiring whether he wanted another. He had no idea how the evening would pan out and, for all he knew, Johnson might want a quick drink, grab some food nearby before excusing herself for an early night. In which case another beer now, as long as he drank it slowly enough that he wouldn't force the barman into tempting him into a third before she arrived, couldn't hurt. But, then again, if she was looking to let her hair down a bit, which was perfectly plausible given the few days they'd had, starting so early and being a couple of drinks up when he had no idea of her tolerance might not be a good idea.

'Same again?' The cheerful question from the barman meant McNeil could be indecisive no longer.

As he thought of the appropriate response, a familiar voice called from a few feet behind him: 'Make that two!'

As he turned around to acknowledge Johnson's arrival, the sight before him caused him to gawp. 'Wow' escaped his mouth before he attempted, and failed, to regain his composure.

'Problem?' she enquired with an innocence to her tone that completely contrasted with the mischievous glint in her eye.

'You, er, got changed…'

'Nothing escapes you, PC McNeil.' It was clear that Johnson's trip to the shops, and part of the reason for her being late to the bar, had been much more than picking up a few items for the morning. As far as he could tell, it had stretched to a whole new wardrobe. Her casual jeans of earlier had been swapped for a tighter fitting pair, complemented by some ankle boots with a substantial heel. Her top was a pattern of black and white, the neckline sitting below her shoulders and revealing that, if she was wearing a bra, and the fit of the material made it unclear either way, it was a strapless one.

Johnson suggested that they move from the bar stools to a more comfortable and secluded table towards the side of the room. It was clear from his early attempts at conversation that she wasn't very interested in discussing their case. Part of him regretted not taking the earlier opportunity to get an extra drink in him so he might relax more, but the rate at which Johnson was quaffing her beer suggested that any current awkwardness would soon be replaced by the tongue-loosening effects of alcohol consumption.

'Any thoughts on what you might like to do this evening?' he asked, trying to sound as casual as possible.

'Let's have another here and then see what the rest of this town has to offer,' she said before draining the remainder of her glass.

McNeil moved to get up, but Johnson beat him to it. 'My round,' she called cheerfully, grabbing her small clutch bag and heading back to the bar. A couple of minutes later she returned with a pint in each hand and two bags of crisps clenched between her teeth. As she slumped back down with a satisfied sigh, she slung the snacks into the middle of the table. 'Have whichever bag you like. I thought we could do with lining our stomachs,' she said with a wink.

Chapter Thirty

'Look, I think I'm going to have to eat something soon,' McNeil said. The clock above the bar informed him that it was now 8:45pm. They were in their third establishment since leaving the hotel but this one was much the same as the last two. Having decided that the only premises still open on the high street were the usual chain restaurants, they had ventured down a side street looking for pubs. The number on offer was not the issue, just the lack of variety, and, on a Monday evening, most were quiet. Neither of them had initially seen this as a problem but as they got through more rounds, and their conversations got louder and more animated, they became conscious that the subdued atmosphere was becoming increasingly divergent to their mood.

'I think I'm a little too drunk to sit in a restaurant,' confessed Johnson who, once they had left the hotel, had switched to wine and matched each of McNeil's pints with a large glass. 'Another bag of peanuts?'

'I've had my fill of bar snacks,' McNeil replied, trying to stifle a belch. 'I believe they're still serving food here,' he said, reaching across to the next table to retrieve a dog-eared cardboard menu and offering it to her.

She barely glanced at it before saying, 'Look, we've been in here for at least…' She looked up at the clock and her face contorted in concentration as she attempted to work out the time since their arrival.

'Do you need help with that?' McNeil asked, his voice dripping with delighted sarcasm.

'Piss off!' she replied loudly and receiving irritated glances from across the bar. 'If only it was digital,' she mused still staring at the clock.

Once they had stopped laughing, Johnson leant in towards McNeil.

'We've been here… a while.' She attempted to whisper but only succeeding in lowering her voice to a typical speaking level. 'How many dishes have you seen being served?'

'Er, none.'

'Exactly,' she responded, nodding sagely, as though Confucius himself would have envied her profundity.

It took McNeil a few moments to grasp her point. 'Ah, so what then? Is it too early for a kebab?'

'What?' Johnson replied in mock outrage, once again drawing attention to herself from other patrons. 'This is how you treat a lady?'

'Okay then,' he said good naturedly, taking another swig of his lager. 'At the risk of accusing the lady of being fickle: if she's too pissed for a restaurant, too snobby for a takeaway and too… I don't know what … to eat here… then what would said lady like?'

She leaned in once more, this time much closer. McNeil giggled and turned his head, so his ear was directly in front of her. He could feel her hot breath but heard no words. Instead a smooth hand grasped his chin and gently pulled his face back towards her. She fixed him with her pale blue eyes. Although glassy from the alcohol, they remained as intense as ever. 'Room service,' she whispered.

Chapter Thirty-one

McNeil had mixed feelings about the walk back to the hotel. On the one hand he wanted to get there as soon as possible, lest the moment fade, but on the other he felt more nervous than he could remember in a long time. If Johnson was similarly conflicted, her steady pace suggested otherwise. With her being a stride further ahead, he afforded himself a long look at her body. He had an overwhelming urge to just stop her there in the street and kiss her but, it wasn't so much fear that she wouldn't reciprocate that prevented him, more that he didn't want to appear over-eager. He was very conscious of the age gap and had never been with a woman out of her twenties.

The idea of being with someone older didn't bother him, especially when Johnson's physique looked perfect and she could pass as someone considerably younger. Rather than being concerned that she might be too old for him, he was worried that he may seem too young for her. He had no doubt that the confidence she exuded everyday was replicated when it came to being physical. And whilst the thought of her taking control and being clear about exactly what she wanted thrilled him, at the same time he found it intimidating. He felt caught in the void between the carefree abandon of a one-night stand and the progressive learning experience of a relationship. When he was with a girl he had just met there was the understanding that this wasn't expected to lead anywhere. As such, and whilst his ego had wanted him to perform well, he had known that he could just relax and enjoy himself. When he was at the beginning of a relationship there was more of a focus on intimacy and tenderness; a slowness to the pace and an acknowledgement that it would take time and practice for two individuals to come together as one cohesive entity.

Knowing that he was now over-thinking the concern for what was to follow, he could feel his pace slacken further. This was noticed by Johnson, but she did not seem to misread this as him having second thoughts. 'Come on slow-coach,' she called, turning around and now walking backwards. 'Room service can be terribly slow, so I suggest you order the moment you get back to your room.'

McNeil stopped instantly, slack jawed for the second time that evening. Johnson also came to a halt. Her face looked deadly serious. 'And I bet the tray charge in a place like this is astronomical.' She paused. 'So, I guess it's best we order together,' she said slowly. With that she broke out into a huge grin, grabbed his hand and virtually dragged him up to jogging speed for the final fifty metres to the hotel entrance.

The mixture of cold air, anticipation, anxiety and that final shock on the journey back had done a fine job of sobering McNeil up. Momentarily believing that he had completely misread Johnson's signals had galvanised him into determination that he was going to enjoy himself, come what may. As the doors to the elevator closed and she turned towards him, he could control himself no longer. He placed his left hand on her backside to pull her in and bent his head down to meet her lips. She allowed her mouth to part, and did not object to his right hand finding her breast over the material of her top. But she did not return the kiss. Perturbed, he pulled away to find her eyes boring into him once more. The audible ping, announcing they had arrived at the appropriate floor, punctuated the intensity of the moment. 'Easy tiger,' she murmured, stepping out of the lift. 'We have all night.'

'Your place or mine?' McNeil asked a few moments later, trying to sound sufficiently casual but with his lips still tingling from their recent encounter.

'Mine, definitely mine.'

McNeil waited patiently, and Johnson started to rummage in her bag for the room key. Although small, she had clearly packed as much stuff into it as possible. 'Here, hold this,' she commanded, thrusting her mobile phone towards him, in order to allow her to differentiate between the bag's contents more easily.

As he grabbed it, his touch woke up the screen. Unconsciously he glanced down at the display; an act he would replay over in his mind with regret countless times in the days to follow. 'You have some missed calls,' he remarked absentmindedly.

'Let me see,' she responded, abandoning her search. 'Shit!'

'What is it?' McNeil asked, concerned.

'They're local numbers. Look, I've got a voicemail.' She pressed the icon for recorded messages and then hit speaker so they both could hear.

It seemed to take an age for the automated voice to run through its prescribed preamble. Eventually the message started: 'DCI Johnson, it's DCI Marlowe. We have the murder weapon.' There was a long pause and Johnson's finger hovered over the *End Call* icon. 'I think you are going to want to see this,' she added.

Chapter Thirty-two

Brandt no longer considered himself retired; he very much saw his latest endeavours as a career change. Clearly it was something he had needed to keep to himself, maintaining the impression that he was jobless. This was relatively straightforward considering that his divorce, coupled with leaving the police, had left him with very few regular acquaintances, never mind friends. Yet in the weeks following his retirement party, he had needed to deal with numerous messages enquiring, not without a hint of jealousy, how much he was enjoying his spare time. His responses, sufficiently delayed and short, both implied that he was keeping busy and served not to maintain a dialogue. The occasional phone calls had been more of an irritation, having to answer the usual questions about whether he had taken up golf, found a wealthy divorcee, and if he was missing *the routine of work*. He guessed that he would have been less generous with his responses, had he not wanted to arouse any suspicious as to his well-being. The calls usually ended with non-specific promises to meet up soon but thankfully, they were becoming increasingly infrequent in number.

Except, that is, for Franklin's. DSI Brian Franklin was two years Brandt's junior and busy planning for his own retirement. They had known each other for the past two decades, with their careers progressing at similar rates. However, notwithstanding the fact that they looked similar, with their dark brown hair, average height and medium build, as far as Brandt was concerned, that was where the similarities ended. Whilst Brandt had been satisfied that the job of Chief Superintendent was as far as he could progress without the bureaucracy and politics overtaking true investigative work, Franklin, for so many years, had been hell bent on going higher. Not that he would admit that to anyone now that his proximity to retirement had curtailed his previously minimal chances. As far as Brandt was concerned, Franklin had got as far as he had riding on the back of the success of others. With the spotlight more on him as DSI, he had maintained his position with caution and conservatism, hoping to be seen as a safe pair of hands when further opportunities arose. That Brandt, with a reputation for the unorthodox, had been invited to apply for more senior positions on a number of occasions, hadn't bothered Franklin. Perhaps he saw Brandt's refusal to do so as opening the way for him, hoping that their association would make him a more attractive candidate.

Nevertheless, for all Brandt's maverick tendencies, he knew how to play the game and, whilst not courting opportunities that would lead to him encountering Franklin, nor had he avoided them. Each time he had feigned pleasure in seeing his old colleague, an emotion always reciprocated by Franklin, who was only too happy to use the occasion to pick his brains on whatever case he was currently working on.

Brandt had fully expected his retirement to end their connection, but it seemed that he had underestimated the friendship that Franklin believed they had developed. On one of their recent phone calls, Franklin had confided that he and his wife had recently split and wanted Brandt's advice on how to cope with going through a divorce process. The initial pride he had felt at successfully giving the impression that he had actually coped with his wife's departure soon faded into frustration at, not only having to relive the pain of their parting, but also having to listen to the problems of someone he wasn't in the least bit interested in.

'…and the hardest part is that my children are siding with her.' Franklin was now close to tears. Brandt was pleased; this latest, and somewhat repetitive, monologue had been going on for minutes. Franklin's need to pause in an attempt to compose himself allowed him an opportunity to speak.

'I can imagine,' he said, meaning nothing of the sort. *At least you've got children. The fact that you had children and still managed to fuck it up shows what a complete dick you really are. If we'd had children…* Brandt couldn't, wouldn't, complete the thought. He was allowing this fucker to drag him down and he had been feeling so much better recently. Time to wrap this up. 'Look, hold on in there… buddy,' the last word almost choking in his throat. 'We really must get together sometime.'

'Saturday.'

'What?'

'Saturday. Let's get together this Saturday.'

Brandt's mind was racing. No, not Saturday. Saturdays were his special day. He had so much momentum now…

'Jeff? Are you still there?'

'Of course.'

'Not got plans, have you?'

'Well…' Well what? he thought sarcastically. *Well, aside from my latest serial murder, my diary is looking pretty free that day.* 'Well, sure.' *Think Brandt, think!* 'Look, I've got to go but let's shore up plans later on in the week.'

I'll just avoid his calls and make up a good excuse for when I next have to speak to him, Brandt thought.

'What shall we do?' Franklin asked, as though completely ignoring what Brandt said.

'Er, let's go for a drink that evening.' *Yes, that was it! Keep it to the evening and I can still do both. A few drinks to celebrate my latest triumph and few more for this prick's misery.*

'Perhaps that's not such a good idea. You see, since Louise left I've been er... I've been overdoing it a little. I realise now that it's just making things feel worse. Can we meet for a coffee instead?'

'Yes. Fine.' All the fight had drained out of Brandt.

'Shit, shit, SHIT!' he shouted, smashing the receiver repeatedly against the wall. His conversation with Franklin had only lasted a couple more minutes so that a café could be agreed upon and a time in the early afternoon.

He went and slumped in his armchair, unconsciously reaching for the whisky bottle. As the amber liquid gave the familiar and comforting burn to his throat, he decided that would be the first and only drink of the evening. He would need a clear head to work this out.

About an hour later he felt better. Not just better; really good. Perhaps a drink was in order. Confirming once again to Brandt that he must be following some pre-ordained path, rather than allow his unwelcome date with Franklin to become an obstacle that he would have to work around, he used it as an opportunity to establish how to take his campaign to the next level.

This was the perfect time for a watershed moment; something that would require a bit more planning than the few days between now and Saturday would afford. Leaving the murder weapon in Canterbury did not just allow the connection to be made to his previous acts, but would also mark the transformation to the next stage. He would wait to see what the press made of it over the following days, but he already had a plan formulated.

Central to this was wanting to spend more time with his next victim. It would prevent his actions being pigeon-holed as random stabbings. By this being *more*, it would represent an undeniable escalation that would negate the apparent slow down between incidents and even trump the impact of his reach going far beyond Nottingham.

For a short while he considered deliberately switching the gender of his next victim. A man would serve the purpose of indicating a change in approach, but he eventually settled on his next job being a woman. He wanted to cement the impression of sexual motivation so that, when he switched to a man, it would completely toss into the air all their preconceived assumptions of the perpetrator. Keeping everyone guessing would ensure that he remained one step ahead of his pursuers and, more importantly, serve to keep his actions centre stage in the national consciousness.

A by-product of all this, but perhaps not as much of a secondary consideration as Brandt would like to admit, was that spending time with a female victim would allow him to explore the mixed emotions he had been experiencing. As he reflected on his work so far, his greatest satisfaction had come from the task on the River Trent. He could only surmise it was because he felt a greater synergy with that woman, as a result of spending more time in her company prior to their union. Canterbury had been a unique thrill, partly through relief that, having failed with his initial target, he had still managed to complete his mission, and also because of his decision on how to delay the discovery of the murder weapon. Only a small element was the actual taking of that woman's life, a fact illustrated by it providing him with little *inspiration* once he had returned home. Consequently, his next act would enable him to build up the connection with his victim and, having to simulate sexual assault, rather than deriving genuine pleasure, would prove the purity of his purpose. For whilst Brandt embraced the idea that one should feel satisfaction with a job well done, it was important to him to believe that this all served the wider purpose of waking the people of Britain from their complacency.

Chapter Thirty-three

He liked St. Albans. In a world which he felt had changed almost beyond the point of recognition, the city where he had spent much of his childhood remained familiar, especially in the historical parts like St. Michael's, where he was now parked. Sure, the Roman museum and its gift shop, which he briefly visited in order to get change for his parking ticket, was more recent, but the surroundings of Verulamium Park remained largely the same as when he had visited it so frequently in the 1970s.

Yet, whilst Brandt had allowed time for a touch of nostalgia in his schedule, he was here for a much more specific purpose. The correct way to have prepared for his latest endeavour would have been to make a reconnaissance trip to reduce the number of variables he would encounter on the day. But this would have been too obvious and would have provided the police with an advantage they would surely exploit. When attempting to narrow things down they would be looking for patterns of behaviour and people noticing something similar. Someone hanging around near a train station is unlikely to arouse suspicion but the same person doing it twice may cause something to lodge in someone's mind. The easiest solution would be to carry out the preparatory visit well in advance, long enough ago not to trigger people's memories and, even more importantly, beyond the realistic scope of CCTV footage comparison.

Brandt's timescales hadn't allowed such a luxury. Consequently, he had needed a location he knew, but also one that could not conceivably be linked back to him. The police would be busy trying to establish the connection between Nottingham and Canterbury. Whilst that would prove fruitless, he did not want his third setting to provide any clues.

With sufficient contextual knowledge of the area, Brandt had been able to conduct his reconnaissance using his trusted Google Maps, identifying any changes with the locations he would be using. Moreover, rather than throw up any problems, some of the more recent residential developments beyond the lakes might play to his advantage.

However, the one thing he had failed to appreciate in his time since living in St. Albans was how restricted parking had become in the city streets and how astronomical the charges were in the municipal car parks. Tempted as he had been to simply pop his debit card into the meter, he decided it more prudent to risk breaking a note in the museum. In fact, the lady at the admissions desk seemed far from surprised when he said he simply wanted to pick up a gift for his grandson. Perhaps many visitors to Verulamium found they had insufficient change and followed a similar tactic, or maybe it was because people wanted a souvenir from the historical site without having to inflict on themselves the boredom of viewing a load of old pots and coins.

Regardless, minor hiccup out of the way, Brandt took a deep breath of the late April air, which was turning chilly as the sun made its way towards the horizon. He had allowed himself an hour to make his way across the park to Holywell Hill, a journey that could easily be completed in fifteen minutes if needed. He wanted to go via the lakes, so he set off down the familiar path that took him by the Inn On The Park, which still served as a café.

The path veered off and down a slight incline towards the much smaller of the two lakes. On his left was a low hedge, beyond which was an unkempt field with a few sheep, backing onto an enormous Edwardian house. For the first time in four decades Brandt wondered what type of family lived there and how he had never noticed its front when walking through St. Michael's. Whereas once there had just been parkland on his right interrupted by the occasional large oak tree and sections of the old Roman wall, there was a splash zone, closed until the warmer summer months arrived. The various pipes and spouts, painted in a variety of gaudy colours, clashed with the natural tones of its surroundings. Brandt could just imagine all the middle-class mothers and nannies attempting to navigate their expensive pushchairs down this path one handed, holding their obligatory coffee in their other, before unleashing the offspring to charge around the fenced areas whilst they got back to checking Facebook, Twitter and whatever else was on their precious mobile phones.

He stopped by the first lake; more a pond really, fed by the overflow of the main one; cunningly housed under the bridge that linked one side with the other. Although it was only home to a few ducks and a coot, he remembered Sundays where the still conditions would be used by young, as well as old, radio-controlled boat owners to navigate the still waters, whilst drawing an audience from passers-by. Brandt wondered whether that still happened, but suspected that a combination of ridiculous health and safety laws and kids being more interested in sitting at home on their games consoles had conspired to kill the tradition.

Saddened, he continued, rounding the smaller lake and taking the path by the larger one that had the River Ver running parallel on the left. Half way along, and still with plenty of time to get to his destination, he rested on a bench for a while, perpendicular to one of the lake's two islands. The silhouette of its trees was imposing with the sun's weak rays behind them. Save for the occasional honk of Canadian geese, and pedestrian footsteps, there was a peacefulness here that Brandt found enriching. He felt his mind, so often overcrowded with thought, begin to quieten.

It occurred to him that he could stay in this very spot until either the sunset or the growing chill forced him from the bench and simply return home. He could find a new direction, perhaps something that would allow a permanence of the serenity and tranquillity he now felt. But he knew that was just a selfish pipe dream. Even if he could accept denying the people the new-found respect for life that his actions were provoking, he could not allow the sacrifice of his three women to go unrewarded. He owed it, not just to them, but also to their families' suffering. Whilst he never expected them to understand his actions, much less accept them as the necessary part of restoring society's humanity, he was content to play the bad guy if it meant he could die in the knowledge that he had done good.

He roused himself from his thoughts, left the bench and continued on his way. There was more purpose to his walk, partly through his renewed determination and partly seeking to eradicate the cold which had permeated his body. As he rounded the top of the lake and saw the small bridge leading to the Fighting Cocks pub, he turned right along the treeline and followed the path, more heavily populated with people walking from the city centre to the King Harry housing estate, until it opened to allow him to cross the field that led to the Westminster Lodge leisure centre and the main road beyond. Brandt remembered when the pool there had first opened, and it was where his father had taught him to swim. Although it was a conventional rectangle, and the subsequent water flumes had yet to be installed, the diving boards had been a source of fascination to Brandt. He had only seen people use the medium board, but the top 10 metre one, a concrete shelf rather than a spring-loaded plank, had held his gaze on many occasions.

He had sworn to himself that one day he would scale it and launch himself into the terrifying space between it and the water below. It was a promise he had never kept but, in the particularly dark times when he considered how he would like to end his suffering, he came back to thoughts of plunging. In the weeks and months after his wife had moved out, he had often drifted into alcohol-fuelled unconsciousness; fantasising about the rush of air to his body as he stepped off from whatever ledge had entered his mind that night.

That a place that had once held so much enjoyment and hope for the future, now represented a life unfulfilled and tinged with regret, both upset and angered Brandt in equal measure. He resolved not to even glance in its direction on his way back and, instead, to revel in the moment of what he will have soon achieved.

Chapter Thirty-four

It had been a long day; the only comfort being that it was still light as she left the office. Lily James supposed that people dealt with stress in their own way. Whilst a number of her colleagues had decided to head into town for a few drinks, what she was looking forward to most was getting home and shoving something simple in the oven, which she would eat watching last night's recording of MasterChef. Once she had eaten, she would give her mother a quick call and have a bath; maybe treating herself to some of the scented candles that had been bought for her last Christmas. Then she would tuck herself up with her book and have an early night. Sure, the others would probably have unwound even before she had got off the train, but Lily knew who would be better able to cope with another day of ridiculously short deadlines and outrageously demanding clients tomorrow.

'Are you sure we can't tempt you, Lil?' Steven, a guy from her department, called as they went through the automatic door exiting the building. She hated being called *Lil*, almost as much as she hated how, after roughly two drinks, Steven would start patting her leg as he spoke to her. 'We could even start at The Flag in case you change your mind,' he said, pointing down the road in the direction of the pub next to Watford Junction station. It was a large establishment designed to house bands at night but, during the day, was too big for its catchment – mostly the sort of people who couldn't bear the thought of going home to what awaited them without having at least one drink inside them.

'No, you're alright, Steve, if I hurry I should make the next train.' Most of her colleagues lived in and around Watford or in nearby towns like Hemel Hempstead where rent and house prices were comparable. Lily lived in St. Albans and, although in her mid-twenties, had only been too happy when her comfortably-off parents had offered to buy her a place, convenient to the station, in the town in which she had grown up. It wasn't that she was a snob; in actual fact she went to great lengths to mask the privilege of her upbringing. Whereas some people have a telephone voice, a tone that is more well-rounded than their natural way of speaking, Lily masked the quality of her elocution; small things like dropping the occasional *t* at the end of a word or sometimes pronouncing *th* as *f*, in order to better fit in with her colleagues. What's more, when asked about her weekend, she sometimes swapped things like horse riding with going to the cinema.

Lily didn't see her charade as deceitful, just a way of being allowed to concentrate on her work without sticking out. She had also fallen victim to a few failed relationships where men had viewed her as a potential meal ticket, having judged her by the way she spoke and the expensive but conservative way she dressed. The fact was that all her potential inheritance, save for the share of her parents' property, which would have to be divided between her four siblings, had been pumped into her small terraced house, and her job paid nothing more than the typical decent graduate could expect in this economic climate. Maintaining a horse, with all the various associated costs, had meant forgoing a car; something even her closest friends found incomprehensible. However, living a short walk down Holywell Hill from St. Albans city centre, and only a few minutes from the train, meant she had little need for a car.

The station entrance was packed with people milling about; some finishing off a cigarette, others either being collected or dropped off by cars. As Lily attempted to navigate the throngs, any hope of making the earlier train faded. She still had a couple of minutes until its departure time but its position on the furthest platform meant she would have to run, something she had no intention of doing. Instead, and against her better judgement given the time of day, she ordered a coffee from the station barista and browsed the shelves of the newsagents for a suitably vacuous female-interest publication for her bath.

As she waited in the platform's sheltered area, refusing to while away the tedium by starting her magazine, it wasn't for the first time she mused that the term *Abbey Flyer* could be considered false advertising given the near fifty-minute wait between trains. Lily now wished she had run earlier and risked the twisted ankle her shoes posed. Many of her fellow commuters wore trainers, with their smart footwear poking out of their bag waiting to be swapped at work. Lily came from the mind-set that trainers were for sporty pursuits and, although she owned a pair, a barely used example purchased to coincide with an ill-fated gym membership, donning shoes that so obviously clashed with the rest of her clothes was against her better nature.

Knocking up a quick stir-fry would see her in front of MasterChef far quicker than waiting for a packet meal to heat up in the oven. With thoughts of supper firmly in her mind, she noticed that some of the other passengers had started moving outside in anticipation of the train's arrival. Keen as Lily was to get a seat, despite the relatively short sixteen-minute journey, she moved to the back of the platform. She knew the front of the train would be less busy and she had unconsciously balanced out the risk of not gaining a seat, and thus being unable to rest her weary feet, with being more susceptible to suffering the effects of a head-on collision or derailment.

With the sun setting on her journey which, not only had seen her sit down but also remain without someone neighbouring her, it was decidedly gloomy as she exited the train. It also seemed much cooler now and she buttoned up her coat to keep out the chill. St. Albans Abbey Station was little more than a platform at the end of a gravel car park, in stark contrast to the sprawl of platforms at Watford Junction and even St. Albans' main station on the other side of town. With only four coaches, the number of people also getting off were relatively few and, as Lily started to get left behind, her progress slowed by the uneven ground, she did wonder whether she would eventually have to relax her stance on footwear.

She came out of the station and turned right onto the slight incline which would soon become the steep Holywell Hill. At the second junction she headed into a narrow side street and, further down, she could already see her window box jutting out from the front of her bedroom window. This was always the sign for her to start rummaging in her handbag for her keys. It was merely out of habit but, on a cold evening such as this, it would also serve to allow her into the warmth of her house with minimal delay.

She already had the key selected and pointing forward, ten yards before reaching her property. With it now inserted, she twisted the lock and the door released with a squeak from the top where the wood was slightly too large for the frame.

Although she wasn't aware of anyone else in the street, it didn't surprise her when she heard a voice. Seemingly these days there was always one courier or another delivering something; if not addressed to her then requesting she accept it on behalf of a neighbour.

'Yes, is it for...?' The words died in Lily's throat.

Chapter Thirty-five

It was fortunate that Brandt considered himself a patient man because events hadn't gone as smoothly as planned. Having arrived at his destination early, through wanting to clear Westminster Lodge and all its negativity quickly, he had perched on one of the benches outside the Duke of Marlborough pub, which sat across the road from the station. From here he would be able to see when the passengers disembarked, and it would provide him with plenty of time to cross over and pick his target.

When the train arrived, he was pleased to see that there were a number of potential candidates, and it was just a matter of using his instincts to select the right one. Of the eight he spotted, two made their way back to their own cars, one was being picked up, and a further two were waiting for taxis. That left just three. One was more casually dressed than the other two but, as far as Brandt was concerned, all were viable. He hesitated a moment when the group split, with two heading right, one of them the casual woman, and the other heading left. Although selecting the pair would keep Brandt's options open, he went for the lone woman because she was walking away from the town centre. This meant she was far less likely to be stopping off somewhere before going home.

Satisfied he had made the right decision, and with his hands in his pockets, he followed at a discreet distance. If luck was with him, she would live alone but whilst Brandt would rather avoid the complication brought on by others, he had no doubt he could deal with the situation. Through surprise and sudden, overwhelming force he would knock down the woman to allow him to deal with the unwelcome addition quickly and decisively. Ironically, he thought to himself, not dissimilar to when the police storm a location.

Therefore, it was with mixed feelings that Brandt observed the woman pass the entrance to the luxury apartments and carry on. A flat would have meant she was more likely to live alone but, instead, would provide other complications. Her next move was left, onto the main road that led to some retail outlets on one side and a supermarket on the other. Given the size of the store, he would get plenty of warning if she were electing to go there, and he would hang well back and look to pick her up again when she exited.

Believing fortune to continue to be with him, he was pleased to see that the woman quickly crossed to the other side of the road and, ignoring the shops, headed up a residential street. These were semi-detached 1970s built houses with their ugly white PVC front panels. Switching to the other pavement, he knew that she must either be nearing her house or looking for another turn off. His preference would be the latter because the road was a little busy for his liking, but the sun was well behind the buildings now and the light was murky.

The properties technically possessed front gardens, but most people had elected to pave or gravel over them, either to make them easier to maintain or to provide additional off-street parking. As the woman turned into one of these, Brandt was not alarmed by the house having lights on inside. These days most people were wise enough to use timers and it made sense for them to be active now, especially as they were still likely to be on their winter settings.

It was with annoyance he observed that this particular front garden had been gravelled, but the upside was the absence of a car. His move would have to be quick because his footsteps would be audible. He was poised and ready, when something made him hesitate. He noticed a flicker. As he looked directly into the sitting room window, he heard the faint sound of the key being inserted into the lock. He was wasting time; missing his opportunity. There it was again; that flicker. Instantly it registered that it must be a screen of some sort, most likely a television. Brandt could feel his heart thumping in his chest. *Do it, DO IT!* But his legs were frozen with indecision. As he looked back towards the woman, he saw the door was wide open. If he didn't go now, this very instant, she would have sufficient time to hear him charging up the path and be able to slam the door behind her.

He carried on walking up the road. In total he must have been stationary for only a few seconds and he pulled out his phone to give the impression, should anyone have observed his behaviour, that he had felt it vibrating in his pocket. This part of town was unfamiliar to him, but he guessed that once he made it to the top of the road, he could find a way to loop around and make his way back down to the station. A glance at his watch told him that it was fifteen minutes since the train had pulled in. That gave him a good half an hour before the next one. That should leave him plenty of time to get there and, just as importantly, calm himself down.

Once Brandt knew he was heading in the right direction, he slowed sufficiently to avoid being at the station early. Knowing that waiting outside would be equally as unwise as going to the Duke of Marlborough for a second occasion, he needed to time it right. As he passed the block of flats again, he cursed his misjudgement when he saw the first people emerge from the station. He sped up his pace knowing that if he blew it again he would have to abandon, and devise a different plan for another time and place. Similarly, and against his judgement from earlier, he would have to select someone heading towards town to avoid having to double back on himself. With a good fifty yards still to cover, the number of passengers exiting was beginning to thin. His brain was a whir, attempting to deal with a multitude of possible scenarios at once. As he got closer and the last trickle was leaving, the one that seemed increasingly best was to abort.

Already turning towards the pedestrian crossing that would take him back to Verulamium Park, he noticed a lone figure stumbling slightly. A woman. However, any thoughts that she might be drunk, and what advantage that would give him, exited Brandt's mind as her walk steadied as she started in the direction of the hill.

He admonished himself for his previous lack of faith and swore that, if her next destination was a property, he wouldn't chicken out, even if she arrived to a whole welcoming committee. If the worst came to the worst, he would quickly stab her whilst she was still in the doorway and take flight.

Oh, this is good, he chuckled to himself as the woman turned into the second side road. He rounded the corner and saw that she was already reaching into her bag. All the houses were small, reducing the number of likely occupants.

As she turned to open her door, the streetlight between them provided a clear profile of her face. *Pretty*, he thought, not without a little satisfaction. He was only a couple of yards away as she started to push through the entrance. He slowly withdrew the knife from his pocket.

'Madam?' Brandt called in a neutral tone, making sure that he didn't allow the adrenaline that was coursing through his body to affect his voice too much.

She turned instantly but without the speed of surprise. She started to respond but before she could finish her sentence, he clamped his empty hand over her mouth and used his body to push her into the house.

Brandt needed to establish two things, and quickly. First, if there was anyone else in the property and, second, if he could get the door closed without having to gag her.

He held the knife in front of her right eye; she flinched but didn't try to pull away. That was a good sign. 'If you make a noise, other than to answer my questions, I will blind you. Do you understand?' She nodded slowly. 'You're not going to scream, are you?' She shook her head, more vigorously this time.

Brandt gradually removed his hand. Lily gasped, and he could detect the scent of coffee on her breath. He was increasingly anxious to get the door closed but knew he had to do this properly. 'Is there anyone else here?'

'No.' He believed her; there was nothing he sensed about the place to suggest otherwise.

'Is anyone going to come back?'

She looked at him blankly. Her mouth flapping open as though she wanted to say something but didn't know what.

'Does anyone else live here?' he growled impatiently.

She shook her head.

Brandt turned to shut them in, pleased to see the door had a security chain. Applying it meant that he would be warned of anyone else returning. Just a precaution but it paid to be cautious, even though he believed the woman was telling the truth.

Facing her again in the dark hallway, he paused for a moment to consider his next steps. All his planning up to this point had concerned finding the right woman and getting to the stage where he had her alone.

'What are you going to do?' Lily asked, trembling. Brandt found it amusing that she had voiced his very thoughts.

'I want you to take off your coat, move slowly into the sitting room and draw the curtains.' She immediately turned and, shrugging off her coat, walked through the first doorway. As with most houses in city streets, it had netting in the window, but Brandt couldn't be sure how much would be visible from outside once the lights were on.

'Sit,' he commanded, indicating to the nearest chair. He instantly regretted selecting the two-seater sofa opposite for himself; his frame sinking into the foam more than he expected.

'I don't have much cash,' she said, her hand bag clutched in her lap. 'But I have some credit cards. I can give you my PIN.' She started reaching into it. 'The same one works for all of them.'

'Stop!'

Lily instantly froze.

'Keep your hands where I can see them!'

'Erm, how about some jewellery? I have some nice stuff. I don't wear it to work but I could go and get it for you if you'd like.'

Brandt didn't like this. The previous women hadn't spoken to him. Rather than increase the intimacy of the situation, this woman was unnerving. More unsettling was the way she was looking at him. It was similar to how his wife had done, on the occasions when he used to return home drunk. He had never really understood what it had meant; in fact, all it had done was anger him but, in the cold reality of sobriety, rather than being deliberately awkward it was the look of someone desperate to say the right thing but not knowing what that was.

He felt sick.

'Are you okay, sir? Is there something I can do to help?'

The woman's question seemed to snap Brandt awake. 'Yes, yes, you see I do need your help with something.' His tone was light, almost conversational. 'I'm doing something really important. It's hard but it's really important. Do you understand?'

'Erm, I think so,' Lily replied willingly.

'That's good. No, that's really good. I've had to do some things… some things that people think are wrong. But I've done them to do good. Have you ever done that?'

'Well, yes, of course.'

He was feeling happier. The woman had calmed down and seemed genuinely willing to help. Perhaps this could still sort itself out. 'I have to make this look like something it's not,' he explained.

'Okay. Like what?'

'I need to… I need to do some things…'

'Sure, take as long as you need. If you need to make a call, I have a mobile or, if you prefer, you could use the land line.'

'No, no,' Brandt said, shaking his head. Anger crept into his voice. 'I have to do some things… some things… to you.'

'What?' Lily called out loudly. 'I don't understand, what do you mean?'

Brandt hefted himself out of the sofa. Whereas the woman hadn't recoiled when he put the knife to her eye earlier, now she was attempting to push back her chair with her feet, as though to maintain the distance between the two of them.

He held up his hands in an attempt to reassure her. Seeing her eyes glance to the knife, he dropped it, so it was just his palms on view. 'See, I don't want to hurt you. I promise to be gentle, but they have to find evidence.'

'Who? What evidence? Gentle?!'

She's going to scream, Brandt thought suddenly and launched himself across the room, knocking her off the chair. They both landed together on the floor. With his left hand he found her mouth again and with his right he started pulling at her shirt. It took a few tugs before the material ripped to reveal a plain white bra underneath. She was writhing, and he positioned himself so he could pin her down with his legs. Now sitting on top, he could feel her continued movement in his groin. He was surprised but not displeased that his body was reacting positively to it. *Perhaps this won't be as difficult as I thought*, he smiled to himself. As he began to paw at the bra, unable to move it into a position where he could see her breasts, he considered whether a punch to her face might knock her unconscious and allow him to use both hands. But although her struggling was weakening, he didn't want to deny himself the feeling of her body moving underneath him. No, instead he would go for her pants. If he couldn't manage to rip the material, he was sure he could yank them sufficiently away or just push them to the side. Reaching behind him he managed to pull the skirt halfway down her thighs, but he couldn't get at the knickers themselves.

Brandt leaned to one side, attempting to reposition himself. Lily must have interpreted the lightening of the pressure on her as presenting her with her only chance. She swung her left arm up to meet with his shoulder. The force was enough to tip him off balance and he fell to the side, smashing his head against the window ledge.

Lily rolled onto all fours, the material of her skirt bunched up around her knees, causing her to slip a little. She shuffled forwards in the direction of the door before trying to gain her feet. Her skirt ripped as she planted one shoe on the floor and, as she rose up and put down the other heel, her ankle twisted, and she collapsed to the ground, falling on to her back.

Brandt was dazed but could not allow the woman to escape, with her back on the floor he managed to pull himself up and crawl onto her; gripping her throat as soon as his hands reached it. She brought up her hands and, unable to loosen his grasp, reached up to claw at his face. Brandt leaned back and her flailing arms only managed to brush his nose.

It was some time before Brandt released his grip. His fingers seemed locked in place and unwilling to extend. He knew he had to go but the shock of what had just happened was preventing him from getting up. He moved her head to the side to stop her sightless eyes looking at him. Her tongue lolled out of her mouth, which he found even more appalling.

The act of standing up brought a little clarity to Brandt's thoughts. He was bound to have left some physical evidence here, but he was equally sure that he hadn't with his other victims. If he stuck to his old methods with the next one, there would remain nothing to connect him to this. He certainly doubted those hapless idiots in the police would realise without him leaving any clues. You only receive what I choose to give, he thought smugly.

Feeling reassured he decided to turn out the lights but leave the curtains drawn. He was already outside and pulling the door to, when he felt a moment's hesitation. For some reason he had an urge to check his pockets. Propping open the door with his foot, he patted down his front. Nothing. *Nothing!* He pushed back through into the hallway, unconcerned at the slamming noise behind him. He flicked on the lights in the sitting room and frantically started scanning the floor for his knife. 'Shit! Where is it?' Brandt cursed out loud. He hadn't checked under the sofa yet, but suddenly became aware of a more likely location.

He could scarcely believe how hard it was to move her; this body that had felt so energetic beneath him just a few minutes before. Rather than manage it in one go, and with no sense of irony whatsoever, he went through the stages of putting her in the recovery position. The relief of spotting the knife where she had lain was short-lived as the panic that it might have punctured her skin took hold. Frantic moments of checking her still-warm skin revealed an imprint of the hilt but no wounds.

He left her on her side in the hope this would be more likely to aid the indent to disappear and, besides, he preferred how she looked in this almost foetal position.

Satisfied that he hadn't overlooked anything else, Brandt exited the house.

Chapter Thirty-six

DSI Potter sighed. 'Look, is this because I said that unless we made some progress soon we would have to scale back resources?'

'Not at all, guv,' Johnson replied. She was telling the truth. When he had first warned of this earlier in the week, she had fought her corner, but reluctantly accepted the situation. He had agreed to let her continue to use PC McNeil and knew that she could get the whole team to be redeployed if they uncovered some crucial evidence.

'Look, I backed you on the Canterbury thing but this... I just don't see it.'

'But I was right about Canterbury, wasn't I!?' Johnson knew she was starting to sound like a sulky teenager and, from experience, when Potter had made his mind up he wasn't easily swayed. However, equally she knew that if anyone could change it, it was her. They had worked together long enough for him to know that her flights of fancy sometimes paid off.

Not today it would seem. 'But that was completely different.'

'What you said at the time, guv, was the absence of a direct link didn't mean that there wasn't one. Remember when I called you from Canterbury? You said that we needed to keep our minds open until we found evidence that discounted our guy?'

'Look,' said Potter, leaning forward on his desk. 'With St. Albans, everything seems to discount our guy…'

'She's a young woman…' Johnson knew this was a feeble response.

'But everything *else* is wrong. Wrong location, wrong method, wrong motivation… even the wrong day of the week for Christ's sake.'

'I think I can explain all that.'

Potter sighed again. 'Okay, I'm listening but I think we're just going round in circles.'

'The leaving of the murder weapon in Canterbury symbolised the end of the first phase. He has established that he was targeting women and that he could strike anywhere. It makes sense that the next one would be different.' Johnson was frustrated with herself for not being able to explain it better. 'The only constant would therefore be that it would be a young woman.'

Potter sat for a moment thinking. 'Do you really think it's him? I mean *really* think it's him?'

It was her turn to pause. She didn't feel this was the usual question that, if answered with a positive, would lead to being told that he trusted her instincts and that she could follow this up. It felt more than that; it *was* more than that. She knew the pressure he was under, the constant phone calls and even visits from the top brass. He would have considered all this even before she came to see him to argue the link and, if he even had the slightest belief this could be their guy, he would have jumped on it; if nothing else but to look like they had some leads and thus buy them more time.

Her answer to this question could have deep ramifications for her. If she pushed this and, as was possible, it turned out to be false, then it would undermine her credibility and, more importantly, his trust in her.

Maybe being completely honest and admitting to all the doubts she had, might not only restore his confidence in her but allow her a little leeway in terms of what they did next. 'No, guv. I still believe it's possible that he is changing his approach, which may explain the delay from what seemed a well-established weekly pattern, but this isn't like him. It's messy. Plus, he would have left some kind of calling card. Why go to the effort in Canterbury of showing us the murder weapon only to do something radically different and provide no link?'

'Yes, I do have some thoughts on that. Perhaps he thought we might be onto him with what he did here and so he did the Canterbury murder to throw us off the scent.'

'But we don't have anything, guv. What would make him think that?'

'Well, firstly it could just be paranoia. Who knows what drives someone to commit such terrible crimes, but clearly they are not of sound mind and judgement. Alternatively, his decision to go elsewhere and then lay low might be based on fact.'

'You've lost me, guv.'

'He did something wrong here in Nottingham and left some evidence that he was worried about.'

'But we don't have anything,' she repeated but, in doing so, realised what Potter was getting at. 'You want us to rework the evidence, don't you?'

'It's the best we have to go on. Unless he strikes again all we can do is go over what we have so far, rather than try and introduce something like St. Albans which may only serve to contaminate what we have.'

'But…' Johnson felt deflated and yet, at the same time, knew what the DSI was saying made sense.

'Maybe, Stella, you never know, going back over everything might throw up some DNA which might match with what was found in St. Albans?'

If this had been an effort to placate Johnson and to motivate her into the joyless task of revisiting all the previous evidence, the look she returned Potter showed it had failed.

'What's the alternative? I hold a press conference where we talk about a link which you and I both know doesn't exist?'

Chapter Thirty-seven

There was no press conference; but that wasn't to suggest there wouldn't be one. There had been no link made in the national newspapers; but that didn't mean there wouldn't be one. If Brandt had thought the days following his trip to St. Albans waiting for the news to break had been agonising, this was worse.

He had not slept since Lily James' parents had gone around to her house and discovered her dead body on the sitting room floor. The only emotion Brandt felt towards them was anger. Apparently, they had become worried when she hadn't made her usual phone call to them that evening. And yet it had taken three days, *three whole days*, and only then after being contacted by her employer to express concern that she had failed to turn up yet again without explanation, for them to make the short trip across town to find her. Lily's mother, interviewed by a local television station, explained, through tears, that she had hoped Lily had found a nice young man and had been swept off her feet.

Brandt had spent those three days waiting and wondering, with increasing paranoia, why there was nothing. By the end of the second day, by which time he was certain she would have been reported missing, he became convinced that the police must have ordered a media blackout. That could only mean one thing, they knew it was him and were about to pounce. Twice he had gone to his car and sat there, key in the ignition, willing himself to flee. But where? If they knew it was him, all the sea and airports would be looking for him and he couldn't hope to travel anywhere in Britain by road without being tracked by the network of ANPRs.

No, the time for escape had passed. That would have needed to be done before the connection was made. Brandt had two choices: allow himself to be captured or kill himself. He favoured the latter because, much as he still believed that he had been acting in the best interest of the country, he didn't think he could cope with the humiliation of arrest. Having spent a lifetime catching, interviewing and locking up criminals, he didn't think he could cope with being on the other side.

The only way to maintain some kind of control of the situation would be suicide. Whilst he always imagined the grand gesture of plunging to his demise, where he lived was nowhere near the coast, nor did it have the sorts of mountains or even hills where that would be possible. It would be too much of a risk to travel, with the police just waiting to pounce. Brandt knew, if he put his mind to it, there were plenty of options: find a tall building nearby or even a sufficiently high bridge over a road, but he favoured an alternative method given the circumstances.

He wanted the satisfaction of imagining all that pent-up anticipation, something he had felt so many times in his career, of the officers waiting for the order to storm the property turning into the bitter disappointment of finding his lifeless corpse slumped in the armchair.

Between the plentiful supply of whisky and all the various pills and capsules his wife had left behind, he was sure he had enough to finish the job. He never understood how so many people were cited as attempting to take their own life and failing. To Brandt that was just confirmation of how pathetic they were and consequently how frustrating it was that they had been unsuccessful. If you were so useless in life that you couldn't even manage death, then there really was no point in living.

As he had sat there that evening, forty-eight hours after being in St. Albans, he convinced himself he had until the small hours of the morning to swallow the pills. The police, knowing how dangerous he was, would be waiting until then to increase the chances of him being asleep. He didn't know how long the pills would take but if he left it until midnight he would be long dead before they burst in.

Brandt had awoken the next morning with the light around the drawn curtains confirming that it was day. A confused stare at the clock on the mantel piece told him that it was after 7am. With the pills counted out and still sat on one of the nest of tables, it would seem that the serenity Brandt had found in deciding on the only logical course of action had sufficiently relaxed him that he fell asleep, ironically into an uninterrupted slumber that had lasted far longer than he could remember in years. What's more, there had been no pre-dawn raid and, as he pulled back the front curtains, he was met with a view outside no different from any other day.

He slumped back in his chair and switched on the news. There was still nothing about the woman, and although he took the precaution of bringing in a knife, in case he needed to slash his throat quickly upon hearing his door being burst open, he became less and less sure that the police were just around the corner. By lunchtime he even made the walk to the local shop to collect some supplies and, paranoid as he was, he didn't spot anyone who could even conceivably be keeping him under surveillance. Feeling much better he considered how he should have put more thought into what to do if things went wrong. The first thing he would require was money, and plenty of it. Once being chased, something as simple as walking into a bank and withdrawing it was a sure-fire way of getting captured. One of the very first things done by the police is to trace any transactions. Brandt resolved that as soon as he was certain he was in the clear, he would ensure he had enough cash to make his getaway. Given the surveillance would extend to public transport and his registered vehicle, he would need to have a sum large enough in case he needed to buy a second-hand car. Stealing one could only ever be a last resort because, as soon as the theft was reported, the police would be able to trace him through the vast network of ANPR cameras.

The other thing Brandt wanted was a gun. He had absolutely no desire to use it on any of his *jobs* because, notwithstanding the immediate attention firing one would bring, they were inelegant, cold, impersonal weapons. Anyone could pull a trigger, but it took proximity and a certain strength of character to use a knife. But Brandt was willing to forgo the symmetry afforded by ending of his own life with a blade. If he found himself in a similar situation to earlier, where plunging to his death was not an option, he would rather blow his brains out than cut his throat. That way there was no chance of him bungling it sufficiently that someone could stem the bleeding until the ambulance arrived. Similarly, if on the run, the gun would be a more effective deterrent for any potential have-a-go heroes who considered intervening. It would also enable him to quickly get what he needed from people. Clearly obtaining one was going to present more of a challenge than getting hold of his savings, but a career working the streets made Brandt confident he knew the right places to go.

When the report finally came through that Lily James, as they had named her, had been murdered, it wasn't so much relief he felt but anxiety. Much as fear of being caught had brought him to the brink of suicide, it was something he had known was a possibility from the first Saturday he headed to Nottingham. The dread he now felt was different. Now that he no longer was concentrating on the likelihood of being arrested, he had to focus on the much darker reality of what he had done. Whilst he waited for the connection to be made with the St. Albans murder, he contemplated how this would be presented by the police and how it would be perceived in the press. Every hour that passed without him being provided with the answer was torture; an agony fuelled by snippets he found on social media whilst constantly searching for the news to break.

Previously Brandt had never understood the attraction of sites like Twitter; much less their use, except for famous people to write in haste what they would later regret. Yet he had become aware of what people had been saying since he had embarked on his new career. Initially he had stumbled on comments whilst completing internet searches linked to his actions, but he soon realised that they were a barometer of people's perception of what he was doing. He had originally gauged reaction from what was in the news, but social media allowed him to bypass much of that and get straight to the national consciousness. This was because there were always a few people, if you read enough of the replies, that approved of what he was doing. It would seem there was a small section of society that believed women's liberation had gone too far and that the way many women now acted and presented themselves was inappropriate. They said that what he was doing was reminding women of the need to be more conservative. Although this hadn't been Brandt's actual motivation, he could see some sense in what they had been saying. He thought back to the situation with his wife. If they had been married decades ago, she would have stood by him and provided him with what he needed; for that would have been her job, rather than focusing selfishly all the time on what she wanted.

It wasn't those who seemed in support of him that gave him the greatest strength. Conversely, it was the vast majority of those who commented. They were quite vociferous in their condemnation of his actions and, from that, he drew comfort. An increasing number of women were posting about concern for their safety and being more careful where they went, especially if unaccompanied. For Brandt, their perception reflected the reality of what he saw day in and day out when he was in the police. The streets had become more dangerous; Britain had become less safe and yet the Government, the media and, to a certain degree, the police itself had chosen to ignore this; relying on the public's apparent desensitisation to violence and crime to leave the truth unspoken. What Brandt had managed, even if it was just on a small scale at this stage, was to cause it to be spoken about and make people sensitive to what was happening. He considered some of the nature documentaries he so enjoyed on television. What better way to attempt to illustrate the impact of global warming, something that most people know is bad, but few do anything about, than to show a polar bear unable to feed her new born cubs because the seals they would look to feed off are resting on ice that has become detached from the mainland. It matters not to the filmmakers that what they are observing may just be because the region has entered the summer months and there is something of a natural thaw; the perception is that global warming is melting all the icecaps so they make the perceived reality of what they are shooting fit that view. What Brandt was doing was artificially magnifying the horrors in British society to the point where they could no longer be ignored.

But the link to St. Albans could undermine all that. Social media was already speculating on what kind of a person killed Lily James. With the news of some bungled attempt at rape, or however they chose to describe it, the focus would switch from the victims to the attacker. Until this point there had been the odd random speculation as to his identity, each as fanciful and fantastical as the last, and none had been latched on to by the media. Of course, with them being women, there was some talk about a sexual motivation but there had been no evidence for that. Clearly Brandt had planned for this in St. Albans but whilst he had seen sexual violence as something for people to fear, the apparent notional quick fumble was going to be ridiculed.

As Brandt waited and waited, and with that delicious and enriching sleep of a few nights ago a fading memory, he became certain he would be described by the papers as impotent. In the limbo that seemed to exist solely for those on the point of exhaustion, he was visited by memories of his wife asking him, with a mixture of pity and frustration, whether he needed to see a doctor.

On one particular evening she had cooked a special meal; special in the sense that it was half-way edible. He knew something was up when she watched him closely as he poured his first measure of whisky, which, as was typical back then, came almost before he had removed his coat. Feeling her stare on him, he only half filled the glass; her smile that followed telling him that he had done the right thing. She had bought wine to accompany the dinner in order to add to the mood, but kept the bottle on her side of the table so as to be in control of its dispensing. That she had drunk the majority was a source of curiosity to Brandt, the reason revealed when she announced she had also prepared dessert but, rather than going to the fridge, excused herself and went upstairs. Unsure what to do next, he had remained seated, listening to the creak of the floorboards and the associated noises of his wife's movements to give clue as to what was happening.

She returned in lingerie that had clearly been bought for the occasion. A black lace bodice with pink fluff around its edges, along with stockings and suspenders and a pair of shoes with heels way too high for her. Brandt had only seen such an outfit in his increasing internet usage. Whereas before it had made the models look sultry and seductive, here on his wife it just looked contrived. It served to hold in her stomach and accentuate her curves but the cellulite on her substantial thighs stood out in stark contrast. Nevertheless, whilst not being a turn on for Brandt, nor was it a turn off. In fact, as he sat there gazing at the sight before him, something his wife took to mean he was impressed, it was more the implication of the outfit than the look itself that provided him with hope. If she went to this much effort, in a slightly misguided attempt to aid her appearance, it surely meant she might actually *do something* in the bedroom besides lying there motionless. Not only might she put some effort in herself, but she might be willing to engage in foreplay designed to do more than just make him sufficiently hard that he could enter her.

When she held her hand out to him, Brandt stood up. Nothing had been said in those moments since she had come downstairs. He looked at his wife with genuine longing for the first time in years. As he had stepped forward to embrace her, she suddenly pulled away, reminding him that he had yet to have his dessert. Brandt, in his best attempt at an alluring voice, had suggested he thought she was dessert. As she moved into the kitchen, he suddenly had some kinky thoughts about whipped cream and chocolate sauce, but she did not return with a bottle or a can. Almost reverentially she held in both hands a side plate with a small silver cloche on top; evidentially another purchase. She nodded to indicate that Brandt himself was to unveil its contents.

Without hesitation he lifted the lid, keen to see what was there, given it was too small for either of the foodstuffs he had considered earlier. Initially baffled by what lay before him, Brandt leaned forward to take a closer look.

It was a pill. A blue pill.

Without looking at his wife, he turned and walked out the house. This wasn't the last time he saw her; in fact, she didn't leave for nearly another year, but this was the last time she had initiated sexual congress.

Chapter Thirty-eight

'You okay, McNeil?' Johnson said as they approached the building.

'Yeah, but… well, last time I was here it didn't exactly go smoothly…'

'Ah come on, that was an honest mistake. Could have happened to anyone.' Her wink, rather than prove reassuring, suggested to McNeil that she only half-meant it.

'Sarah Donovan. It's DCI Johnson and PC McNeil. May we come in?'

A long pause. Johnson and McNeil looked at each other. 'Er… sure, but I have… I have company.'

'That's okay,' replied Johnson in as light a tone as she could manage. 'I'm sure this won't take long.'

'Erm, okay. Come on up.'

As they took the stairs up to the flat, McNeil couldn't help but relive those horrible moments of a few weeks ago when, first, he thought he was too late and the attacker was going to get Sarah, to be followed by the realisation that they had only caught her old boyfriend instead. What was his name? McNeil wondered.

'Josh,' Johnson called out in surprise.

McNeil looked round in confusion. *How did she know…?* They had only just pushed through the heavy fire door into the corridor. Josh Ramage was exiting Sarah Donovan's flat, clearly in a hurry. Perhaps he had hoped to make it to the stairwell before they arrived in the lift.

'I must say I am a little surprised to see you here.' Johnson's voice was somewhat mocking, suggesting impropriety.

'I'll leave you to it,' he responded, more to Sarah than Johnson. 'Call me when you're done.' With barely a glance up he made his way past the police officers. McNeil noticed that Johnson was slow to move to one side, and wondered whether she had been thinking about standing her ground to see how he would react.

'Miss Donovan,' Johnson said, much more formally than when she had introduced herself on the intercom. 'Thank you for agreeing to see us. May we come in?'

What followed was an interesting but ultimately fruitless conversation. Johnson had been careful not to reveal any more about the investigation than was already in the public domain. Sarah was surprisingly sketchy on the details; having only picked up a few things here and there. McNeil asked her why she wasn't more concerned about her attacker being captured. She countered by saying that there was nothing more she could do to help and that the best thing for her was to try and move on. As if to illustrate this, she said that she was currently negotiating with her school when to start her phased return to work. Despite this, Sarah agreed to go through the events of that fateful Saturday in as much detail as she could remember which, as it transpired, wasn't much, and no more than she had been able to provide in the days following the attack. Johnson had been keen to explore any physical contact, no matter how fleeting, that in any way could indicate a sexual motivation. It would seem, certainly from what Sarah remembered, there had been none. McNeil was hardly surprised. Given the location and the crowds outside the railway station, it would take an attacker far more brazen than theirs to attempt to grope her first.

'Any good?' he asked as they made their way back down the stairs.

'Nope, as expected really. With nothing sexual on the bodies of the three victims this really was a long shot, but it was still an interesting visit.'

'Ah, Josh you mean.'

'Yes. By the way, what did you two talk about when I went to the bathroom?' Johnson asked, trying to sound casual.

'Nothing really.'

'Oh.'

McNeil burst out laughing. 'I knew it.'

'Knew what?'

'That was deliberate!'

'Yes, it was a conscious decision to empty my bladder.'

'You know exactly what I mean. You wanted to leave us alone in the hope I would ask the question.'

'I did no such thing,' Johnson protested. 'Did you though?'

'Yes, she said that her and Josh were together.'

'Go on,' she said impatiently.

'If you wanted to know more, you should have asked her yourself.'

'McNeil!' she shouted, punching his arm. Thankfully they were now exiting the building and well out of Sarah's earshot.

This small bit of playfulness felt good to McNeil. The last few days had been difficult, not so much because of the seeming pointlessness of revisiting evidence that had been thoroughly interrogated first time round, but because Johnson had become increasingly withdrawn. If this had happened immediately following their trip to Canterbury, McNeil would have taken it as her regretting how close they had come to being more than just work colleagues, but the discovery of the murder weapon had enlivened her; for a short time at least. For McNeil, establishing the link between Nottingham and Canterbury had been bitter sweet. Although he had never met the owner of the car garage, he disliked him intensely. If the man had been lazy enough to wait until after the whole day of trading before handing a knife into the police, *a blood-stained knife for fuck's sake,* he could have waited for the next day, allowing McNeil a few brief moments of happiness.

It made him even more desperate to catch the killer. He knew that his best chance with Johnson would be the inevitable celebrations that would follow the arrest. But he wasn't sure he could wait that long, especially as it had seemed that Canterbury might have signalled the end of the murder spree. Yet McNeil knew that if he made a move at the wrong moment he might ruin his chances altogether. And, so far, their days had only seemed to be a series of wrong moments with Johnson's increasing sullenness. If it hadn't been for what had happened in Canterbury, he could have suggested they go for a drink to drown their sorrows, but he knew Johnson was sharp enough to realise the suggestion would not be as innocent as presented.

McNeil understood that there were only two ways this cycle was going to end. The first was that they would run out of evidence to re-examine and, with the investigation being scaled back, he would return to normal duties. The other was for the killer to strike again and provide Johnson with the boost she needed – they both needed. Acknowledging it would mean the death of another innocent person. He resented the growing part of him that wished for the latter.

He need not have worried, for, whilst he was in the midst of these dark thoughts, Brandt was on the move again.

Chapter Thirty-nine

He felt better; much better. The pills had been put back in their various bottles and he had abstained from drinking for the last couple of days. He was even managing a fair amount of sleep each night. As if to prove to himself how far he had come since the abject despair of a week ago, Brandt had decided to meet Franklin once more.

The previous encounter had been as bad as he had expected. Over an hour sat in a coffee shop, hoping that no one could overhear the pathetic whining of his former colleague. When the tears had eventually come, Brandt made his excuses and left. Phoning Franklin had not been an act of guilt, seeking to apologise for his swift exit. Attempting to make it up to him would prove to Brandt that he was sufficiently recovered from the shock of St. Albans that he could resume his work again. However, Franklin had taken some convincing. His tone was ice cold when he first picked up the phone and, for a few moments, Brandt thought he would hang up. Even his subsequent apology appeared insufficient until Brandt claimed that the reason why he had needed to leave was because all the pain Franklin was suffering was serving to bring back the pain he felt; he *still* felt about his own divorce. Brandt would not admit to himself how much truth there was in this statement, instead choosing to focus on its apparent success. The positive effect had been immediate. Franklin offered his own apology; for being insensitive; for being so wrapped up in his own misery that he hadn't considered the impact that it would have on Brandt. They resolved to try to avoid discussing women, and agreed to meet for a walk along the canal near where Franklin lived.

Although the warmth of the afternoon had been in stark contrast to the chill he had felt in St. Albans, the parallels between those two days did not escape Brandt. He had never been good at small talk and with Franklin determined to avoid the topic of spouses, something he was clearly preoccupied with, the conversation was laboured; punctuated by frequent, awkward silences. Attempts to focus on previous encounters similarly failed with the realisation that they had few shared experiences worthy of recollection. Instead they swapped stories of old cases, something Brandt found himself more comfortable doing. They had a number of anecdotes worth sharing, although he became aware that some of Franklin's were far from authentic; often claiming to have said or done things Brandt knew for a fact had been different or should be attributed to others. Not that it bothered him, Franklin seemed much more comfortable and he had to admit that just being out of the house was doing him some good.

Nevertheless, it came as surprise when Franklin suggested they pop into the pub by the locks a bit further up. He had reiterated on the phone that he was still trying to lay off the drink and with even the past stories starting to dry up, there seemed no reason to prolong their meeting. It was purely out of curiosity that caused Brandt to agree.

He made a point of declaring that he was buying the first round, keen as he was to see if Franklin would select something non-alcoholic. Indeed, Franklin made a point of asking the bartender what soft drinks they served, but all the while was unable to take his gaze from the selection of beer pumps. Trying to sound helpful, Brandt had even suggested a shandy, but the response, which had been a pint of Stella, had come as no shock. Moreover, the greedy way in which Franklin had watched it be poured spoke volumes in itself.

Ordinarily, Brandt would have followed suit but conscious that the last thing he needed was to be pulled over for drunk driving, and have his prints matched to those in St Albans, he settled for a coffee. Any disappointment Franklin had felt by his partner's choice seemed forgotten as he took three large gulps of his beer, even closing his eyes to better enjoy the sensation.

With Franklin more relaxed than Brandt had ever seen him, the conversation, admittedly somewhat one-sided this time, soon began to flow. Franklin had insisted that he return the favour and buy them another drink, even though Brandt had little more than sipped at his coffee whilst waiting for it to drop to a more palatable temperature. Brandt had agreed but resolved that this would be their last. Yet something changed that made him decide to stay a bit longer.

Franklin, with the effects of the Stella starting to take hold, struggled to keep his promise of not talking about his wife. However, he managed to keep it to only the odd coarse and venomous remark. But what held Brandt's attention was his starting to refer to current cases he was overseeing. None of these meant anything to Brandt, but he was intrigued by this uncharacteristic lack of professionalism. Seeing little risk in it, he steered the topic to what had happened in Nottinghamshire and Kent. Although Franklin worked for Thames Valley Police, a force covering a relatively large area that ranged from Oxfordshire and Buckinghamshire in the north of the region, down to Berkshire in the south, and consequently not connected to either investigation, it came as no surprise that Franklin claimed to have operational knowledge.

Beneath all the bluster and bullshit, Brandt detected that Franklin had no real understanding of what was going on, other than what had been made available to the public, but there seemed to be a genuine link between him and the DSI there, Robert Potter. No doubt Franklin had met him at one conference or another and had attempted to brown-nose him in the same way as he had Brandt, looking for yet another way to get a leg up in the force.

Brandt exited the pub later that afternoon, pleased that Franklin had not accepted his half-hearted offer to drive him home, claiming instead that he would get a taxi later. An idea had formulated in his mind that he needed to think through.

Chapter Forty

'It's now or never,' Johnson said. They were sat in a coffee shop waiting for the extra uniformed officers drafted in, almost purely for appearances sake, to be in position.

'Huh?' McNeil responded, not for the first time surprised to hear her vocalise something he was thinking. But his thoughts were more of a personal nature. He assumed Johnson was referring to it being Saturday and, with it marking four weeks since the murder in Canterbury, if their killer didn't strike today the chance was he had decided to quit. McNeil held the same view. He knew from brief references she made to the DSI that things were to be wound down on Monday. In truth, he could understand why. They had been going round in circles for the past fortnight looking for new clues that simply weren't there. Whatever had motivated the man to target some women in Nottingham and then switch to Canterbury, before stopping altogether, remained a complete mystery.

'Won't be here though,' she said, raising the last dregs of her coffee to her mouth before thinking better of it and putting her cup down.

'Unless Canterbury and the gap since was to make us complacent.' McNeil instantly regretted saying it, thinking that Johnson could view this as a criticism.

If she had, she didn't show it.

'It still doesn't make sense to me. He's targeting women; young, attractive women. There is a clear motivation there, so why stop? Also, why change areas as well, only to then stop? What has he achieved by that? It just doesn't make sense,' she said.

'Maybe he wasn't planning on stopping but something made him stop. He got ill, or run over or something.' McNeil realised how unlikely this sounded but he was desperate to contribute; to have Johnson converse with him, even if it was to tell him he was wrong, rather than just share her own thoughts out loud.

'Unlikely but possible… He must have enjoyed what he was doing, and he was clearly good at it. To commit a murder in broad daylight without being seen and leave no real evidence is hard, but to manage it multiple times takes skill. If nothing else, he must have got off on the thrill of being successful.' Johnson was becoming more animated now. 'And we know this because he had the arrogance to want us to know they were all his work.'

'So why not carry on? Kill a new girl each Saturday, picking different locations to keep us guessing?'

'It wasn't enough,' she said thoughtfully. In the long pause that followed McNeil wanted to ask for clarification, but he could tell by Johnson's expression that she was concentrating. Eventually she continued, this time fixing McNeil with that hard stare of hers: 'The act of stabbing Sarah Donovan wasn't enough for him. He made sure that he killed his next victims by ensuring he opened the wound with a twist of the knife. But perhaps the thrill of that wore off too. A bit like how they say heroin addicts are always chasing that feeling from their very first hit. The only way they can do that is to up the amount to try and compensate for the body's growing tolerance of it.'

'Oh yeah, like you hear of some alcoholics drinking a bottle of vodka first thing in the morning just to be able to make it through the day.'

'Precisely. So, what does our guy have to do to chase the thrill of that first kill?'

'Up the dosage. So, what, kill more frequently? But he hasn't.' McNeil wasn't sure Johnson's line of logic was working out.

'Yes that, or go for a bigger hit.'

'Like what?'

'That I don't know. Why don't you get me another cup of coffee whilst I think about it?'

McNeil was happy to oblige. Anything to ensure that, if these were the last couple of days working together, it wasn't filled with Johnson moodily stalking around Nottingham with a look of hurt resignation etched on her face.

'St. Albans!' Johnson virtually shouted at McNeil as he carried the two cups back to the table. 'Why didn't I think of that before?!'

McNeil was now genuinely confused. 'But you did?'

'No, I thought it might be; perhaps I just wanted it to be him. But I couldn't make the connection, at least not in a way that I could convince the DSI.'

'What *is* the connection?' McNeil asked, still not hopeful.

'Look, it makes sense. Right, so alcoholics and druggies need a bigger hit each time to have the same feeling as before. So how does a serial murderer with a fixation on young women get a bigger hit?'

'Erm, I guess he takes more time with the killing and perhaps he…' McNeil felt uncomfortable verbalising the end of his thought.

'Exactly!' Johnson said, unconcerned. 'He rapes his victim either pre- or post-mortem.'

'But that didn't happen in St. Albans.'

'No, something must have gone wrong.'

'Like what?'

'I don't know.' Anger flashed across her face. 'Something; *anything*! Who knows what is going through this sick bastard's mind? Perhaps he couldn't get it up. Perhaps the phone rang; it doesn't matter!'

'Doesn't it?'

'No, because it all makes perfect sense. There was no calling card in St. Albans because the killer didn't want us to know it was him. He wasn't successful. He messed up.'

'Well he did kill her…'

'No!' Her anger was now replaced with frustration that McNeil wasn't following quickly enough. 'He could have done that anywhere. We know she had a short walk from the station, where I guess he first found her. This was meant to be much more than before. And we can see that at the crime scene: there's evidence of a struggle and her clothes were ripped. She even had a busted ankle, presumably from trying to escape.'

McNeil nodded slowly. As he processed everything Johnson had said, what she was arguing seemed to make sense. However, there were still some unanswered questions.

'And think about it,' she continued. 'The method fits too. What better way to up the ante from stabbing than to killing with his bare hands? Like an alcoholic moving from beer to neat spirits or a junkie from smoking crack to injecting heroine!'

'Okay, so he doesn't want us to make the link because he doesn't want us to see his imperfections. I get that. So what, he just quits?'

'No, that doesn't feel right,' Johnson said, calming down. 'I think if he were to end it, it would have to be on a high. Perhaps, he realised that he needs more thorough planning…'

'What now, do we take this to the DSI?'

'And do what?' Johnson replied, not unkindly. 'Like he said to me, we can hardly hold a press conference based on this theory. We'd look stupid.'

'What then?'

'We just wait,' Johnson said, solemnly. 'We have to wait until he strikes next.'

Chapter Forty-one

If Brandt could have overheard the conversation in the coffee shop, his emotions would have been mixed. First there would be the fear that DCI Johnson had made the link he had been so desperate to avoid. There might even have followed a brief moment of admiration for how she had managed to get into his head in the same way he had managed with so many killers before. Then would come the anger. The brief suggestion that he may have been unable to complete the physical element of his mission would have enraged him. He already hated Johnson because of the way she looked at him with those cold, calculating eyes in the press conference; and for her to then, like his wife, suggest he might need a little blue pill to do what any self-respecting man should be able to manage unaided, would tip him over the edge. Nevertheless, what would follow would be the reassurance that he was still one step ahead of them. For all her insight and understanding that he was to strike again, what she was expecting would prove wrong. *Very wrong.*

Brandt did not feel the thrill of anticipation as he followed the signs for Milton Keynes. Today was just a job, one of those necessary tasks that would put him back on track with his work and provide him with a chance to push on from there. Done correctly, it would serve the dual purposes of bypassing what happened in St Albans by making the link back to Canterbury, and also allow him a closer insight into the workings of the investigation.

Brandt hated Milton Keynes, even more so as he hit the grid system of roads with its characterless, countless, and ostensibly identical roundabouts. Fortunately, he knew most of the area quite well; his wife had insisted that she be taken there a few times each year for a shopping spree. Brandt wouldn't have minded, anything to keep her happy and stop her moaning, if it didn't always require a return trip a week later so she could get a refund on all the clothes she'd bought and no longer wanted.

This time he wasn't heading for the shopping centre with all its CCTV cameras. On one of the trips with his wife, a particular occasion close to Christmas, he had become so frustrated with all the cars queuing to make their way back to the main roads that he had insisted on finding an alternative route. He had tried to sound knowledgeable, pompously explaining to his wife that the A5, which ran all the way from London to North Wales, was also known as Watling Street, being based on an ancient Roman road. Over recent years planners had, in places, deviated the A5 from Watling Street to allow for the creation of dual carriage ways to alleviate congestion. Brandt had contended that they simply needed to pick up the old Watling Street somewhere on the western side of Milton Keynes and follow it south until it reunited with the A5 again.

Somewhat inevitably he had become completely lost and ended up in Bletchley, one of Milton Keynes' constituent towns, looking for directions back to the main road. They had stopped by the parade of shops with the relative depravation of the area highlighted by the absence of major chain stores and the prevalence of charity shops and bookmakers. Having been provided with some vague instructions which, perhaps more through luck than judgement, enabled them to get back to the A5, Brandt had been sure he would never consciously visit Bletchley again.

As usual, Brandt had spent some time on Google Maps learning more about his surroundings. He had decided to park at the edge of somewhere called the Lake's Estate, which some simple research had suggested was sufficiently rough that, if his escape on foot was noticed, his direction of travel would be in keeping with people's expectations as to where the likely culprit might reside.

As he turned into the side street, Brandt mused that, at first glance, the area seemed perfectly decent. If it wasn't for the couple, who could be no more than fifteen years old, walking past in matching tracksuits pushing a pram, Brandt would have double checked on his phone that he had come to the right place. All doubt was removed when another youth on a scooter designed for primary school children, nearly took him out as he shut his door before shouting behind him: 'Watch out, you old twat!'

'Hope you're off to the shops,' Brandt muttered to himself, putting his hand in his pocket to feel the familiar warmth of a wooden knife hilt. Despite being identical in every way to the one he had used before, having come from the same set bought as a wedding present that his wife hadn't deemed sufficiently valuable to take with her, it didn't quite feel the same. However, he suspected it would within the next hour or so.

He exited the side street and crossed the road, passing a small Co-op on his left and an independent off-licence on his right. The couple he had seen earlier were stopped outside the latter seeing how much change they could pool together. Brandt would bet his mortgage they were looking to buy either cigarettes or alcohol, despite being too young to legally purchase either.

It was surprisingly busy with cars; exacerbated by the road furniture, designed to calm the traffic, but only serving to cause them to aggressively accelerate once they had cleared the obstacle. It was much more peaceful when Brandt turned off in the direction of the main shops, a tranquillity matched by an appreciable improvement in the quality of the housing. Although far from large, the tidiness of the gardens and the condition of the front doors suggested residents who took some pride in their property.

Arriving at the crossroads at the top, Brandt observed that both left and right routes ran behind the shops, as indicated by the large metal doors leading into the buildings and the industrial sized rubbish bins next to them. Just to double check he was in the correct area, he carried on forwards and within a hundred yards arrived about a third of the way along the parade. Brandt was surprised by the number of shoppers, given the lack of what he saw as anywhere worth visiting. He couldn't help but sneer at the Polish supermarket opposite, flanked by an electronic cigarette shop and a barbers advertising gentlemen's haircuts for £6.

A look up at one of the lampposts confirmed that there was CCTV along the front of the stores, so he turned right along the shorter section. Apparently stopping to browse a charity shop's window display of tired children's board games, Brandt was actually looking down the alleyway that ran from front to back. This is what he had been looking for. Every second shop had it, to enable access to the flats above on either side.

Satisfied that everything was as he had expected, Brandt reached the end of the parade and followed the road back round to the junction from earlier. He now carried on behind those shops that he had not walked in front of, briefly glancing down each alleyway until, at the fourth one, he spotted what he wanted. The relative darkness of the narrow path meant he could only observe the silhouette of a figure; a glowing ember lighting up the gloom suggesting it was someone who had popped outside for a smoke. If Brandt was quick enough, the person should still be in the same place by the time he reached them. Of more interest was that the silhouette's short hair and relative height suggested it was a man. This was ideal, so, quickly glancing at the back of the shops either side to check they didn't have their own security cameras for deliveries or potential break-ins, Brandt moved towards him.

He had anticipated that, once in the alleyway, the sound of his footsteps echoing off the walls would cause the man to notice him. Now out of the direct sunlight he could see more easily his features. He was Asian, approaching forty years of age, and wearing a uniform for a company he didn't recognise.

'Got a light, mate?' Brandt asked in a friendly manner. As the man patted the top of his trousers to determine where he had placed it, Brandt reached into his pocket as though to pull out his own packet of cigarettes. Holding out the lighter, the man didn't notice that what Brandt had withdrawn was very different.

'Sorry about this mate,' Brandt said, maintaining the tone from earlier, before launching at the man and burying the blade in his stomach. The man grabbed his shoulders, staring into Brandt's eyes in shock. Brandt pulled out the knife and thrust it forwards a further four times, twisting the handle on each occasion, just to be sure. The man didn't so much as fall down, as slowly sink to his knees, releasing his grip to put his hands to his belly. They could do nothing to stop the flow and, with blood pouring from between his fingers, the man slumped to the side, only to remain propped up by the wall; his eyes never leaving Brandt's.

In what he hoped was an obvious enough gesture, Brandt wiped the blade on the man's upper arm but, just to be sure, tucked into his top pocket a printout of the logo of the car garage where he dumped his last murder weapon.

Transfixed by what was in front of him, Brandt realised that he hadn't once checked the top of the alleyway to see if any of the shoppers had noticed what had happened. He was relieved to see the entranceway was clear and that the few people who passed in the time he looked were completely oblivious.

Gazing back down at the man again, he was shocked to see him blink, but the next time he closed his eyes, they didn't reopen. Having seen enough, he turned around and made his way back in the direction he had come, pleased to find that no cars passed until he reached the relative safety of the crossroads once more.

In the fifteen minutes it took Brandt to return to his car, he had failed to hear a single siren. The absence of any physical feeling, and with his pulse rate having long returned to normal, meant that, if it wasn't for the sticky knife in his pocket, Brandt could almost believe that he had imagined the whole thing.

There would be no celebratory Chinese takeaway tonight. Sure, he may allow himself a drink or two but, despite his recent abstinence, that was hardly out of the ordinary. He doubted he would even bother trying to catch the local news for the area; the stabbing of an Asian man in a rough part of Milton Keynes was not worth getting excited about. No, conscious in the knowledge that it would be Monday before the police would be ready to hold a press conference, he would just get on with enjoying his weekend. He could give his old pal DSI Franklin a call, but he suspected the man was likely to be busy this evening now that the circus had come to one of his towns. The very thought caused a wide grin to spread across his face.

Chapter Forty-two

McNeil was waiting for Johnson at one of the desks in CID. She had been in DSI Potter's office for a while now. Between the slats of the Venetian blinds he could see her becoming more and more animated. This didn't look good. Confirmation had come through quickly that the body found in Milton Keynes was connected to their case. They knew it wasn't a copycat because the name of the premises where the knife had been left in Canterbury had not been released to the public. Not that it would have been a very good copycat, what with the victim being a middle-aged Asian man. The initial euphoria that had followed the news quickly subsided. McNeil had thought it was because Johnson, like him, realised how inappropriate it was to greet the murder with excitement. Perhaps she had, but McNeil felt it was more than that. She had hardly said a thing until Potter arrived in the office. Judging by what seemed to be going on in the office, she had been bottling something up.

When Johnson left, she didn't even glance in McNeil's direction, much less tell him where she was going. He had a pretty good idea though, which proved to be correct as he smelt the cigarette smoke as he pushed through the back door into the secure car park.

'What is it, ma'am?'

'He's just so blinkered… so… frustrating!' She was pacing up and down.

'Who is?' he asked, already knowing the answer.

'Potter!' she replied. 'Look, I get it and if I was in his position, I guess I would be similar but if he just listened… truly listened, he would know I am right.'

'Right about what?' McNeil felt he might be getting somewhere.

'Have you ever believed that if something is too good to be true then it probably is?'

'Er, yes…'

'Well this is it.'

He gave a nervous laugh. 'Look, Johnson, if you want me to understand what you are going on about, you're going to have to be a little less cryptic here.'

'Okay,' she said, taking another long drag from her cigarette and stopping to compose herself. 'It's too obvious.'

'You're saying this wasn't him?'

'No, no, no,' she cried, but her frustration seemed more with herself than McNeil. 'It's as though he was desperate for us to make the connection. We would have done that with just the swipe on the shoulder. Although it only contained the victim's blood, it is far too obvious a reference to the second attack to be anything else.'

'So why put the garage logo in the man's pocket?'

'Exactly!' Johnson beamed. 'It's too much, too… desperate.'

McNeil paused for a few moments, thinking. 'Perhaps, what with it being a bloke and the gap since the last one he felt the need to emphasise the link?'

'Well possibly,' Johnson conceded but an almost imperceptible shake of the head suggested she felt otherwise. 'That's what Potter said. But that's what also troubles me. Why a man this time?'

'Why also Milton Keynes? It seems to me that he is just trying to mess us about. You know, now switching the gender to go with switching the locations. Toying with us.'

'I know… I know it looks that way and maybe he is but there's more to it than that. I just don't know how to explain it to you.'

'You don't have to,' McNeil said, grabbing her shoulders to stop her pacing and so that he could get her to look at him. 'I'm not the DSI, you don't need to convince me of anything. Stop worrying about trying to put forward as strong an argument as possible and just tell it to me as you see it. For what it's worth, I can then tell you what I think.'

'Okay, let's sit down though.' Johnson looked around before shrugging and sat down on the tarmac with her back resting on the police station wall. McNeil did the same and waited patiently whilst she lit another cigarette.

'The murder in Milton Keynes seems simplistic. Certainly, it should have taken no more planning than the ones here and in Canterbury.'

It did not escape McNeil that Johnson hadn't just said no more planning than *the others*, instead referring to Nottingham and Canterbury as though they didn't represent all the previous murders.

'So that doesn't explain the gap in time. Also, the method of killing was the same, using a similar knife, but why did he get rid of the old one in Canterbury? Before you say it, there were plenty of other ways he could have shown it was him in Canterbury, not least his tell-tale swipe on the shoulder.'

Johnson looked across at McNeil to see whether he had a comment on her last statement. 'Okay, go on,' he simply replied.

'And then there is the reason for switching genders. I could understand if he had done that here, in order to change it up a bit, but he achieved that by moving location. Which he does again with this one.' She paused. 'I have considered whether it was just coincidence that the first four were women, especially because, aside from being young and attractive, they are not exactly similar looking.'

'No, even I don't buy that, ma'am. Just look at Sarah Donovan. She's at the station surrounded by mostly male football supporters. He deliberately picked her out, whether in advance or there and then.'

'He has a thing for attractive women, yes?'

'Don't we all though?' McNeil replied. Correcting himself he added: 'I mean what's unusual about that, given he is a bloke and all?'

'If he gets off on young women, why isn't he doing more to them?'

'Erm, because it's too risky. He'll leave DNA. It'll take too long; it's just more *complicated*.'

'Exactly, it is complicated! Like I said to you in the café the other day, it would take a different approach, as symbolised by him getting rid of the knife. But by being complicated it has more chances of going wrong. And it did go wrong.' Johnson deliberately paused waiting for McNeil to speak.

'Like in St. Albans?'

'Yes! This attack in Milton Keynes only serves to confirm that it was him that killed the woman in St. Albans.'

'What, by the stabbing of a man in broad daylight somewhere different?' McNeil hoped his voice had sounded more incredulous than sarcastic.

'Precisely! What better way to distance himself from St. Albans altogether than to do something, not only completely different to St. Albans, but also something that seems to be reverting to type.' She stood up again. She had been so wrapped in the conversation that she hadn't noticed her cigarette had burned down. She absentmindedly tossed it in the direction of a drain.

'But if he's reverting to type, wouldn't he kill a woman again? Perhaps back in Canterbury or here even?'

'Yes, that's the logical thing to do.'

'You're agreeing with me?' McNeil asked, confused.

This time it was Johnson's turn to laugh. 'No, it may be logical but remember we are dealing with a serial killer here. He's cold and calculating, sure, but that doesn't make him rational. No, by trying to cover up his mistake in St. Albans he has gone on to make more mistakes. It's back to the garage logo. Just like he was too obviously trying to make the direct link back to Canterbury, thus bypassing St. Albans, picking a man this time is too obviously trying to imply there is no sexual motivation to his actions. Like you said yourself, McNeil, it was no coincidence that he was selecting women in the first place...'

McNeil stood up too. His mind was struggling to cope with all this. 'Right, let me get this straight, what you're saying is that, rather than the obvious explanation, he is switching it up again by changing gender as well as location and he's keen to show us the link because it's been a while since the last one, and this is an elaborate way of distancing himself from the murder in St. Albans, something no one had linked him to.'

'Precisely,' said Johnson, grinning.

McNeil shook his head and laughed again. 'Well, ma'am, you're either completely mad or completely amazing.'

'Oh, I am amazing,' Johnson said punching the number into the keypad to regain entry to the station. As she stepped through the doorway, she added: 'And soon I'll prove it.'

McNeil remained stationary, allowing the door to close behind Johnson. He sincerely hoped he wasn't reading more into that last statement than had been intended.

Chapter Forty-three

Johnson couldn't remember the last time she had felt this nervous. She had contemplated discussing it with Potter, but she knew he wouldn't allow it. It was better for him that he didn't know. She hadn't told McNeil either because he would try and convince her out of it. As far as Johnson could see, this was the only way. Unless she intervened, there was a good chance they could be chasing this killer indefinitely. It seemed he was way ahead in the game and if she didn't switch it up, they had little hope of catching him. She had found a weakness and she was going to exploit it. One day Potter might even thank her for it. *Not today though*, she thought to herself.

After all this, I really am going to cut down, she promised herself, stubbing out the cigarette on the overflowing metal container. She entered the building and noticed that members of the press had already gone through and taken their seats. Lurking inside the double doors was McNeil, who happened to turn at that moment, spot her, and offer a thumb's up. As she went around the corridor to the side entrance, she saw DSI Potter talking to someone unfamiliar.

'DSI Franklin.' He introduced himself before Potter had the chance to do so. 'DCI Johnson, I have heard so much about you.' There was a smarmy quality to his voice. 'Listen, Potter and I have been talking and we think between us we have it covered. However, for the sake of continuity it wouldn't do any harm to have you up there.' His wink at Potter brought a shiver to Johnson's spine even before he added, 'Bring a bit of glamour to proceedings, eh?'

Johnson could see Potter was about to say something in reply. Credit to him, much as they had disagreed recently, she admired his commitment to not being caught up in the old-boys' club misogynist bullshit that still went on in the force, albeit much better hidden than it used to be. She put a hand on his arm to stop him and received a quizzical look in return. 'No problem gentlemen,' she replied. Then indicating at the door, she continued, 'Shall we?'

There was the familiar flash of cameras as soon as they entered the room but the number of them suggested a far bigger gathering than Johnson had encountered before. As she took her seat, she noticed her hand shaking slightly when she reached out to the glass of water in front of her.

Johnson wasn't surprised that it was DSI Franklin who started the press conference. From the brief encounter with him it was obvious he would want the limelight, despite DSI Potter having led the investigation since this had all begun. Franklin introduced himself and explained that he would read a short statement regarding the most recent murder, before passing over to Potter. He added that there wouldn't be an opportunity for questions. *Shit!* Johnson thought.

What Franklin said about Milton Keynes was the typical speech under the circumstances: giving some basic details about what had happened and that they were following up a number of lines of enquiry. But the way in which he delivered it was curious to Johnson. She felt she could detect a sense of pride in his statement, as though he was pleased that Thames Valley Police was getting its share of the publicity. Similar in a way to a newly announced host city for the Olympics or World Cup looks forward to the gaze of the world falling upon them.

Potter played with his usual straight bat, explaining that they believed this to be the work of the man responsible for the attacks in Nottingham and Canterbury. Johnson noticed that he had been careful to avoid the words *serial killer*. From that point she largely zoned out from what was being said, her mind ablaze with thoughts of how to get her opportunity. These thoughts were met with others attempting to reassure her that *it was probably for the best* that she wouldn't.

DSI Potter had been brief; so much so it seemed to come as a surprise to the whole room when he finished. There followed a pause that felt like an age to Johnson, who was still wracked with indecision. In unison both Franklin and Potter leaned forward, ready to push their chairs back and stand when a voice called out from the middle of the room.

'Why a man this time?'

This is it! Johnson knew that if she wasn't the first to speak then the moment would be lost. Out of the corner of her eye she could already see Franklin's hand being raised in a dismissive gesture.

'I'll take this one,' she blurted out as quickly as she could.

She could sense the two heads swivel towards her and could imagine the shock on their faces.

'We believe this shows the same...' Deliberate pause. '...motivation as in previous attacks.'

'Yes, thank you,' Franklin called loudly. 'We said there would be no questions.' With that he stood and then so too did Potter and Johnson. She was relieved that it was her who would have to lead them out but, even with her back to her DSI, she could feel his stare bore into her.

Anxious to delay the inevitable chastisement that was to follow, she headed round the corridor and back to the main entrance. 'I hope that wasn't too subtle', she murmured to herself whilst apparently stopping to look for something in her bag.

'DCI Johnson, do you have a moment?' It was Gail Trevelly, reporter for one of the red tops.

'If you can walk and talk,' Johnson said, trying to sound casual, despite her heart going ten to the dozen.

Stepping outside she did not even hold the door open. If Trevelly was offended she didn't show it. 'I wanted to ask you about that comment you made in the press conference.'

'You do?' Johnson replied, as innocently as possible, pausing her walk to face the journalist.

'Yes, what did you mean when you said *same motivation*?'

Johnson had to turn away again, hiding the smile of delight that had formed on her lips.

Chapter Forty-four

'For Christ's sake, Johnson, Potter is going to kill you!' McNeil was sat in the same coffee shop as before, but this time was waving a newspaper around. 'And if he doesn't read this, all the others will have latched on to it by tomorrow and it will be everywhere.'

'I didn't say that,' Johnson responded, though with a knowing look in her eyes.

'*There is speculation that the attacker's switch to a male victim is the result of his own conflict with his sexuality. Perhaps he is bisexual or, at the very least, bi-curious,*' McNeil quoted.

'I didn't say that,' Johnson repeated.

'What did you mean by *motivation* then?'

'Oh, that was just an accident.' She looked down in mock shame. 'I forgot that DSI Franklin had said there were to be no questions.'

'Bullshit! Save that for Potter. I know you and I know that, however impetuous you appear to be, behind everything is cold calculation.'

Johnson was about to respond; genuinely concerned for the first time in the conversation by something McNeil had said. But his face caused her to pause. It was as though she could almost hear the cogs whirring.

Suddenly his face lit up. 'You really are amazing!'

'You don't know the half of it,' she replied, placing a hand on his knee, this simple gesture causing a slight flutter in his chest.

'I can just imagine,' he said in a low whisper.

'Perhaps you won't have to much longer,' she purred. Then an instant later she was on her feet and marching towards the exit.

'Where are you going?' McNeil called after her, deciding whether he could comfortably stand up.

'Back to face the music,' she replied over her shoulder.

Chapter Forty-five

'You cunt!' Brandt roared, throwing the newspaper across the room; the individual sheets separating before falling to the floor. 'You did this!'

Brandt had watched the press conference the previous day and had been satisfied with how it went. That was until the very end when that bitch piped up. Although she was shut down quickly, he had been keen to see what the press made of it. Arriving at his local shop the next morning, he was pleased to find his exploits on the front page of all the tabloids and even some of the broadsheets. He could think of nothing that would give him greater pleasure that day, than to pick up a copy of each one and spend the morning poring over them. He quickly devised a route that would take him to two other newsagents and would see him back home within the hour. Purchasing two papers from each shop wouldn't arouse any suspicion and he would use the walk to build up the anticipation by imagining the flurry of activity that morning in the relevant police stations.

Once home, Brandt had decided to start with the broadsheets, knowing their more measured style to reporting would stick closer to facts than opinion. Whilst he enjoyed reading the snippets in there, it was the sensationalist nature of the tabloids that he was really looking forward to. The first one didn't disappoint, suggesting that Britain was in the throes of its greatest serial killer since the Yorkshire Ripper. Brandt knew that the comparison would cause fear amongst some of its readers although, if he were feeling particularly egotistic, he would point out that the Ripper had been preying on a particular type of person and in a relatively localised area. It started Brandt thinking about what he should do next to ensure that the wide-ranging nature of his exploits be fully appreciated.

It was with such thoughts that he turned to the next publication. With an absent mind he scanned the front page, with its now familiar description of Saturday's murder and the police confirmation of the link to the Nottingham and Canterbury killings. He followed the link at the bottom to page 7 which introduced an editorial by their columnist Gail Trevelly. Brandt briefly glanced at her photo which he knew would have been professionally taken but did show her to be not unattractive. He was amused to find that she was claiming a unique insight into the murderer. *Oh, this should be good*, he chuckled to himself knowing that anything dramatic would serve his purpose of generating more fear among the public. But slowly his excitement had turned into shock, which was then replaced by fury.

With his legs shaking he made his way to the house phone, sat in its charger in the hallway. He forced himself to take a few moments to compose himself before punching in the number.

'Brian, how are you buddy? It's Jeff.'

'Oh hello. What can I do for you?'

Brandt was slightly taken aback by the purposeful tone he was met with. In his state of high emotion, he hadn't considered that ringing Franklin during working hours would be very different than the evening.

'Oh, I er… I just heard about what happened in Milton Keynes.'

'Yes, you can imagine what a furore it has caused.'

Brandt detected a little pleasure in Franklin's tone.

'Listen, we're quite busy here, what with everything, is there something specific I can do for you?' Franklin said.

'Oh no I just… I'll give you a call later once you're finished.'

'Are you okay, Jeff? You sound different.'

Shit! Just tell him you're fine and that you wanted to wish him well with the investigation. 'Fancy meeting up at the weekend?'

'Er sure, I could probably do Sunday assuming nothing else happens here on Saturday.'

It won't, Brandt thought to himself with a smile.

'I'll give you a call later on in the… Oh wait, I just remembered that I'm going to my Uncle's to watch the Arsenal game,' Franklin said.

Shit! Think, Brandt, think. 'That's just it: I've been given a couple of tickets to the match and wondered if…'

'Mate, that's awesome. Count me in. Look, I've got to go. I'll give you a call tomorrow night.'

The line went dead before Brandt could reply. With the receiver still to his ear he stood there motionless for a while, attempting to process what he had just done. On the one hand he was pleased that he had managed to provide a suitable reason for phoning at such an unusual time. Similarly, he had found a way of getting Franklin to agree to meet up when it had seemed he would be too busy. But on the other hand, he didn't even know what Arsenal game Franklin had been referring to, much less had tickets for them. Brandt hated football; ninety minutes of watching massively overpaid prima donnas falling to the ground and writhing in mock-pain as though they had broken their legs, only to jump up and celebrate scoring a goal like they had just discovered the cure for cancer. And that was watching it on television from the comfort of his armchair. The only enjoyment it had ever provided him was the fact that his wife had hated it more. Switching it on had been Brandt's way of driving her from the sitting room; something he found all too tempting in the latter years of their marriage.

Now, not only would he have to go to a game by choice, but he would have to pay for the privilege. As Brandt headed into the kitchen to fire up his laptop, he tried to reassure himself that he had made the right decision under difficult circumstances, and what he would gain from the day would be worth the hassle.

After twenty minutes on the internet and a frustrating phone call, he realised that the effort required to make this work was far greater than he had imagined. His initial relief at discovering they were playing at home, rather than somewhere like Newcastle, was tempered by who their opponents were. Even Brandt's limited knowledge extended to an appreciation that a game between Arsenal and their north London rivals Tottenham Hotspur was likely to increase demand for tickets. The website said that the match had been sold out weeks ago and a call to the ticket office confirmed this. The man at the other end of the line explained that, for a fee, Brandt could purchase two membership packages which would entitle him to purchase seats made available by season ticket holders who were unable to attend. However, he admitted that there were thousands of other members trying to do the same and that the chances of being successful were, at best, slim. Somewhat unhelpfully, he suggested keeping his money and using it to watch the game at the pub. Brandt attempted to hide his increasing annoyance and, rather than tell him what a stupid idea that was, said he might do just that.

Chapter Forty-six

Keep it simple. Say as little else as possible, take the bollocking and get out of there as quickly as you can. Despite this attempt at reassuring herself, Johnson felt queasy as she approached the door to Potter's office and was unable to hide her irritation when her path was blocked by DI Fisher and DC Hardy.

'Can't it wait? I'm busy,' she barked.

The look that passed between them made it clear that it wasn't a chance encounter. 'Ma'am, have you seen what the newspaper is saying?' Hardy asked.

Fucking little weasel, she thought to herself, instantly knowing that Fisher had made him raise the concern.

'What, do you need me to read it out to you? Explain what the big words mean?' She didn't have time for whatever stupid game he was playing and used their shocked expression to push past them and burst through Potter's door.

'Ah, Johnson, I've been looking for you!' The haste in his voice seemed to speak volumes.

'Oh really, guv, how come?'

'Look Stella, I don't have time for this. I don't know what you were playing at in the press conference but something more important has come up,' he said.

This was not at all how she had expected this to play out. Whatever it was, she hoped it was good news for a change.

'Before I tell you, for what it's worth I wanted to apologise for not trusting your instincts.'

'Er, go on, guv.' She was really confused now.

'Thames Valley Police found a foreign fibre in one of the stab wounds. Turns out it was a small piece of carpet thread.' Potter was being very calm, but Johnson could see the excitement in his eyes.

'Yes?'

'Well I was thinking about what you had said. And I thought that there was no harm in checking…'

'What is it?' She was becoming impatient.

'Well I asked them to cross reference to the carpet in St. Albans…'

'Fucking hell, I could kiss you right now!' Johnson exclaimed.

Potter looked shocked; her reaction being far from what he had expected. Rather than carry out her threat, she slumped into the chair opposite his desk.

He coughed, composing himself. 'I wanted to discuss with you what we should do with this information. I was thinking we…'

'We sit on it,' she interrupted.

'But this is big, it's…'

'It's massive,' she agreed. 'But now is not the time to reveal it.' *Oh shit, here goes.* Far from attempting to cover up what she had been up to yesterday, she was going to explain it all to Potter. 'We've already got something in play, so we need to hold this card back until we need to use it.'

Potter looked entirely confused with what Johnson was saying, so she proceeded to tell him what was in the paper that morning and her conversation with the journalist outside the press conference. She frequently paused during her explanation, partly to consider her words carefully but also to try and read Potter's reaction to what she was telling him. He had remained stony faced throughout.

Having finished, she was alarmed that he remained motionless for a while. *Oh God, what have I done?*

'So how does this play out?' he asked, calmly.

'Well, assuming he reads what is in the article today or sees what others make of it tomorrow, it will influence what he does next.'

'Go on…'

'Now his sexuality is being called into question, my guess is one of two things. He'll either stop…'

'Why?'

'…because he won't want what he is doing next to be misinterpreted. The alternative is he will want to remove suggestions of homosexuality by attacking a woman again.'

'So, we're back to where we were before…' Potter put his hands to his head to massage his temples.

'No, guv, he's making mistakes now. By inciting him into doing something more… complex again this time, we are going to ensure he continues to make mistakes. And that's how we will catch him.'

'This doesn't sit at all well with me, Stella.' His tone was one of admission rather than criticism. 'I don't like the idea that we are just waiting for the next murder, much less seem to be provoking it.'

That Potter had said *we* did not escape her. 'Me neither, guv but, if it's any consolation, I think he would have done it anyway. Knowing what we know about St. Albans, the killing of the man in Milton Keynes was just there to suggest a direct link back to Canterbury. Something made him want to spend more time with his female victims; an urge he would revisit at some point. I don't think he can help himself.'

'Why is that?'

'Because I don't think targeting a man was just for our benefit. I think he was trying to convince himself that it's just about the killing. But it's not and St. Albans proves it's not.'

'And so, the speculation about his sexuality…'

'Will make him confront it.'

Silence descended in the office with both of them lost in their own thoughts. 'Okay then,' Potter said eventually. 'I don't know if it will make me sleep easier tonight thinking that we are just accelerating the process rather than making it worse…'

'How are things, guv?'

The frankness of her question caused Potter to pause.

'Oh well, you know… Actually,' he continued with an ironic laugh. 'The pressure from above seems to have eased since Saturday. With it being in another police authority it has kind of spread the load.' His face became serious again. 'It doesn't really make it any easier though.'

'No,' Johnson agreed. 'And yesterday?'

'It seems that no one was surprised by your apparent impetuousness in the press conference.'

This time Johnson laughed. 'I should have told you, guv…'

'No, you shouldn't,' Potter replied. They both knew what he meant by that.

Chapter Forty-seven

Brandt waited for the train and reflected on his visit to London two days previously. As promised, Franklin had called on Wednesday evening and Brandt had persisted with his story about being given tickets for the weekend's match. That was despite him remaining unsuccessful in his search for any. The next day he had resorted to the box office worker's original suggestion of purchasing club membership. Having cost £35 to get registered, he found out that it only entitled him to purchase a ticket for himself so he reluctantly bought an additional one. Spending most of the day refreshing a digital stadium plan until sections turned from red to yellow to indicate a ticket had been made available was as tedious as it was ultimately fruitless. Except for on one occasion, he found they were just singles and had to go back to the main screen. As the afternoon had worn on, and just as he was about to give up hope, two arrived on the upper tier, positioned near the half way line. Brandt had been taken aback by their individual cost of nearly £150 and the pause meant that when he clicked on the seats a message appeared to say they were no longer available. Now entirely frustrated with the whole thing, he slammed down the lid of his laptop and left the room.

The next morning, whilst sporting an awful hangover, searches on the internet revealed websites claiming to have tickets. Advertising themselves as travel operators, they tapped into the foreign market for tourists who wanted to take in a big game whilst in the city. Brandt saw them as little more than legalised touts, an opinion strengthened by the astronomical prices they were charging. Promising that orders before 3pm would be sent out for next day delivery, Brandt had come close to clicking the button to purchase. After agonising for a while, he decided it too much of a risk to rely on Saturday's postal service. Instead he took the last desperate step of travelling to the stadium itself.

It had been a miserable trip to London with a delay on the line leading to his train being late and packed with other passengers. To cap it off, the rain he was greeted with when emerging from Highbury and Islington tube station only intensified on the mile or so walk to The Emirates. Despite the weather, there were quite a few people wandering around the outside of the stadium, stopping to take pictures of themselves with the various statues of former players dotted around. Yet more people were in the huge club shop picking up gifts and souvenirs. Brandt didn't go in, but he could see through the windows that the merchandise stretched far beyond the typical replica kit. People could even purchase a tour of the stadium for prices more than Brandt had originally expected to pay for a match ticket.

The only area that seemed empty of people was the box office. Approaching one of the kiosks, he wasn't surprised to see a sign confirming that the match was sold out, but persisted with asking the attendant anyway. As he left to start on his alternate plan of looking for spares around some of the local pubs, he noticed that someone was now waiting behind him. Pretending to check his phone, Brandt remained in earshot to hear that the man was collecting the tickets he had ordered when they had originally been on sale. As he left Brandt had tried to buy them off him but, despite offering twice their face value, he was unsuccessful. He knew that it was probably better to leave the pubs until they got busier later in the day, so he hung around the stadium at a distance that wouldn't arouse suspicion from anyone inside, waiting to see if more people would collect their tickets. It was a slow and frustrating couple of hours, getting increasingly wet and cold, and having to go through the humiliation of pleading people to part with something they clearly had no intention of giving up. Resolving that he would make one last attempt, he noticed the final couple leaving the ticket office seemed to be arguing.

Brandt could not believe his luck when the snippet of their conversation he caught as they passed him seemed to revolve around the man's shift pattern at work. Pouncing on his opportunity he apologised for interrupting them and enquired what the problem was. Receiving a look from the man that suggested he should be minding his own business, the woman, clearly angry with the situation, blurted out that he had gone and spent money they couldn't afford on football tickets that, it turns out, are for a game when he is working. She went on to explain that if he had got his lazy arse here a couple of days ago the club might have been able to resell them but, at this late stage, they had said it wasn't possible. Brandt, putting on his best concerned voice, offered to take them off their hands and said he would give them an extra £20 so they could make up whilst having a drink on their way home.

Delighted with the outcome, Brandt still had enough time to undertake one further task before heading home. An hour later, and back at the station platform, he withdrew his hand from the bulge in his pocket to slowly caress his cheek; the place where the delighted woman had kissed him. She had been beautiful and, in Brandt's opinion, far out of her boyfriend's league. The way she had spoken about him made Brandt believe that his intervention was just a stay of execution for their relationship.

With nothing else to prepare in advance of the match, Brandt had spent most of Saturday fine tuning the plans for the day and what he was going to do with the information he obtained. The key to everything was alcohol, and more specifically Franklin's growing dependency on it. The fixture was an early kick off, so he knew that his best chance was after the game anyway. Nevertheless, he wanted to test the extent of Franklin's resolve to stay on the wagon so, having agreed to meet him at the station, he then texted to say he had arrived early and was waiting for him in a bar just above the concourse.

Positioning himself a few tables inside and with a view of the entrance; Brandt wanted a chance to appraise Franklin before he was spotted. The way Franklin paused at the top of the escalator, causing the people behind to have to walk round him, amused Brandt. He looked nervous. The cause of those nerves was clear when, having finally clocked Brandt, his eyes were immediately drawn to the drinks in front of him. One pint was half empty but there was a full one sat opposite.

'Sorry buddy, I didn't know if you wanted a beer, but I didn't want to look like Billy No Mates.' He smiled to himself as Franklin continued to look at the drinks. 'Look, if, you know, you'd better not I could just…' He theatrically moved his own glass out of the way and slowly reached for the other.

'No, no that's fine,' said Franklin in a voice that was an octave too high. 'One for the road eh?'

'Yep, can't beat a beer and some football,' Brandt lied. 'We'll just have this one and head on to the stadium, shall we?'

Franklin didn't respond, so consumed was he with taking a couple of large gulps of the beer. Brandt could see him force himself to then slow considerably, and the conversation was as stunted as when they had first walked along the canal. *Give it time*, Brandt thought to himself.

'Er, do you want another?' Franklin asked, noticing that Brandt had finished his whilst he still had half left.

'Nah mate, if we hurry we can get one in before the match starts.' With that he rose, enjoying the look of disappointment on Franklin's face. That he then chose to down the remainder of his beer in one go made Brandt turn to conceal his grin.

Fifteen minutes later they emerged from Arsenal tube station into a flurry of activity. They turned off Drayton Park Road and up some steps leading to a bridge. The now familiar outside of The Emirates came into view.

'Stunning, isn't it?' Franklin commented.

'Sure is,' said Brandt, irritated by the crowds of people blocking his way. He glanced at his watch. It was only half an hour to kick off. Thankfully turnstiles were dotted all around the stadium perimeter and it only took them a further five minutes to gain entry to the lower tier. Inside was a hubbub of chatter, with screens mounted high on the walls showing the highlights of recent games.

'Shall we see them finish warming up?' Franklin asked excitedly.

'I thought we might er…' Brandt didn't finish his sentence, instead cocking his head to the nearest bar.

'Oh yeah, sure,' Franklin replied politely. 'My round isn't it?' He reached for his wallet.

'Great. I'll just go for a piss,' Brandt said. He couldn't bear waiting whilst Franklin queued. He knew that he would have further chances should he return with a soft drink for himself, but Brandt would be able to relax, perhaps even enjoy the game, if the right decision was made now.

Brandt had managed to squeeze into a gap in front of one of the long troughs but had been unable to urinate. His bladder was sufficiently full, but the close proximity of other men alongside him, and knowing that people were waiting impatiently behind, put him off. Frustratingly, the urge returned as soon as he passed the sinks on the way to the exit which only angered him further. For a moment he had completely forgotten about Franklin and the bar but, not only was he greeted with the sight of him holding two bottles of lager, he could also see that one was already a third empty.

'Cheers mate,' he said, taking his drink and listening to the dull thump of the plastic as he hit it against Franklin's.

'No mate, thank *you*. I haven't been to a game in ages. What with the week I've had and everything… you know, with the wife and all. Well, let's just say, it's good to let your hair down once in a while.'

That last statement was music to Brandt's ears.

Chapter Forty-eight

'How long do you think the DSI is going to last?' McNeil asked. They had been watching CCTV footage from St. Albans for hours and Johnson's ability to stay focused never failed to amaze him. He knew that being in the police was more than a job, but this seemed bordering on an obsession for her. When she had come back from seeing Potter, he had been genuinely touched that she had confided in him about the carpet fibre, though it appeared she was under strict instruction to not let the information leave his office. What had impressed McNeil the most was the way she hadn't spoken about it in terms of vindication. She could have used this as an opportunity to laud it over everyone else; to emphasise that she knew the link that all others, McNeil to a certain degree included, had dismissed. He'd often wondered, as clichéd as it seemed, whether Johnson's apparent confidence and bravado was a mechanism for covering up her insecurities. What he now believed was that it was a more intrinsic part of her; designed, consciously or not, to promote her beliefs. Therefore, when she was proven to be correct she could dispense with the dramatics in the knowledge that she had been successful.

'What's that?' Johnson replied, her gaze not leaving the screen in front of her.

'I asked how long Potter is willing not to go public with St. Albans.'

'Oh that, well I think we've got the rest of next week,' she said, almost conversationally.

'You mean if our guy doesn't strike again in that time?'

'Yep.'

McNeil waved his hand in front of her face to break her concentration. 'Hello, Johnson? You don't seem concerned by this.'

'Nope,' she replied, refusing to be baited and pretending she could still see through his hand.

This time he reached out for her chair, one of those on wheels, and started swivelling it towards him. Johnson didn't resist, allowing her body to twist but keeping her head resolutely trained on the CCTV footage.

He burst out laughing. 'You're such a piss-take, ma'am.'

'And you, PC McNeil, are an irritant. Just because you have the concentration levels of a goldfish, it doesn't mean us humans should similarly suffer.' The lightness of her tone designed to soften the impact of the words.

'I'm just worried that your refusal to accept that you need glasses will soon have your nose touching the screen.'

McNeil had learned by now that any reference to her age, however dangerous that might be, always served to provoke a reaction. He just hoped to God it was the right one this time.

Johnson turned towards McNeil, enjoying the look of apprehension her cold stare was having on him. 'I need fucking glasses you say?' For effect she squinted slightly and leaned towards him, as though to get a better look. Quick as a flash she reached out and grabbed the sides of his chair and wheeled him towards her so quickly it bumped into hers. Before McNeil could recoil in shock, she planted her lips on his. Unlike in the lift in Canterbury, this time she was the one doing the work; her tongue darting into his mouth to meet his. But just as he reached out to embrace her, she planted her legs firmly on the floor and pushed her seat away, with her backwards movement soon breaking the kiss.

McNeil remained motionless, still leaning forwards, his mouth puckered and with his eyes remaining closed. Johnson crossed her arms. Eventually and slowly he opened one eye and then opened the other to look at her with mock shock. 'Oh, had you stopped? Sorry I hadn't really noticed.'

She tried to resist giggling but when McNeil closed his eyes again to resume the exact pose as before, she couldn't help herself. 'Fuck you!' Was all she could manage before his laughter set her off again. Eventually calming down, she said, 'Look, just get me a cup of coffee or something and I'll try and get this last tape finished.'

'You didn't say please.'

'Excuse me?' Johnson said, rising out of her seat.

'If you expect me to be your servant as well as your… your plaything, the least you can do is ask nicely.'

'Oh really?' she said menacingly, approaching him slowly. 'And what if I don't want to be nice?'

McNeil went to reply but Johnson reached forward and put her index finger on his lips. 'Shhhh,' she soothed. With her other hand she hitched up her skirt, so he could see her slender thighs. She removed her finger from his mouth, but when he went to speak she put it back, slowly shaking her head and placing her other hand high up on his leg, edging close to his groin. She could see him harden at her touch. Leaning round to whisper in his ear, she pulled his head close. 'Now,' she said, allowing her warm breath to fall on him. 'Be a good little boy and make me a cup of coffee.'

Johnson remained there for a moment, impressed that he hadn't attempted to grab her this time. He was learning patience. That was good. Slowly she rose and enjoyed the anguish on his face. She took a step backwards, slipped her right foot out of her shoe and used it to part his legs. She placed it on the seat, inches from the front of his strained trousers and leaned forward, but only so her leg could bend and, with an almighty shove, she pushed him so that he and the chair went wheeling backwards; crashing into the door behind.

Johnson stood watching the astonishment on McNeil's face, and used a quick shimmy of her hips to encourage her skirt to drop back down into place. 'And get me a fucking biscuit,' she commanded.

Chapter Forty-nine

If this was going to work, Brandt would need him sufficiently inebriated so that he was unlikely to recall their conversation. So far, the signs were good. The match had started off well and a quick goal for Arsenal lifted the crowd, Franklin included. Spurs had scored an equaliser at around the half hour mark, but any concerns Brandt had that this would dampen the mood were instantly eradicated three minutes before half time when Arsenal smashed in a second. As the home fans celebrated, Brandt suggested he nip to the bar to get the drinks in. Franklin enthusiastically agreed.

Exiting the stadium, with an injury time goal for Arsenal making the score 4-3, Brandt was going to wait until they saw the queues for the tube before recommending they stop somewhere to allow the crowds to die down. He need not have worried.

'Mate, that was amazing. I've never seen a game that swung so back and forth.'

'It sure did,' Brandt replied. Even he had to admit the action, combined with the electric atmosphere in the stadium, had conspired to make it enjoyable. Perhaps not enjoyable enough to justify all the hassle and expense he had gone through to get hold of the tickets, but satisfying nonetheless.

'Are you sure I can't give you the money for my ticket?'

'Nah, mate, my treat. Honestly.'

'Well, how about I buy us a late lunch somewhere?' This sounded promising to Brandt but would depend on what type of restaurant. 'Besides, it would be wrong not to celebrate such a fine victory.'

Bingo! 'That sounds splendid. I think I might know just the place,' Brandt replied diverting them from their current path.

That the pub was packed with Arsenal fans and all the available seats were taken, didn't seem to faze Franklin. 'I'm sure we'll get a table once some of these people go. Let's have a couple of pints at the bar whilst we wait.'

'Great, I'll keep a look out,' Brandt nodded. With Franklin busy purchasing their drinks, he deliberately positioned himself so he would be the one viewing the seating area. With the three beers they'd had already working their way out of their system Brandt wanted to ensure they remained standing for as long as possible. Holding a pint, rather than having it propped up on a table, always worked to encourage one to drink faster. That, in combination with their empty stomachs, was sure to get Franklin drunk quicker. Brandt wanted that overloading of the brain caused by fast intoxication to cover his tracks.

If anything, the pub got busier during the first hour they were there. Brandt identified a couple of tables during that time but acted sufficiently slowly enough that other drinkers got there ahead of them. Franklin did not seem concerned in the slightest. He was maintaining a strong pace, the effects of which were illustrated by often cutting himself off mid-sentence to join in with the various football chants that occasionally erupted from the other customers.

Brandt was no light-weight and had honed his ability to drink copious amounts over the last decade but, a preferred whisky man, he was starting to struggle with the sheer volume of liquid they were consuming. Selfishly he didn't want to suggest a switch to spirits because of concerns that this may lead to him having to help Franklin home. Resolutely, he stuck to beer.

Just as he was starting to feel nauseous from the effects of the alcohol combined with his empty stomach, he saw his chance arrive. Franklin was enthusiastically recommending they challenge some thugs in the corner to a game of pool. 'Yeah, in a minute mate. There was something I wanted to ask you…'

Chapter Fifty

The percolator had needed refilling and McNeil planned on using the time to attempt to calm himself down. As he tried not to read too much into what had just happened, he was startled from his thoughts by DI Fisher entering the small kitchenette, claiming he was looking for a spoon for his yoghurt. McNeil had grown used to their supposedly coincidental encounters. Fisher had long since moved on from being hostile towards him, and was instead trying to act like a mentor. McNeil had been suspicious of the turnaround and, when Hardy had let it slip in conversation that Fisher had applied for the DCI position when Johnson had got it a couple of years back, his motive had become clear. With the enemy of my enemy being my friend, Fisher wanted to glean whatever information he could in order to jockey for position should Johnson be unable to catch the killer. McNeil felt uncomfortable with knowing a member of the team wasn't fully on board, perhaps even glad that things weren't going well, but would keep his concerns to himself for the time being. Johnson seemed to have enough on her plate at the moment.

With the coffee finally brewed McNeil made his excuses to leave, deciding not to bring along the packet of biscuits that sat next to the machine. Holding a mug in each hand and using his foot to push open the door he hoped, with a smile, that his defiance of her instruction would lead to some form of retribution that may rekindle their earlier lack of professionalism.

Yet Johnson appeared not to notice his re-entry, much less what he had failed to bring. Something about the furious way she was flicking between different images suggested to him that no amount of provocation would lead to a reigniting of their earlier intimacy and, with a sigh, he placed the coffee on the table nearby.

'What have you got?'

'Ah good, you're back,' she said, continuing to stare in front of her. 'Hardy picked this up earlier. See this man here?' She tapped the screen to show who she was referring to. 'He crosses in front of the station twice in an hour.'

'So, it's near the town centre; surely there are lots of people that go back and forth.'

'Yes, and that's probably why no one flagged him up before. Let me show you the two sets of images and you can tell me what you think.' Johnson stood up to allow McNeil to sit down. As she leaned over him to use the mouse, he could smell her fragrance once more. He had to close his eyes for a second to try and regain focus on what she was asking him to do, but he couldn't help feeling unsettled by the apparent ease with which she could switch between work and play.

Trying to push all other thoughts from his mind, he concentrated on the man crossing the road. Nothing about his movement was remarkable to McNeil. Presented with the second set of images he could tell it was the same guy; the only notable changes being him walking in the opposite direction and at greater pace.

Johnson swivelled the chair round so he was looking at her. 'So, what have you got?'

'Well, you're right it's the same guy.'

'And…'

'And I bet you've looked at the footage more than once,' he replied defensively.

'You can see it again in a minute, but you have to notice something first to make you want to see it again.' McNeil understood what she was saying. With hours of footage from various cameras to trawl through, you only really had one shot to notice something out of place. Even if you didn't yet know why, you had to have that inkling in the first place to prevent something being missed.

'Well, I would say it is unusual that he is first walking away from town and then coming back towards it.' McNeil could read the disappointment in Johnson's eyes. He opted to continue, 'It would make more sense for him to have been heading into town to pick something up and then returning a short while later.' He could see the disappointment was turning into frustration. 'Naturally he might have been heading away from town to go to the supermarket, or whatever, but then surely we would see a bag when he returned.' He made the last bit sound triumphant and put his best smug face on.

'Yes, yes, yes, but…'

'Oh, one more thing,' he interrupted. 'He's walking much faster second time around.'

Johnson stared at him. 'You fucking tease!' she shouted, punching him squarely on the arm. The irony of the statement didn't escape McNeil. She turned him back towards the camera. 'Now, when we switch to this camera what do you notice?' she asked excitedly.

He concentrated hard on this new footage. McNeil was about to confess that he could see nothing new when, just as the man crossed the front of the station, his pace slowed considerably as he walked out of shot.

'Can you rewind that last bit please?' There it was again; a definite slowing. 'Er, can you show me the first camera view again?'

'Well?' Johnson asked, more patiently this time.

'Have we got a camera further up? McNeil asked, pointing to the left of the screen.

'I'm afraid the next one is towards the top of the hill and he doesn't appear on there.'

'Ok then, here's what I think.' McNeil paused whilst Johnson pulled a chair next to him. 'I think he could well be our guy. He doesn't select his victim in advance and picks one out from the crowd. He's walking slowly in the earlier one because he is in plenty of time for the train. He must have picked out a potential target and followed her.'

'And?' Johnson prompted.

'Something must have gone wrong.'

'Like what?'

He shrugged. 'Could be anything really, she might have met her boyfriend around the corner, she might have parked up the road, she might have gone to the supermarket...'

'Okay, so he comes back...'

'Yes, but he's in a hurry.' He paused for thought. 'So, whatever went wrong with the first target must have happened further on to allow for the time lapse. We can see that he's timed it wrong because the passengers are all leaving before he is in shot. Oh, by the way, which one was Lily James?' McNeil asked, turning back to the screen and expecting Johnson to lean across and wind back the image to the appropriate point. When, after a few moments, she hadn't moved he turned back towards her.

'She was the last to leave the station,' she said simply, allowing the implication of this to hang in the air.

'Fucking hell,' he cursed under his breath, before suddenly sitting up. 'Why didn't the Hertfordshire Constabulary pick this up?'

'Turns out they did but they couldn't get the image to scrub up sufficiently to get a good look at his face and he doesn't appear on any CCTV anywhere in the vicinity. He's like a ghost.'

'*Was* like a ghost…' McNeil offered.

'How come?'

'Because the Hertfordshire guys were only looking at CCTV in St. Albans. If he's our man he'll be on the footage from here, Canterbury, and Milton Keynes.'

'What now, McNeil?'

'Er, go for a drink to celebrate?' he offered hopefully.

Johnson gave a small, wistful laugh. 'Bit premature there. The magnitude of this is overwhelming. We have a blurry image of a fairly non-descript guy that we have to compare with thousands of hours' worth of CCTV cameras. It's like looking for a needle in a haystack.'

'More like a needle in a stack of needles,' he replied thoughtfully. 'Tell you what, let's start with Milton Keynes and Canterbury as they will have the fewest cameras to check.'

'That's the spirit, McNeil,' she said, slapping him on the back. 'Tell you what, before we get started, why don't you get us some coffees. I think this is going to be a long night.'

'Er, ma'am, I already did,' he said, nodding in the direction of the mugs.

'Oh yeah,' she responded casually. She then turned to glare at him. 'But you forgot the fucking biscuits!'

Chapter Fifty-one

Brandt's hangover was unpleasant but not so debilitating as to prevent him being up and washed early. His instincts had told him that he couldn't afford to wait. What cheered him up was imagining the state that Franklin must be in, no doubt attempting to hide his symptoms whilst delivering his Monday morning briefing. The information he had managed to extract wasn't as detailed as he would ideally have liked but, with just about enough to go on, he'd decided that to push things any further would risk his persistence lodging something in Franklin's inebriated mind.

Brandt had feared it would take some persuasion to remove him from the pub, but he had been helped by the pool playing gentlemen taking exception to his claim that they were a bunch of pussies for not wanting to accept the challenge of a game. Suggesting they had better move on to another establishment, Franklin didn't complain when Brandt steered him towards the tube instead. Back at King's Cross, he had waited by the ticket barriers whilst watching Franklin totter unsteadily along the platform and onto one of the carriages.

Satisfied, he had decided that the walk back to Euston would do him some good and, by the time he had devoured a Burger King before boarding his own train, he had been feeling much better.

That was the last time he had eaten, and Brandt detoured his route to get some breakfast before picking up his car. As he sat in the café waiting for his fry-up to be served, he scanned a newspaper left behind by a previous customer. There was no mention of his killings, which suggested to him that all had remained quiet since those unfortunate articles the previous week.

As he used his last round of toast to mop up the tomato sauce left on his plate, he considered once more the structure for the day. He knew that, this far into the game, revisiting a previous destination was particularly risky and had decided that he would cut down on CCTV exposure by driving the entire journey. Brandt had always wondered to himself who would be stupid enough to buy one of those cars you occasionally saw parked up on a verge somewhere, with nothing more than a price scribbled onto a piece of paper, along with a mobile number. And yet, leaving the café, he started punching into the cheap pay-as-you-go phone the digits for one he had spotted a few days earlier.

'Hello there,' came the heavy Irish accent through the receiver.

Fucking pikeys! Brandt laughed to himself. *Perfect.* Any concerns that the vehicle might be traced back to him evaporated.

'Good morning,' he responded cheerfully. 'I'm telephoning to enquire about the car.'

'Now which one might that be?'

'The Vauxhall Astra parked on, er, by Church Street.'

'Ah, that one. Sure, it's a fine motor there.'

'Can you tell me a little about it? Does it run okay?'

'Sure does, my fella. Sound as a pound. One lady owner and just sixty thousand miles. Barely run in.'

'And how much do you want for it?'

'Ah now, see, that's the thing. You notice that little sticker in the window with three numbers on it?'

Brandt hated this man already. 'Oh, I see,' he replied trying to hide his contempt. 'In which case I think I might like to buy it.'

'Would ya now? And when would that be?'

'No time like the present…'

'Sure enough, my fella. I'll be right over.' The line went dead.

Despite the man's promise, and even with the fifteen-minute walk, Brandt was at the car first. Having used the time to check it had no damage more superficial than the usual scrapes and parking dings, he was about to phone the number again, when a large white Porsche SUV came around the corner and parked up next to him. With the window dropping to reveal an unshaven man with a mop of unruly black hair, and a tasteless gold chain sat over the top of his checked shirt, Brandt put his phone back in his pocket. 'I see I'm in the wrong business,' he said, looking along the vehicle's flanks.

'So, you got the money then?'

Brandt was pleased by the man's unwillingness to engage in conversation. The less he knew about Brandt the better.

'Here it is,' he said holding up a roll of notes. 'Would you like to count it?'

'Not at all, my old fella, I trust ye,' he replied with a wink. 'Would you like a test drive?'

'Nah, I trust you too. I need the paperwork though.'

'Of course, of course,' he said reaching into the glove compartment to pull out a fresh looking V5. A quick scan revealed that the car had five previous owners, the last a man called Oscar Miles. Rather than raise complaint, Brandt was satisfied to see the address was in Yorkshire and clearly not the man sat before him.

'Want me to fill it in?'

'Up to you, fella,' he said, shrugging.

'I'll get it in the post today,' Brandt replied, handing over the money.

'That's the spirit, I'm sure you'll have many years of happy motoring.' The man tossed Brandt the key, gave him a wink and set off, window still retracted.

Walking up to the car Brandt pressed the button for the central locking system. *So far, so good*, he thought opening the door. Unperturbed by the unfortunate looking stain on the driver's seat, he lowered himself in. With the key inserted, he nervously waited as all the warning lights on the dashboard came on; relieved to see each one subsequently disappear. Making the final twist he heard the starter motor try and fire the vehicle into life. Turning over longer than it should, the engine finally caught before settling down into a reassuring thrum.

He reached over to the passenger side of the windscreen to tear off the car's amateurish advertisements, only mildly irritated by the residue left over by the Sellotape. He was about to toss the crumpled-up pieces of paper over his shoulder into the rear seats when it suddenly dawned on him that leaving the traveller's mobile phone number inside was far from a good idea. Anxious to get moving before drawing any more attention to himself, he placed it in one of the cup holders and resolved to use the car's cigarette lighter to destroy it, along with the V5 document, when he found somewhere secluded.

Putting the car into gear, and having to raise the clutch more than was healthy to find the biting point, he rolled steadily off the verge. There was the merest creak from the suspension as the wheels met the road. Here we go then, he thought, following the familiar route to the motorway.

Chapter Fifty-two

'I think that's him,' McNeil said, pointing to the screen. Never mind Johnson needing glasses, he felt he should go for an eye test the way he had to keep blinking to stop the image appearing blurred. They had both worked long into the previous night before finally admitting that, with so much to sift through, they would have to call on extra support. With exhaustion pushing thoughts of an amorous nature out of his mind, he had gone home to get a few hours' sleep. Johnson had promised to do the same and, although she was wearing different clothes now, he wouldn't have put it past her to have a change of wardrobe in one of her office cupboards that she used for occasions such as this. Certainly, the dark circles under her eyes didn't suggest otherwise.

'Okay let's run with this,' she agreed. With the images from St. Albans providing them with so little to go on, in terms of a possible description, they had been struggling to narrow down the huge number of men that passed the cameras in the relevant time windows. They were looking for someone middle-aged; the nature of the crimes had suggested a calmness and maturity that came with time, and the images of St. Albans neither showed the sprightliness of youth, nor any symptoms of being elderly. However, this had still left an unfeasible number of possibilities. The sheer mass of people at Nottingham railway station for the first one was proving prohibitive; there was no CCTV in the vicinity of the second attack and the third, on the river path, was hard to narrow down in terms of where the person would have joined or exited. Milton Keynes had been more promising because there were cameras on Bletchley High Street, but they didn't show anyone enter or even stop to look in the alleyway, much less go down it.

In each case they neither knew from which overall direction their man had approached, nor which way he had left. Except, that was, for Canterbury. Following the attack, he had walked north along the Whitstable Road to the mechanics where he dropped off the knife.

Knowing his direction of travel had allowed them to greatly reduce the number of cameras that needed checking. With the little they knew already, and with assumptions like he wouldn't be carrying any shopping, they had narrowed it down to one individual.

'Put St. Albans on the other monitor and let's run these images side by side,' Johnson suggested. They both sat in silence, flicking their eyes between the two screens. 'I couldn't say for certain that it is the same person but...'

'...then again there is nothing to say it isn't.' McNeil finished the sentence for her.

'Exactly, we need to speak to this man,' she said enthusiastically. 'Right, get the IT guys to follow him back and get the best image of him for us to work with.'

'So, what's next?' he enquired.

'Well hopefully he's on our database because Potter is never going to let us make a public appeal.'

'Er, how come?'

'Based on what? We found someone who might, *might*, have something to do with St. Albans. We have then found a man in Canterbury who we can't say looked like this man, only just that he doesn't *not* look like him. And that's even before we consider the fact that we haven't even gone public with the connection to St. Albans yet.'

'Oh, I see,' responded McNeil, lowering his head.

'Hey,' she said, lifting his chin up gently. 'This is good. More than that, it's the first decent lead we've had. If this guy has got previous, and let's face it people don't tend to start their career of crime with serial murder, we'll have his address within a few hours. You never know, we might be celebrating cracking the case tonight!'

'I'd like that.'

'Me too,' she replied softly. 'Right,' she continued, standing. 'Let's get this over to the IT nerds and order an early lunch whilst we wait. What do you fancy?'

McNeil didn't answer. What he was thinking he didn't dare say out loud.

'I want pizza,' she continued, unconcerned by his silence. 'One of those greasy ones with extra cheese.'

He laughed. 'I didn't think you did carbs, ma'am.'

'Today's different. Special, I think.'

I hope so, I really do.

Chapter Fifty-three

Brandt didn't mind waiting. It was to be expected. Given some of the unsettling noises from the car on the journey up, and the way it pitched alarmingly to the right under heavy braking, he was just glad to be there at all. *Perhaps I'll do a pikey next*, he chuckled to himself. Still full from the substantial breakfast, he hadn't yet touched his meagre packed lunch. With longer to plan, he would have definitely picked up some more appetising supplies, especially because he had no idea how long he would be sitting there. Brandt knew there was a strong possibility that he might not even see his target today but, with his Milton Keynes murder making St. Albans seem like little more than a bad dream, he felt luck was on his side again.

One thing he hadn't given much thought to was what to do with the car afterwards. He would need to dump it somewhere but clearly far enough from his house that it wouldn't lead the police straight back to him. *It's not too late to go home and think this through a little more clearly*. Brandt hated that voice, always trying to make him doubt himself. Whilst he had to admit that this had been a little rushed, and perhaps events had conspired for him to be less measured, less dispassionately calculating, that wasn't to say he was doing the wrong thing. If he developed the habit of listening to this voice, he very much doubted he would get anything done. Brandt was put in mind of a quote he had read once about fools rushing in where angels feared to tread. He knew he was no angel, but he was far from a fool either. *Calculated risks*, he reassured himself, manually reclining the seat to relax his posture.

Chapter Fifty-four

'What if we were able to get a clearer image?' Johnson asked without waiting for a reply. 'McNeil, perhaps we can see if we can pick this guy up on a camera somewhere else and get...'

'Look, ma'am,' said the IT guy whose name Johnson didn't know or couldn't remember, pointing at the screen. 'These dots show where the facial recognition software has picked up specific points for comparison. It found enough to work its way through the database.' He was pointing at a slightly blurred still of Brandt's face.

'Well clearly not, because it hasn't found anything!' Johnson fumed.

'No,' he responded calmly. 'It's just that there were no matches.'

'This is bullshit,' she said, storming out of the room.

'Thank you for your help,' McNeil said sincerely but only receiving a shrug of acknowledgement before he set off after Johnson.

She was already half way along the corridor when he tried to gain her attention. When her pace didn't slow, he jogged to catch up. Concerned that she was still ignoring him, he held his hand out to prevent her being able to pull open the next door.

'What the fuck?' she snarled, turning to glare at him.

He could see her eyes were watery; whether through rage or disappointment, he couldn't tell. 'What is it?' he asked, trying to sooth her. 'Tell me.'

Johnson released the handle and slumped against the wall. 'I really thought we might have got him.'

'And we might still have,' he ventured hopefully.

She shook her head.

'Seriously, Johnson, we just need to go back to the other footage and identify him at each of the other crime scenes. Potter is bound to sanction the public appeal in that case.'

'That's assuming this is our guy…'

'What?'

'Like I said before, the chances of this being his first criminal offence are slim. We have to accept the strong possibility that we may have picked out the wrong guy.'

'Where, in St. Albans?'

'No, I'm convinced he's the one, but we need to double check that we didn't match it up with the wrong one in Canterbury.'

Although McNeil was pretty sure no one similar had been missed, he was encouraged by this. Johnson had moved on to thinking about their next steps, however laborious and tedious they might be.

'Okay, let's grab some coffee and start on that,' he said in as enthusiastic a voice as he could muster.

She slowly nodded and stopped leaning on the wall. McNeil had already turned to open the door when he felt a hand on his shoulder. 'Thank you,' she said quietly.

'No problem,' he replied breezily. 'We're both tired; neither of us got much sleep last night.'

She looked up at him guiltily.

'If any at all,' he said, correcting himself. 'Are you sure you don't want some kip now and we start on this tomorrow?'

'No,' she said firmly. 'I just need to be more certain this is the right guy first. At least then I can send it around to the different police stations, including distributing it here. Okay, he's not on our database, which means he might not have actually been convicted of something, but that isn't to say he isn't known to someone.'

Chapter Fifty-five

DSI Franklin felt dreadful. He should have taken his falling asleep on the train and having to wait at the end of the line for another to take him back to his station, as a sign that he had drunk enough. Instead he had staggered home via the off-licence and picked himself up a four pack of lager to help wash down the kebab he bought at the takeaway next door. This had been the first night he had been grateful to return to an empty house. His wife would have been apoplectic with rage given the state he had been in.

Waking up the following morning, fully clothed and lying on the sitting room floor, the first thing he had done was to rush to the kitchen sink to vomit up his partially digested supper. The improvement to his symptoms this provided was only a brief respite and, as he showered a few minutes later, he began retching again until all he was throwing up was the yellow bile from his stomach lining.

Regretting having told so many of the department that he had been going to the football yesterday, an absence from work would only confirm the suspicions he knew some held that he had hit the bottle since his wife left. Gambling the risk of driving against him being spotted arriving in a taxi, Franklin decided on the former. Stopping in a layby to involuntarily purge himself of the water he had drunk in a vain attempt to combat his dehydration, he vowed that he would invent an off-site meeting for the afternoon and return home early.

Having sweated his way through his morning briefing of CID, he had retired to his office, pretending to be on the phone whenever anyone had tried to come and see him. Despite the way he was feeling, he had enjoyed yesterday. It seemed that, in retirement, Brandt had become far more interesting than Franklin would ever have expected. He certainly had kept his love of football a secret. And what a game it had been! All the drama of Arsenal continually being pegged back by equalisers, only to then finally win in added time. That was enough excitement to light up any match but for the last game of the season, against Spurs of all teams, it was something Franklin expected to remember for a long time. He decided he must ask Brandt who his mate was that gave him the tickets, because he'd love the opportunity to go again next year. He doubted anything could live up to that game, but perhaps it was something they could do together once in a while. The fact that it was something his wife wouldn't have approved of only made the thought appeal more to Franklin.

He couldn't remember whose idea it was to go to the pub afterwards but that had been an inspired choice too. The atmosphere in there was almost as good as the stadium, what with the chanting and everything. Franklin thought it a shame that those idiots by the pool table hadn't seemed as friendly as everyone else. He assumed they were regulars who resented the extra people that match day brought in. Seeing yet another person walking towards his door, he decided he would give Brandt a call.

With his call going unanswered, Franklin assumed that Brandt must still be in bed, yet another benefit of retirement, and hung up. Reminiscences of yesterday's enjoyment had caused him to feel a little better, deciding that now would be a good time to risk lining his stomach. He left his office in search of a bacon roll.

Feeling slightly guilty for having guzzled two of them, along with three cups of coffee, he returned to work believing he could last the day without having to invent a meeting elsewhere. However, and although his late breakfast had managed to settle his stomach, he started to flag in the early afternoon. Franklin couldn't remember what time he had gone to sleep last night but the combination of being laid out on his hard sitting room floor, along with the effects of the alcohol, had conspired to leave him weary. With the stimulation from the caffeine having worn off, the headache he felt that morning seemed to now be approaching a full-grown migraine. Staring at his laptop hadn't helped. The initial optimism of discovering a blister pack of paracetamol in one of his desk drawers was replaced by the frustration of finding it empty. Concerned of the suspicions that asking his colleagues if they had some might arouse, he decided that he would just make some excuse and leave for the remainder of the day.

After a quick tidy of the papers on his desk, none of which he had actually read, he went to shut down his computer. As he was just about to close his emails the alert for an incoming message sounded. It was from the Nottinghamshire Constabulary. He shifted his cursor over to it, but with his head now throbbing, he moved the mouse back to the small cross in the top left-hand corner of the window. It can wait until tomorrow, he thought.

Chapter Fifty-six

'All done?' McNeil asked.

'Yep, that's the last of them sent,' replied Johnson, closing the lid of her laptop. It hadn't taken them long to revisit the footage from Canterbury and confirm that there weren't any other middle-aged men who had arrived from the same direction and turned off the high street at the correct point without having bought items from any of the shops.

'I guess we had better start looking at the cameras from here again,' he sighed, reaching in the box for the last remaining slice of pizza. It had long gone cold and the cheese topping looked rather congealed, but he assumed he was in for a long night.

'That can wait until the morning,' she said, stretching. 'We're both knackered and could do with a good night's rest.'

'I'm not sure I could sleep...'

Johnson laughed. 'Oh God, don't start turning into me. I can assure you, being this highly strung is not fun. It certainly ruins your social life.' She turned towards him. 'Walk me to my car?'

'Sure,' he replied, dropping the pizza slice, having taken only a bite.

They didn't say a word to each other as they exited the building; both deep in their own thoughts. McNeil was about to say goodbye and veer towards his old blue Ford Fiesta, a hand-me-down from his mother, when Johnson stopped and grabbed his hand. 'I'm sorry.'

'Oh, don't worry, believe me I am as frustrated as you are that the man wasn't on the database...'

Johnson laughed again but this time nervously. 'No, I mean... erm, I mean...' She shook her head. 'I don't know how to describe it but clearly there's something there; something *between us*.' She looked into his eyes to see if he was following what she was saying. 'The truth is I don't know how I'm feeling and it's hard with all this other stuff...'

'I get it,' McNeil replied, trying to offer a reassuring smile.

Johnson shook her head again. 'No, I need to explain it.' She paused, taking a deep breath. 'I don't care about the age gap...'

McNeil opened his mouth to speak.

'Please let me finish,' she said softly. 'I don't care about the age gap. I don't even care that I'm much more senior than you.'

McNeil giggled, notwithstanding knowing how unfortunate his timing was.

'Oh, for fuck's sake! I meant senior as in higher up than...'

'I know, I know,' he managed, despite having yet to regain his composure.

Johnson couldn't help but smile at his ability to always take the tension out of a situation. 'Look, what I'm trying to say is that I'm not hiding away from what's developed between us. I just want you to know that I'm sorry it's taken this long. I promise you that when all this is done I want to see how this, *our* this, whatever *this* is, plays out.'

McNeil nodded.

'I just need you to be patient for a little while. Do you think you can do that?'

'Yes, I think so,' he lied.

Sat in his car he guessed that, by now, Johnson was busy lighting a cigarette. He regretted the way he had handled the situation, particularly with his laughter. He could have done more to reassure her that he felt the same way about her, and that he understood the reasons why things hadn't progressed. The truth was, as awkward as she had appeared, he was equally as unaccustomed to discussing his feelings. What he had really wanted to say was that, if nothing else, the last few weeks had taught him how precious life is and, rather than wait for the *right time*, whatever the hell that was, people should embrace the chance of happiness whenever it presented itself.

Not wanting to drive off before she was ready and, perhaps, give suggestion to the frustration he was feeling, he waited to hear the rumble of her car starting, accompanied by the activation of her daytime running lights. Waving for her to go in front of him at the gates he saw her bow theatrically before mouthing the words, *thank you, kind sir*.

Wistfully observing the red sports car accelerate up the road McNeil failed to notice that the tired-looking Vauxhall Astra parked on the other side of the road wasn't unoccupied.

Chapter Fifty-seven

Perhaps this time, thought Brandt as he watched the solid metal gate retracting once more. He knew it was only mid-afternoon but sometimes fortune favours the brave. Having already filled two bottles with urine, and nibbled a few bits of his lunch, he was ready for some action. The nagging, doubting voice in his head had gone away and all he felt now was a calm serenity.

It's red. The gate's slow movement had revealed the car's flank. *It looks small and sporty.* He could feel the excitement swelling. He could see the front grill; four interlocked rings. *It's an Audi!*

Go, go, go! He reached for the ignition. *Hold on, is it her?* The voice had returned; that pernicious cunt. But Brandt did look up again and the person he saw in the driver's seat was unmistakably DCI Stella Johnson. He could feel goose bumps break out on his arms. Just seeing her in the flesh was thrilling. *Franklin, you old bastard, you were right!*

The spell was soon broken, with her car pulling out as soon as there was a gap large enough for it to squeeze through. *Go, go, go!*

'Not now, you fucker,' Brandt shouted as the ignition turned over but failed to fire the engine. 'Come on!' A panicked glance up saw that she was already halfway down the road and another car was now pulling out of the police station.

Don't flood the engine, the voice warned. Perhaps it was on his side after all. He turned the key back to the original position and took a long deep breath. Trying again was only met by the same whining sound but then, suddenly, the motor roared into life. It was lumpy and irregular, and Brandt was sure that any second it would conk out. *Give it some beans.* He prodded the accelerator harder than intended and caused a sudden flare of revs. Shocked by the noise, Brandt unconsciously pulled his foot away and the car settled down. It still sounded rough but no longer at risk of cutting out. *Next time maybe start it up as the gate retracts.* Brandt could sense the mocking tone.

'Fuck you,' he muttered and slammed the gearstick into first. The engine roared again as he failed to remember how high he needed to raise the clutch before it would engage. Moments later, and accompanied by the screech of wheel spin, Brandt set off in pursuit, now cursing Franklin for being able to tell him little more about Johnson than that she had a flashy red Audi. *A fucking fast Audi he should have said.*

He lost sight of her, but he knew that Radford Road was long and, if he could make up some of the gap, particularly with her car being so distinctive, he should be able to spot her again. Sure enough, as the traffic queued for the major intersection with Gregory Boulevard, he saw she was three vehicles in front of him, indicating right. With the traffic lights having turned green he was pleased to see that, in advance of the junction, his lane split into two and both of the cars between him and Johnson were moving into the left hand one. However, the blue Fiesta was slow to complete the manoeuvre and, stuck behind it, and with Johnson already making her turn, Brandt felt a moment of panic as he saw the lights flick to amber. With nothing else for it, he lurched into the oncoming traffic to round the obstructing vehicle and, although the lights were on red by the time he reached the junction, he made it before the other lanes of cars were released.

Johnson already had a lead of a couple of hundred yards but, with nothing else between them, Brandt selected a pace that would gradually close the gap. This was still resulting him exceeding the speed limit by a good 10mph but, in his anonymous car, he wasn't concerned by the prospect of speed cameras.

The rest of the journey passed without incident and, with her finally turning into a residential street, he was relieved that she seemed to be going straight home. Franklin had told him that she wasn't married because he claimed to have checked to see if she was wearing a ring as soon as she had come over to discuss the Milton Keynes case. Brandt had forced a laugh and told him that he was a sly old bugger, which, in his drunken state Franklin had taken as a compliment. Naturally that didn't mean she didn't have a boyfriend, but she didn't look the type to be supporting some freeloader so, at this time of day, he assumed that any partner would still be at work somewhere.

She stopped in front of a property and Brandt quickly pulled into a space of his own, a few houses down. There were plenty to choose from. He opened his door ajar whilst waiting for her to get out of the car. He wanted to make as little noise as possible and wouldn't fully close it when exiting. He doubted anyone would notice it wasn't shut, much less be interested in a shitty old banger, given how nice the area was.

After what seemed an age, he finally saw her legs swing out and then stand up. As she stretched wearily, he slipped out of his vehicle and started walking slowly down the pavement. If she was aware that she wasn't alone, she didn't show it, and made her way to her front door without turning to look back. He waited patiently whilst she found her keys, observing that the house was detached. *We can afford a little noise*, he smiled to himself.

'DCI Johnson,' he said in an official voice as soon as she pushed open the door. She started turning and he closed the gap. Whilst peering at him with a vague look of recognition crossing her face, Brandt punched her squarely in the jaw.

Chapter Fifty-eight

McNeil knew it was largely down to tiredness but, all the same, he felt miserable. The day had been such a disappointment. From thinking they might have solved the case, not least the opportunity it might have given him to make his move on Johnson, he was now on his way home to his grotty shared house. Rather than focus on all the positive things she had said confirming her feelings for him, all he could think about was her appeal for him to be patient. Patience had never been a strong point of his and he didn't see how he could be expected to be patient now, when faced with the prospect of something he wanted so desperately. He would try and respect her request, but that didn't mean he had to like it.

His mood wasn't helped by some idiot nearly going into the back of him when jumping the lights. Rather than give him the finger, which was his usual response to poor driving, he had called up the road, 'Why so impatient?' His poor attempt at ironic humour had given him little satisfaction.

The house was thankfully empty, and McNeil guessed that if he went to bed now, the way he was feeling meant he would most likely sleep until morning. But with his pizza long digested, he made his way to the fridge. The last thing he wanted was to wake up hungry in the middle of the night and then find he couldn't get back to sleep with all the thoughts whirling around in his head. He would eat the left-over takeaway he had from a couple of nights before.

On the middle shelf was the large Tupperware box with his name clearly written on in permanent marker. However, as soon as he felt the weight as he lifted it up, he knew that something was wrong. Opening the lid revealed that the pork balls were gone, as was the half portion of the chow mein he had put in there. All that was left were the sticks from his chicken satay. 'Greedy bastards,' he cursed loudly as he threw the box into the sink.

Momentarily consumed with thoughts of retribution, he frantically searched for something; anything he could eat from the remaining contents of the fridge. He didn't care whether it was the wrong housemate's food but all he could find were various dubious looking jars of pickles and gone-off packets of pasta sauce. They each had a cupboard allocated to their dry and tinned foods but, revenge or not, the last thing McNeil wanted to do at that moment was start cooking.

Muttering various swearwords under his breath, he grabbed his keys and stomped out of the house. Tomorrow night, when everyone was in, he would call a meeting. The first thing on the agenda would be finding out the identity of the thoughtless, disrespectful, and selfish thief. The next thing would be the re-establishment of clear ground rules. These would go beyond just food and would address all the other things that irritated McNeil. As he started reeling off lists in his mind, that included replacing the toilet roll after using the last piece, remembering to double bolt the door when last to leave, and not running a bath without checking whether anyone needed some hot water left for a shower, he realised he was already at the small parade of shops.

No sooner had he walked through the door of the kebab shop, he was asked by the owner what he would like to order. *Just give me a fucking moment to have a look at the menu, will you?* McNeil had wanted to reply. 'Oh, I'm not sure yet,' he said, in as polite a tone as he could muster. Nodding, the man went back to chopping lettuce.

Whilst staring up at the various options, a thought entered his mind. *Why not get something for both you and Johnson.* He supposed he could phone and ask her. But she might already be asleep. *You could take it round as a surprise.* But she might be asleep. *You could knock quietly so as not to wake her if she is.* And what if she isn't asleep, what then? She doesn't even like kebabs, she told me so in Canterbury. *So why not...*

McNeil's thoughts were interrupted by the ring of the bell above the door announcing the arrival of another customer. 'Are you in the queue?' the woman asked.

'Oh, er, yeah,' McNeil said, turning back to the kebab shop owner who was now looking at him again. 'Small doner and chips please.'

Chapter Fifty-nine

Brandt just sat there looking at her, enjoying the blissful discomfort of his erection being strained by his trousers. *You could just take them off, it doesn't mean you have to touch it*, the voice inside his head teased. But Brandt knew the truth. He was so aroused at this moment that he feared even the slightest movement of the material on his shaft may cause him to orgasm.

Still unconscious, Johnson was tied to her bed in just her underwear. Brandt had conducted a quick scout of the house whilst she lay in the hallway, knocked out cold. Her house was minimalist and with neutral colours. There was a feminine quality to it, but Brandt had quickly checked the drawers and wardrobes upstairs to make sure that no man stayed there. What he had found in the main bedroom had caused him to let out a little squeal of delight. She had a wrought iron bed. Brandt had known he had wanted to tie her up, bringing the twine to do so, but thought he may have to settle for just binding her to render her immobile. His discovery meant he could arrange her in a far more inviting pose, tying each limb to its own corner of the bed.

In his haste he had completed the knots with her still fully dressed but, rather than go to the effort of untying them, he used the steak knife to clumsily hack away at her outer garments.

She was beautiful; far more so than he had believed her to be from the images on the television. Her black matching underwear was a delicious contrast to her smooth white skin. The only thing Brandt had found slightly off-putting was the smell of cigarette smoke that clung to her hair. He had rummaged in her bedside cabinet to find some perfume and had been shocked but, on reflection, not surprised to find some more intimate items. 'Perhaps once I'm finished,' he promised her, shutting the drawer.

In the days following those despicable newspaper comments, Brandt had contemplated exactly what he would do with Johnson. His thoughts had ranged from a quick death all the way through to an entire night filled with pleasure for him, and pain for her. Sitting there, watching her motionless body, he realised that he needed her awake. He wanted her to know who he was and why he was doing it. Most of all, he wanted her to tell him how it felt, both emotionally and physically. He would only use a gag if necessary, and render her unconscious again as a last resort.

A few minutes later Johnson started to stir. Brandt remained sat next to the bed wondering what would unfold. She let out a small moan as she tried to change position and found she couldn't. Gradually opening her eyes, she squinted against the light and the pain in her head. Rocking her jaw from side to side she attempted to bring her hand across to where Brandt had punched her. Finding her movement restricted, her eyes opened wide in panic. Suddenly she was shaking the bed as she attempted to move all her limbs at once. Unsuccessful, she raised her head to try and see what was preventing her. She stopped.

Brandt could tell she had spotted him out of the corner of her eye and he reached across to put his hand over her mouth before she could scream. 'There's nothing to worry about,' he said, speaking over her muted cries. 'You're safe now,' he chuckled.

Her noises stopped. He removed his hand. 'Good, I want you nice and calm. Now, let's get the ground rules out of the way. You scream? I knock you out. Clear?'

'Fuck you,' Johnson spat at him.

Brandt leaned forward, holding up his blood-stained knife. 'Recognise this?' But her eyes didn't leave his and he could feel them defiantly boring into him again, like they had at that first press conference.

He didn't like it and was about to punch her again when her expression suddenly changed to one of recognition. 'It's you!'

'Yes, I thought the knife…'

'No,' she interrupted. 'Your face. We were right!'

'What?' He didn't like this. She was the one who was supposed to be confused, not him.

'We found you… on the cameras. You sick…'

Before she could finish Brandt saw her expression change once more, as she began to fully comprehend the situation she was in. He smiled and relaxed back into his chair. He'd find out what she meant later, much later, but for now it was time to get the conversation back on track. 'Do you know why I'm here?'

'How… how do you know where…?' Johnson stammered.

'Shh,' he said, soothingly. 'All in good time. The reason I am here is because you have been spreading lies. *Nasty* little lies. You have gone way beyond police protocol and if I were your guv'nor, I would have disciplined you long before now. I didn't mind that you were chasing me; of course that was to be expected, but you haven't played fair. Spreading vicious rumours…'

He paused, noticing that the defiance had returned to her eyes. 'We know about St. Albans…'

'Bollocks! I've never even been to St. Albans.'

To his surprise, she laughed. A loud, fulsome hoot that reverberated around the room. 'Now who's telling lies?'

'Stop!' he shouted, waiting for the anxiety to envelop him. But it didn't. And nor did he feel any rage. Instead he realised that he had maintained his erection throughout their exchange. He felt calm. Ready. He stood up and smiled at the flinching reaction. Reaching down to unbuckle his belt he whispered, 'No more talking…'

Chapter Sixty

McNeil switched off the engine and rested his forehead on the steering wheel. 'This is stupid,' he muttered. *Well, you're here now so you might as well.* He shook his head. He needed to wait; he needed to think about what he was doing. Rather than exacerbate his hunger, the combined smell of the kebab and the Chinese takeaway was conspiring to make him feel nauseous. *You can't eat all that by yourself, so what are you going to do, put the leftovers in the fridge for those greedy bastards to steal again?*

Still wracked with indecision he looked towards Johnson's house. Having only been there once before, he was worried he might struggle to find it, but the presence of her car confirmed it to be the correct place. It was too early for lights to be on in the house, but the curtains were drawn. He guessed she could easily be asleep by now but decided to send her a text anyway, hoping that, if she was, it wouldn't wake her.

He didn't know what to write. In the minutes that followed he must have typed, deleted and retyped the message half a dozen times. In the end, it rather pointlessly asked: *Are you asleep?*

As he waited for a response he gazed up at the window. At one stage he thought he could see the flicker of a shadow but, when no message followed, he assumed he must have imagined it. A further five minutes passed with no reply and he put the key back into the ignition and started the engine. Selecting first gear he checked his rear-view mirror to see if there was any traffic behind him and reached for the indicator. He stopped. 'This is stupid,' he repeated.

He got out the car this time, taking the Chinese but leaving the kebab, and made his way gingerly through the front garden. McNeil promised himself he wouldn't use the doorbell and would give a slight knock instead. One that would only be perceptible by Johnson if she were awake and alert. It also meant she could choose to ignore it if she guessed it was him and thought his visit inappropriate. With his hand pulled back just a couple of inches from the wood, he thought he heard a noise. He put his ear to the door to listen. It was her. She was laughing. He wasn't sure whether that was a good or a bad thing. She was awake, which was good, but she might also be on the phone.

His heart sank as he considered a further option. *What if she has company?* He heard a deeper voice, a man's voice.

McNeil was devastated, he couldn't believe he had been so stupid. All that bullshit about waiting for the right moment, when all she had been doing was stringing him along. Just something to keep her entertained through the boredom of the case.

He turned to walk down the path back to his car.

Chapter Sixty-one

This felt amazing. He was on top of her, ripping away her bra whilst his penis, now free, was poking at the material of her knickers. He didn't care if he ejaculated straight away; he had all night and could have as many goes as he wished, but was pleased to find he had a little more self-control than he expected.

Johnson was thrashing underneath him in a way Brandt found most pleasurable. With her breasts now released he leaned down to suck on her right nipple. He couldn't resist biting it instead. She cried out in pain. Brandt sat up and raised his fist to punch her for breaking one of the ground rules but then shrugged. *Fair enough, I suppose.* He bent over again to kiss it better.

There was an almighty crash from downstairs. Simultaneously Johnson stopped wriggling and Brandt raised his head to stare at her in confusion.

'Police, stop right there!' commanded the voice from below.

Brandt spun off the bed with an agility that belied his advancing years. He reached over to the dresser, grabbed his knife and made for the stairs; almost tripping over her discarded clothes as he went.

Exiting the bedroom, he covered the short journey across the landing in two strides and rounded the top of the bannister. With a thump he collided with the intruder and, feeling his balance going, he instinctively tried to steady himself. With his left hand Brandt grabbed the side of the man's jumper and, forgetting in his panic that he was armed, unwittingly drove the knife into his ribcage with his right.

For a few fleeting moments it appeared they had successfully stabilised but then the intruder fell backwards down the stairs; his grip taking Brandt with him.

He felt collision after collision slamming against different parts of his body as his spinning vision told him he was falling down the stairs with increased momentum. As he reached the bottom, his body continued to rotate, and his head smashed against the solid brick wall behind him. His brain didn't have time to register a coherent thought before unconsciousness enveloped him.

Chapter Sixty-two

In the distance he could hear something. Faint, almost imperceptible, but certainly there. It was growing louder; still unidentifiable but definitely more noticeable. It was a scream; a woman's scream.

McNeil opened his eyes as reality hit him. It only took a few moments of staring up at the unfamiliar hallway ceiling for everything to become clear. It was Johnson upstairs screaming, much louder and more frantic than the one he had heard outside. He attempted to call back to her; to tell her it was okay, and he was here, but as he pulled in a deep breath he started coughing. Blood was mixed in with his spittle and he reached towards the searing pain in his chest to find the hilt of a knife. McNeil didn't remember being stabbed but he assumed it must have been done by the man lying slumped against the wall, blood pouring from the back of his skull.

He reached out to prop himself up but when he placed his left arm down it collapsed under him, having been broken in the fall. As his body involuntarily tried to make him cry out in pain, again there was that excruciating burning in his chest, followed by more blood being coughed up.

McNeil knew he had to get to Johnson, so he summoned up all his strength and managed, with just the use of his right arm, to get onto his knees. Blinking hard to try and clear his vision, he crawled to the first step and started his ascent.

She must have heard his shuffling because the screams had been replaced by anxious demands to know who it was. He would dearly have loved to call out to her that it was him; he had come to rescue her, but he didn't dare risk another coughing fit unsteadying him and causing him to fall back down again.

As he reached the top of the stairs, following the direction of the voice from his crouched position, he could only see Johnson's bare feet poking out the end of the bed. The awkward way they were flapping around caused him to see the ropes that held them. Concerned more than ever, he somehow managed to summon the strength required to get him standing and he staggered through to the bedroom, sliding along the wall to keep himself upright.

Horror filled him as he saw Johnson there, spread-eagled and naked except for her black knickers. Hearing her shouting his name brought him back to his senses. Without the wall of the landing there to prop him up, McNeil lurched alarmingly as he attempted to round the bed. Feeling his legs giving way he slumped down next to her.

'My God, what happened to you?' Johnson said, her voice now hoarse from all the screaming. 'Call an ambulance!'

He used his right arm to pat the front of his trousers. He remembered slinging his mobile onto the passenger seat when he thought he was about to drive off.

'No… phone…' he croaked, desperately trying to resist the urge he felt to start coughing again.

'Shit!' she cursed. 'Mine must be in my bag somewhere. Quick, help me undo these ropes.'

McNeil slowly lifted up his right arm and made a futile effort to untie the nearest knot one-handed. 'No… arm…' he spluttered, nodding towards his left shoulder.

'If only I could just get one hand free…' Johnson said, their gaze locking. They looked at each other for a long moment. Her eyes opened in abject panic: 'No!' she shouted, thrashing with all her strength.

McNeil couldn't risk any more words. He just smiled and nodded at her.

He could feel his coordination going but managed to find the hilt after a few moments patting around. Johnson was now pleading with him; begging him not to do it. He tuned her out.

The sound the knife made as he pulled it from his chest; a mixture of squelching and sucking, was hideous. McNeil dared not look but was sure he could feel the blood pouring down his front. He held the blade aloft and realised that she had stopped shouting and was now just staring at him. With his vision closing in, he regretted he didn't have the strength to free her himself. Rousing himself one last time he reached across and blindly found Johnson's wrist. He felt her take the knife, only to return a moment later to wrap her hand tightly around his. Satisfied he had done all he could, he rested his head on the mattress; his now sightless eyes pointing towards her face.

McNeil smiled as he took his last breath.

If you enjoyed this book, please let others know by leaving a quick review on Amazon. Also, if you spot anything untoward in the paperback, get in touch. We strive for the best quality and appreciate reader feedback.

editor@thebookfolks.com

www.thebookfolks.com

On the run, a serial killer lays
a deadly trap

HIDE AND SEEK
DENVER MURPHY

Having discovered Brandt's identity, the race is on to
capture him. DCI Johnson now has a very personal reason
to hunt him down. But Brandt knows she is coming. Can
she evade the traps he has laid?

Book III, coming soon on Kindle and in paperback.

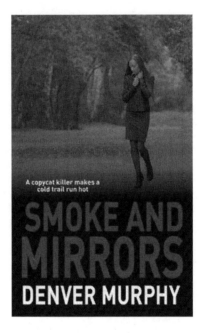

Has Brandt's killing spree come to an end? Is it over? Or have his actions spawned something worse? Will DCI Johnson get her revenge, or will she fall victim to her own rage?

Made in the USA
Lexington, KY
15 April 2019